TESS THORNTON

TAMING THE *Cowboy*

Walker Ranch BOOK 4

EAGLE CREEK
PRESS

Contents

The Walker Ranch Series

A Home for the Cowboy
Cody and Morgan's Story

A Second Chance for the Cowboy
Marshall and Kelli's Story

An Angel for the Cowboy
Dusty and Jess's Story

Taming the Cowboy
Luke and Audrey's Story

A Heart for the Cowboy
Evan and Meg's Story

Chapter 1

Luke

Well, that was it. My little brother and his new wife turned around, hand in hand, and beamed at the rest of us. Mr. and Mrs. Walker. Giddy and excited and about as sure of themselves as a pair of frisky young colts. They weren't even looking at anyone but each other, and I only said what they were probably thinking.

I cupped my hands around my mouth. "Kiss her again, Dusty!"

They were both pink with embarrassment and giggling, but Dusty grabbed Jess and dipped her back for a kiss that made every cowboy in the room whoop and toss his hat in the air. Morgan was standing beside me, crying. Kelli was on my other side, bouncing up and down and taking pictures. But when the new couple finally came up for air and walked down the aisle—practically in each other's shoes, not sure how they could have gotten closer—Morgan and Kelli turned to their husbands.

That left me in the middle, the odd man out. Everyone in the room was talking over each other, laughing about how cute it was that Dusty had almost forgotten to repeat his vows since he'd been just staring at his bride with stars in his eyes. A few were wiping tears over the sentimental vows Jess had written to pledge to Dusty, and I overheard some comments about how the string lights I'd ordered online made our big old drafty barn feel like a swanky, upscale event center.

But no one was talking to me.

Served me right for sitting between two married couples. I ought to have plunked down next to Evan when all the fuss started, but I'd been ushing... is that the right word? Anyway, the seat I ended up with was right in the front row, between Morgan and Kelli.

I was probably supposed to help dismiss people after the new couple walked up the aisle, but there wasn't any point by now. It was like a mob of wandering heifers, everyone converging into one spot and then just standing there talking and occasionally shuffling their feet toward the door.

I looked around and wandered out through another way, but nowhere was safe from the herd of chatty folks. It was a barn, not a cathedral with private halls. Not that I minded people. I like getting out on the town, and I'll shoot the breeze with anyone, but when it's a bunch of crying and gushing, I'm out. I headed for the stable and rolled aside the big door.

Confound it! I wasn't the only one here. A bunch of kids were running up and down the barn aisle, blowing bubbles and shooting Nerf darts. Who on God's green earth bought those stupid things?

Oh, wait. Those were my idea. But they were supposed to be popping them off at Dusty's truck when he left, not spooking the horses! Darn kids.

"Hey, you!" I bellowed. Only one of them stopped. He stared at me, his mouth agape and his Nerf gun dropped from lifeless fingers.

"You, kid! What's your name?" I'd seen him before. He was that kid who'd brought Dusty the wooden sculpture of Duchess, but I'd never talked to him. And he wasn't talking now, either. Just petrified to his spot like a lump of clay.

"I got you, Dustin!" shrieked a girl in a frilly pink dress. She raced by and pinged the kid on the side of the head about three times before she took off toward the tack room. Pretty good aim, actually.

Dustin finally blinked and put his hand to his cheek. He looked down and didn't move again.

"Hey, you alright?" I asked. I remembered a little more about this kid now. This was the one Cody had pulled off the mountain, the one they said didn't talk much. Scary things would overwhelm him. Scary things like girls with Nerf guns who shot him in the side of the face.

This was way above my pay grade.

But no one else was around, and I couldn't just leave the kid glued to the center of the barn aisle. "Dustin? Hey, snap out of it. You want some punch? Cake? There's going to be cake. Come on, let's go find your mom."

He swiped roughly at his cheek and finally looked up, his eyes glittering. "Just leave me alone!" He aimed a savage kick at the Nerf gun, and it went sailing over one of the barred doors, right into Duchess's stall. That gol-durned kid! I'd whoop him if he hit the horse in the head!

But I didn't have time for anything like that because he was running off. For Pete's sake, I didn't know how to talk to him. But Morgan knew the kid pretty well, so maybe I'd message her to check on him. I was pulling my phone out to do just that when I heard Evan's voice across the courtyard, calling Dustin back. I poked my head out just long enough to see that someone was handling things, then I walked back to check on Duchess.

I slid her stall door open, and she lifted her head with the Nerf gun trapped between her teeth. "Hey, Sugar. That thing didn't hit you, did it?"

The toy dropped, she sneezed, then rubbed her face on my shoulder. "Cut it out, now. What'll Dusty say if you get all spoiled rotten?" But I didn't stop scratching her ears. She liked that. The mare was a queen, and it still tore me up that she wasn't the horse for me. She had champion written all over her. I'd just have to keep looking for something that was the same but different.

"Well, old girl, I'm supposed to be back at the party. You stay out of trouble now, you hear?" I picked up the plastic gun and was backing out of the stall, sliding the door closed, when something stung my backside with two quick blasts.

"Gotcha, Aedyn!"

I turned around, and that girl was charging out from the haystack, still brandishing her Nerf gun, but she stopped dead when she saw me.

I pointed at the gun, almost quaking with rage. That little hooligan shot me in the butt! Her mouth fell open, and she froze. "*Drop. It.*" I hissed. "Or I'll break it over my knee!"

Her nostrils fluttered, and her eyes filled with big, syrupy tears. "I-I th-thought you were Aedyn."

"Do I look like a twelve-year-old?" I thundered. "And what are you thinking, anyway, shooting those darned things in the barn? Don't you know animals can choke on those stupid darts?"

Her lip started to tremble, and a puddle big enough to do a crocodile proud slipped down her cheek. "I didn't know," she whispered. "Please don't tell my aunt."

Oh, dad gum it. I couldn't lecture a little girl who was crying any more than I could yell at a horse for making a mistake. What good would it do? I just pinched the bridge of my nose. "Tell you what. You pick up all these darts, and I'll forget you were in here causing trouble."

She sniffed and carefully offered me her Nerf gun. "Can I still shoot it at the newlyweds when they leave?"

I shrugged and threw my hands up. "Sure. You can shoot at his windshield for all I care. Now, get going." I took the toy gun. "Hey, just so I know whose mom to look for if I catch you out here again, what's your name?"

"Lizzy." She bit her bottom lip. "Lizzy Tracy. Only my mom's not here. You can't talk to her."

Something tickled my brain, and I narrowed my eyes. "You James Tracy's daughter?"

She nodded, her wide brown eyes fixed earnestly on mine, and her throat bobbed. I sighed and pushed my hat up. I knew a little about James Tracy, and none of it was awesome. He'd been in Evan's class, married right after school, and divorced just a few years later. He was still around, pulling odd jobs and stuff. But Lizzy's eyes begged me not to ask more about her father.

For some reason I couldn't explain, something about that little girl clicked in my head. I used to be the wild kid like that. And I'd had my reasons, just like I was sure she had hers. I wasn't going to fix her by going and tattling to her mom or her aunt or whoever was in charge of her. Maybe what the kid needed was an outlet. Something that felt amazing and powerful but wouldn't hurt anything.

"Well, tell you what. You pick these up quick-like, and I'll set you up with the water canon instead of one of these silly foam dart guns."

Her face blanched in awe. "Water canon?" she whispered.

I winked and made a shushing motion. "Little surprise for my brother. You keep a secret, now?"

She nodded, her eyes moving up and down in their sockets because they never left mine.

"Good. I'm going to go look in on the party, and when I come back in twenty minutes, I want this barn put to rights. There's a broom right over there. Understand?"

This time, she smiled when she nodded.

I have a thing for chocolate. I always have. My mom used to hide it in a locked case whenever she got some, but I always found the key. And I don't care for fancy chocolate. Hershey's is just fine. Generic is okay. As long as it's sweet and smooth, it hits the spot.

Dusty knew that, and he'd bought bucket loads of chocolate kisses for the wedding guests... but mostly for me, because he figured I'd be the one taking care of the leftovers. And right now, I was filling my vest pockets with big handfuls. They weren't dancing at this wedding because Dusty and Jess weren't into it. It was just cake and toasts and some of Dad's famous smoked brisket, served buffet style.

I'd already missed the main course, but I did my duty, held up my glass, and said the nicest things I could think to say about my kid brother and my new sister. Jess was going to be a killer sister—fun to watch football with, and she could soup up my truck for me. People laughed, but I was serious. Then I filled a plate of leftover brisket, pocketed my goodies, and headed outside. I had the after-party to prep.

I found Lizzy still in the barn, sweeping up the last pile of dirt. I set the plate down and looked around. "I didn't say you had to detail the place. Just pick up the darts. This looks great."

She set the broom aside. "Did you really say water canon?"

I chuckled. "Yep, I sure did. We have a big water truck out back. See, Cody and Marshall thought it would be funny to paint a bunch of pink hearts and stuff all over Dusty's truck before they leave for their honeymoon, but Dusty will die of embarrassment to have smooching signs all over his rig. We'll give them a sendoff to talk about for years to come and wash some of that stuff off the truck into the bargain."

Lizzy came close, sly and smooth as a little cat. "And I can hold the water hose? Is it strong, like a fire truck?"

"Not quite, but that's a good thing. A fire hose would take Evan, Marshall, and me just to hold it. But it's bigger than a garden hose. Trust me, you'll love it. Hey, you hungry?" I offered her the plate of brisket. "I didn't grab a fork, but we're in a barn. Pretty sure bare fingers are legal."

She giggled and dove in. The kid could put it away, and she liked the same pieces I did—the crusty edge pieces with all the flavorful bark to savor. We cleaned the plate slick, and I tossed it in the trash.

"Okay, one last thing. We're missing out on the cake, so I brought some dessert." I dug into my pocket and produced a handful of silver-wrapped deliciousness.

Lizzy's whole face lit up. "Those are my favorites! My aunt won't let me have them."

"Well, your aunt don't need to know. You got pockets in that dress? No? Here, gobble quick, then we'll run out back and drive the truck around before everyone comes outside."

Lizzy unwrapped about five chocolate kisses and shoved them all in her mouth at once. There were so many, she couldn't close her mouth to chew them, and we both laughed at the way she was jawing her chocolate like a cow. Her teeth were bathed in brown syrup, and her lips were covered with sticky goo. Oh, her aunt would know she'd had candy, all right, but who cared? We were at a wedding, and it was chocolate.

She was still smacking her lips, trying to sweep all the chocolate off her gums, and her face was glowing with happiness. "Dis is da bes' wedding ever!"

"And it's going to get better. Need some more?" I gave her another handful, then grabbed my hat off the bench beside me. "Let's go make this a wedding no one will ever forget."

Chapter 2

Audrey

I always cry at weddings. I don't even have to know the couple. It's just the idea of two people plunging into the unknown forever and swearing to do it side-by-side and hand-in-hand... I don't know, it just gets me every time. Usually, by the time the groom takes the bride's hand and looks utterly breath-taken, I'm dabbing tears. And when the bride lifts her sure but trembling voice to pledge her heart to the man she adores, I'm a blubbering mess. I've learned not to wear mascara to these things.

But today, I was in worse shape than usual. I'd gotten to be pretty good friends with Jess. We'd spent many hours together over the past few months, mostly volunteering at White Pines. I had met a lot of great people there, but she was the only person I'd made much time for after hours. It wasn't like I didn't enjoy other people. I used to be a social butterfly, with such a full engagement calendar that I'd hired a virtual assistant just to keep it all sorted.

These days, I had my hands full taking care of my sister Kat, who was in the final stages of kidney failure, and her precocious, energetic daughter Lizzy. Social life? That was a thing of the past. I was just surviving, putting one foot in front of the other, trying to keep everyone's spirits up, and praying against the inevitable.

Jess was the one person I'd gotten comfortable enough with to let her in behind closed doors, on those days when I just needed someone to talk to who didn't try to solve the unsolvable. She just listened. She smiled. She held my hand, brought over some books to read, and she picked up Lizzy from school a few times when I'd been swamped at work. And now, she was moving to Walker Ranch.

What was it about these Walker cowboys? All my friends were dropping like flies for them! First, Morgan—although, I guess Cody was adopted, but that still counts in my book. Then Kelli, who'd snapped up maybe the most handsome of the bunch. From what I could see, they spent as much time "bickering" as they did kissing, and they seemed to thrive on it.

Even Meryl Justice, the retired bank manager who'd approved my loan to buy the dental practice, was engaged to the patriarch of the Walker family. Blake was a good guy. They all were, everyone said. But what was the deal? I honestly didn't understand the obsession with cowboys.

Especially *that* one. I rolled my eyes and counted to three when Luke Walker, the wild one of the family, yelled out for Dusty to kiss Jess again in front of everybody. The man was a yokel.

I was embarrassed for Jess, but she didn't seem to mind kissing her new husband again. Everyone else erupted in applause and laughter. It *was* cute, the way Dusty draped his blushing bride over his arm and shielded their faces with his hat.

I had to admit Jess had done pretty well for herself. Dusty was one of the sweetest men alive, but that didn't mean I intended to follow in her footsteps. The only cowboy to make me swoon was Cowboy Bill, who owned Beaufort's steak house. He made a pretty delicious chili, and it was now one of my favorite comfort foods to pick up in a carry-out box after a long day.

But other cowboys? Nope. I had a type already, and my type didn't include a dusty hat and worn-out boots.

Everyone was wandering out the door and up toward the backyard of the house, where a dozen picnic tables had been set out under shade tents in case it started raining again. Blake promised everyone a plate of smoked brisket, baked beans, cheesy potatoes, and cornbread; nobody minded a little rain with that kind of inducement. Hardly standard wedding fare where I'm from, but it *was* amazing. If anyone knew how to smoke a brisket, it was the Walkers.

I waited in line for my turn to fill my plate and glanced around. My niece was nowhere to be seen. I stood nervously on my toes and swept the wedding party with a worried glance. Lizzy had a bad habit of getting into trouble.

She wasn't a bad kid. She was high-energy and sharp as a whip at the same time—a dangerous mixture combined with the boredom that was her life. A kid with a terminally ill mother did a lot of waiting around.

I'd been taking care of Lizzy for over a year and a half now, and I'd watched with dismay the slow unraveling of her behavior. She got in trouble at school for making too much noise and not turning in her homework, even when I'd checked it the night before. She got dropped from the girls' volleyball team for showing up late to practices, even though she was at school by the proper time.

Also she had trouble making friends because nobody quite knew how to take her. The more she was left to her own devices, the worse things got. And I hadn't seen her since the vows were spoken.

"Hey, Morgan," I asked, sidling over to her at a table, "have you seen Lizzy? She promised not to run off this time."

Morgan winced and gave a guilty smile. "Sorry, Audrey. Luke bought a bunch of Nerf guns for the kids to shoot at the newlyweds' truck when they drive away, and I told them they could all go get ready."

I felt my entire face drop. "He bought *what?* Who does that?"

Morgan chuckled. "Luke does. Come on, they can't hurt anything, and they'll have a ton of fun with it."

I closed my eyes and shook my head, searching for that calm center that would keep me from doing or saying something unreasonable. I tried. Honestly, I was trying. I counted in my head a lot these days. "You're not kidding. They're really going to fire a bunch of darts at the truck as it drives away?"

She shrugged with a helpless grin. "Guess so. But keep it quiet, please. The surprise is part of the fun."

"Oh, I just bet it is."

Lizzy would love it. I wasn't personally crazy about the idea, but Morgan was right. Where was the harm? It just wasn't what I was used to, and I wouldn't want someone pulling a surprise like that at *my* wedding.

Weddings should be classy, beautiful affairs. The new couple had just sworn to love each other for their whole lives! That deserved a little respect, a little decorum. But here we were, eating brisket and baked beans on paper plates in the back yard, and waiting for a bunch of kids to pepper the honeymoon vehicle with Nerf Darts.

Yeah. Not at all what I was used to.

I wasn't as sociable as I should have been at dinner. The food was incredible, and people were going back for seconds and thirds. Everyone was having a great time, laughing and talking nonstop.

But I was more worried about what Lizzy had gotten up to. I hadn't seen her in over an hour. When we were at home, and things got quiet, that was when I got nervous. She was an imaginative, mischievous kid with a lot to deal with, and sometimes things... happened.

The worst of it was that most people didn't realize why she acted out. Instead of guidance and understanding, Lizzy's behavior was usually met with frustration and punishment. I spent a lot of time trying to shield her from the typical corrections meted out by the school because to Lizzy, they would only make things worse. But I couldn't let her just run wild, either, so I tended to be a protective mama bear to her in public, but I overcompensated with more correction at home. Which wasn't working, either.

My fears came to a head when I saw Evan Walker escorting Dustin Truman up from the barns in search of Meg, his mother. He was crying. And somehow, I knew before I even walked over to find out what had happened.

Lizzy.

"She shot him in the side of the head with the Nerf darts," Meg whispered. "But I don't think she meant to. It was just a game."

"Lizzy knows better, especially when it comes to Dustin. Either she wasn't watching where she was pointing, which is bad enough, or she *was,* and she hit him on purpose. "

"He's okay. I'll just keep him with me until he can calm down. I'm just impressed that he was playing with the other kids at all. Really, Audrey, I think they were just having fun, and it got out of hand."

I blew out a breath. Meg Truman was one of the few people who *did* get it. Of course, she got it. She faced some of the same challenges raising a bright, autistic son alone. "Thanks, Meg, but she still needs a consequence for that one. I'm going to have to tell her she can't shoot at the truck as it's leaving. Any idea where the kids are?"

Meg shook her head with a laugh. "There are so many barns and outbuildings here. They've probably already moved from the last place I heard about! I'm sure they'll turn up for cake and ice cream."

Oh, great. Sugar. Because that was *exactly* what Lizzy needed. Every time she visited her dad, she came home bouncing off the walls. I'd spend the week detoxing her from all the junk food he fed her, and then the weekend would roll around, and she'd come home berserk again. "Yeah. I'm sure she'll turn up for that. Thanks, Meg."

But Lizzy didn't appear when Dusty and Jess cut their cake. And I was actually starting to worry. I didn't stay for the toasts but headed for the last places I'd heard the kids playing. The problem was, this place was huge. I was crossing the lawn again to try somewhere else when someone called me.

"Audrey, there you are!"

I turned around to find Kelli Walker carrying a serving tray of coffee cups. She lifted it toward me. "You look like you need a pick-me-up. I have a super dark roast for the guys who want to put some hair on their chests and a medium-roast crema blend for the rest of us humans. Care for a cup?"

I reached for one of the lighter-colored cups. "I can't resist a good crema. Thank you."

"Of course. I noticed Kat didn't come today. Jess wasn't sure if she'd make it or not."

I shook my head. "This would be too much for her. I actually need to get back soon. We're doing all her dialysis treatments at home now, and she gets a treatment almost every afternoon."

Kelli blinked. "Every day?"

I shrugged and sipped my coffee. Kelli really did know how to make a proper brew. "Almost. It's easier on her than going to the hospital twice a week. It's three hours or so every time, though. A respite nurse is sitting with her right now, but she can't run the treatments."

Kelli's forehead wrinkled, and she stuck her lip out in sympathy. I used to think she was pouting and being overly dramatic when she made that expression, but it was just what her face did when she hurt for someone. "That's really hard for you, though. Isn't there anyone else who can help? I thought she had some skilled in-home nursing."

"Sure, but Katherine gets upset when I'm gone for very long." I stared down into my cup and let go just a morsel of the awful truth. "It's... it's not good."

Kelli turned and shoved the tray of coffee cups onto a convenient oak barrel that had been set up as a standing tabletop. She came back and rested a hand on my shoulder. "I'm sorry to hear that. Morgan and I were wondering about her. She seemed to think Kat might pull through."

I looked up, met Kelli's deep brown eyes, and bit my lips together.

"Oh, Audrey. I didn't know it was that bad," she whispered. "How long?"

I shook my head and sipped some more coffee. "I don't know. The doctors say a few months, but what do they know?"

Kelli's mouth trembled, and she swallowed. "Does Lizzy know?"

I huffed and blinked away the mist from my eyes and looked to the corner of the room. "Oh, I'm sure she knows, deep down. But Kat doesn't want me to tell her anything yet. I think it's wrong because the poor girl's just confused, and nobody's giving her any answers. But what can I do? I'm just her aunt."

"You're all she's got. That's what you are."

I rested my gaze on Kelli and wished I had something of the charming flintiness she could brandish whenever it suited her. "Yeah," I agreed softly. "I guess I am."

"Speaking of which..." Kelli pointed to the driveway, where the newlyweds were commencing their farewell march away from the party. "Looks like it's time. Is Lizzy joining the Nerf battle?"

Too late to stop it now. I sighed. "I'm sure she wouldn't miss it."

"Come on!" Kelli dragged my hand from my face and pulled me along with the crowd. "This is going to be fun, Audrey Livingstone, and you deserve five minutes of fun. Look!"

Jess was twirling around, swaying her bouquet to a chorus of cheers. Most of the single girls were clustering around her, hopping, excited, and playfully jostling each other.

"Why aren't you going up there, Audrey?" Kelli demanded as she pushed me forward. I was so astonished I actually let my feet move before I could turn and gape at her. I wanted nothing to do with catching that bouquet. But it didn't matter anyway, because after Jess acted like she was going to throw it, she turned and handed it to Meryl Justice. And nobody could object to that.

Meryl kissed Jess on the cheek, dabbed her eyes, and then the newlyweds walked toward Dusty's truck. Dusty opened the door for his new wife, then knelt in the gravel so she could step on his knee instead of having to jump. And even my stodgy old heart gave a little thump at that. Maybe cowboys could be pretty great after all.

"And... now!" a voice shouted.

I didn't even have to look to know which cowboy *that* was.

Jess had barely gotten her door shut when Luke Walker, leading a mob of short savages, charged the truck, pelting it and Dusty with green and blue foam darts. Dusty laughed, pointed at Luke like he would make him pay for that little stunt, then ducked inside the cab. Even then, they weren't safe because an army of monsters rushed after him for about twenty yards, firing an avalanche of darts.

But the mayhem was just getting started. "Fire in the hole!" Luke cried. I couldn't see him anymore, but there was no mistaking that cowboy drawl. And that was when I realized my niece hadn't been one of the kids wielding a plastic dart gun.

I had a bad feeling about this.

The kids all drew back to the sound of a heavy old truck rumbling around the corner of the nearest barn. It was a water truck, and it turned down the drive to follow Dusty's pickup. And sitting right on top of it was Luke Walker with my niece, wearing her best party dress.

"Oh, no," I whispered. "What is that girl up to now?"

But it was pretty obvious. Lizzy was holding a huge hose, and when Luke flipped a lever, she reared back with the force of the water and proceeded to douse Dusty and Jess's truck as it tried to make its escape.

That thing had some power, too, and my heart stopped. It had almost flipped Lizzy over backward! The only reason she didn't fly off was that Luke made a quick grab for her shoulders to steady her and then had to keep a hand braced behind her.

Yeah, he saved her from falling, but he was the idiot who had put her up there in the first place. That didn't make him a hero.

I followed to the edge of the slope, where I could watch the water truck's progress down the long driveway. There was nowhere to turn around until it got down to the bottom of the hill, and there was nothing for me to do but wait until it got back. And so, I waited.

Seething.

When it did finally roll up the hill, to a smattering of cheers and shouts, I was ready for it. Luke and Lizzy were still sitting on top, laughing like a couple of crazy people. Luke barely glanced over my head—I doubted he even knew who I was. But he'd know in a few seconds, the rascal.

When I got around the corner of the truck, Luke was helping Lizzy down, and she straightened to face me. And she wasn't laughing anymore. "I'm sorry, Aunt Audrey," she said. Oh, her voice was perfectly respectable, but there was a rebellious twinkle in her eye. And chocolate all over her face.

I just stared. "What in Heaven's name? What did you do, drink syrup from a trough?"

Lizzy gave me a weak smile, and I reeled in dizzy horror when I saw that even her teeth hadn't been spared. Her entire mouth was stained brown. "How much did you eat?" I asked in alarm.

Chocolate was the very worst thing for her. Not only was it the onslaught of mass quantities of sugar, which was like a nuclear bomb to her system, but I'd started to suspect Lizzy was lactose intolerant. She was going to spend the night sick to her stomach again, I just knew it. My head exploded with visions of me, running between Kat's dialysis treatment and Lizzy doubled over the toilet. This was just too much.

That was when a tall cowboy jumped down from the truck, his booted feet landing beside Lizzy. I looked up... and up... and into the darkest violet-blue eyes I'd ever seen on a man. I'd never been this close to Luke Walker, and... uh... he wasn't... too bad. To look at. Just to look at, mind you.

"Just a couple handfuls of Hershey's Kisses," he said. "It won't kill her."

"A couple of *handfuls?* That's more than she should have in a month!"

"Hey, come on, sweet thing. It's a wedding! Let the kid have a little fun."

My eyelid started to twitch. "Did you just call me *sweet thing?* Is this a joke to you? Lizzy, go wash your face. It's time to go home."

Luke Walker stuck a flannel-clad arm in front of Lizzy, barring her from doing what I'd told her to. "Now, just wait a second. We were in a hurry, that's all. She didn't get any cake or ice cream because she was helping me, so I gave her some chocolate. What's the big deal?"

"Helping you *what?* You fed her enough chocolate to kill an elephant and then put her up on top of that water truck where she could fall and break her neck!"

He lowered his arm and got a cheesy grin. "Overprotective. I get it. You must be the aunt."

I rolled my eyes. Maybe I *was* overprotective, but raising Lizzy was like running around putting out fires everywhere she went. And he wasn't helping. "Audrey Livingstone. *Doctor* Livingstone to you. And you're Luke Walker, the lunatic."

"Lunatic?" He cocked his head thoughtfully. "I kind of like the sound of that."

"Of course, you would, but trust me, it wasn't a compliment. What on earth were you thinking?"

Luke Walker's cheek flinched, and he stuffed his hands in his pockets. "I was thinking it'd be fun, that's what I was thinking. Dusty was laughing."

"I don't care if Dusty was laughing. You didn't even check with me before you let Lizzy do all that stuff. That's not okay. What is wrong with you?"

He winked and shot me a grin. "You're the doctor. You tell me."

I narrowed my eyes. "The only kind of doctoring you're going to get from me is a dentist's drill with no Novocaine. Come on, Lizzy. We're leaving." I put my arm around Lizzy and marched her toward the car.

"Promise?" Luke called after me.

I turned and glared daggers at him, but he just grinned wider.

"Guess I'll make an appointment for next week, then?"

I straightened. You didn't get anywhere with this kind of guy by rolling your eyes and walking away. You had to challenge them, head-on. "Fine. Next week. I'll sharpen my drill."

Chapter 3

Luke

"Are you busy?"

I closed Duchess's stall door and glanced up at Cody, walking down the barn aisle with a three-year-old stud in tow. They'd just finished a training workout in the arena.

"Yeah, I'm busy. I'm hauling hay up to the broodmares, and then I'm going to circle out to the lower eighty to check calves."

"Oh, not now. I meant later this afternoon." Emily walked up with a freshly saddled horse for Cody to work. He nodded his thanks and switched horses with her. "I'm planning to get three more ridden today, and then Morgan wanted some help later. You're not free to come, are you?"

I shrugged. "Depends on what it is and how many cows are trying to calve today. What, are you doing some construction to the barn?"

"No." Cody threw the stirrup over his saddle to check his cinch. "Morgan's been looped in with a local equine rescue organization. They're always looking for facilities that can house and rehab horses, you know. Anyway, I guess there's a situation over in the next county—a neglect case. They said law enforcement was set to seize about fifty horses today, and they'll need a foster home immediately."

I whistled. "You can't take all fifty, can you?"

"We have the space but not the fences or the help. The rescue organization pays their feed and vet expenses, so at least that part's covered. Morgan and I told them we could take about twenty for now. Anyway, I guess they're supposed to serve papers this afternoon."

"And you need someone to drive a trailer for you, huh?"

Cody grinned. "Nah. You just looked bored without Dusty around. Figured I'd give you something to do."

"Dusty?" I scoffed. "He's a big boy off on his honeymoon. He can do whatever he wants, and I got plenty of my own stuff to do."

"Right. So, ready to leave in about two hours?"

I rubbed my jaw and shrugged again. "Sure."

Cody walked off, and I stood back, watching him go. He'd changed since he met Morgan. He used to be kind of quiet—always thinking, not saying much. Not the same way that Dusty was—with Dusty, it was because he was daydreaming happy thoughts. Cody used to seem almost bitter. Like the guy on every sports team who's hungrier than all the rest but never gets his big break to prove himself.

But Morgan seemed to have unveiled Cody's confidence. He'd walk around the barns whistling now and never passed anyone without saying something cheerful or encouraging. Heck, he'd even scouted Emily as an assistant and bent over backward, trying to help her become a better trainer than he'd ever be. The old Cody would never have done that. This was a whole new cowboy, and I still wasn't used to it.

Maybe it was worth checking out what had turned him around. Because whatever it was that he and Morgan had, it looked like something I'd like to try.

I finished up my chores—extra today because Dusty would be gone for another week—and met Cody in the driveway with a stock trailer. Morgan pulled up a few minutes later with the White Pines trailer, and Cody came to my window. "I'll text you the address in case we get separated. We just heard that law enforcement is on the way, so we'll get there about the right time. Hope you brought your mud boots. I don't know what it will look like when we get there," he warned.

"I've seen stuff," was my simple answer.

Cody grunted and went to join Morgan in their truck. I followed them onto the highway and turned on the windshield wipers against the endless gray drizzle. My phone buzzed with the text from Cody, and I tapped it to see where we were going. It was about fifty miles away. Well, an afternoon drive in my heated truck was better than a soggy ride through the fields with Brandon, checking herds. I cranked up the Willie Nelson and started singing along.

Almost an hour later, I put on my blinker and followed Cody and Morgan's trailer onto a gravel road off the highway. My map said we were still a couple of miles from the place, but it was all washboard and potholes from there on. We slowed to a crawl as we splashed our way through, and just before we rolled over a little hill, I saw two more trailers turn onto the gravel road behind me. Good grief, this must be a bad deal.

But I had no idea how bad.

When the train of trailers finally stopped, we were in front of a tumbling old mobile home with about a dozen broken-down cars parked outside. What fencing they had was mostly crooked posts with old strips of tire rubber stapled to them. Chunks of plywood and loose boards filled gaps here and there, and in one place, there wasn't a fence at all but a dead truck parked in the "gate". I didn't see a barn anywhere, but there was what was left of a shed, housing a single bale of blackening grass hay.

I rolled down my window to get a better look at the property. Then I immediately rolled it back up. The smell was like nothing I'd ever experienced. It was decay and filth, moldy hay and death, and pond scum all mingled together. But where was it coming from? I still hadn't seen anything moving.

My phone rang, and I picked it up, still gaping around at the makeshift corrals. "Awful, isn't it?" Cody asked.

"What the heck happened here?"

"I don't know the whole story. It's going to court, so they're not sharing many details yet. We were just told that the people tried to get a ranch or a breeding operation or something going on here, and it got 'out of hand.'"

"That's the understatement of the century. What a mess! Where are all the horses?"

"Keep looking."

I squinted and rolled down my window again. And then I saw a chunk of mud... walking. I lowered my phone. "Lord, have mercy," I breathed.

The longer I looked, the more "mud" was moving around. But the horrible part was how much *wasn't* moving. I saw three humps huddled together in one area, none so much as twitched. Dead or too weak to get up? I couldn't tell.

"The vet just got here," Cody said through the phone. "And it sounds like they're ready for us. You good?"

I swallowed. I'd thought I was, but now I wasn't so sure. "Yeah." My voice cracked. "Right behind you."

It was hideous. I saw things that would haunt me to my grave—a hulking livestock guardian dog with festering sores and almost zero body fat, snarling and snapping at the rescuers because he had probably never been petted in his life. A starved old mare trying to hobble along on a knee that was clearly broken, and had been for some time. A dozen young horses crowded into a thirty-foot pen, the stronger ones stepping on the weaker ones. The vet got close enough to one of them to see his teeth, and he estimated the colt to be two years old, but he was no bigger than a weanling.

What was wrong with people? Pity twisted in my gut with rage. How could anyone *do* something like this? Yeah, it takes money and work to take care of animals, and I could see how someone's circumstances could change suddenly. This was a lot to manage, and most people would get overwhelmed. But it didn't happen overnight, and it didn't happen by accident. Fifty horses? How could they let it get so bad that animals were suffering this much?

For the next hour or so, we waded through the soupy marsh of the corrals, sorting the horses that could be moved from the ones that couldn't. Three poor horses never left that hell hole because it was more merciful to put them to rest. The first two trailers pulled out, hauling the group of young horses, and the humane society picked up the emaciated guardian dog and five or six cats. There were rumored to be more, but they would have to come back with live traps to rescue them.

That left us to move the biggest and most pitiful horses.

Another trailer backed up to the gate, and a few volunteers were helping weakened horses into it. One old horse looked barely able to stand, but when he saw the trailer, his ears perked up, and he almost ran into it. I guess even horses know how to spot a rescue when they see it. Cody had walked over and was standing beside me as we watched.

"There's a stud in with some broodmares," he said after a minute. "They're not going to let him go to just anyone. Too risky."

"Let me guess. You said you'd take him."

Cody shrugged. "We'll haul him with his mares, but we will have to isolate him after that. I don't know where we'll put him, but I guess we can build him his own pen for now."

"Which one is he?"

Cody pointed. "The big black over there. Not that you can tell what color he is."

I moved that way to get a better look. He was in a cramped pen with five mares, all showing signs of heavy foal bellies under their bony ribs. That was all that stood out about the stud—he was the only one that didn't look pregnant. Every horse in the pen was caked with mud until you could hardly see their natural coats. He was tall and might have been handsome once, but he didn't exactly have the look of the eagles about him now. He just stood with his head lowered against the rain like all the rest—his eyes dull, his lower lip drooping, and his tail so heavy with mud that I doubted he could even swish it.

"They all look like they've given up," I murmured.

"Yeah. So, uh... Hey, I had a thought."

"Why do I have a feeling I'm going to hate it?"

"Oh, I'm sure you will. The quarantine stall in the big barn is open, and I thought..."

"No, Cody. I'm not taking on someone's problem."

"Just till Morgan and I get something built for the stud. It's a liability thing, you know. We'll have to keep him a certain distance away from all the other horses. You wouldn't believe the red tape and insurance stuff she has to deal with."

"No dice. I'm not taking that stud. Why don't you just geld him? Needs to be done anyway."

"Oh, I'm sure that will happen, but the rescue organization doesn't technically own him yet. It has to go through the courts before we can do anything beyond providing basic care. They'll pay for his board and feed until things are settled."

"I'm not worried about that. But if I take that horse back to the ranch, I just know I'll get stuck with him the whole time. How long will that take? Months? Years?"

"Come on. I wouldn't do that to you. It's just for a week or two."

I narrowed my eyes and sighed. I didn't need a charity case around the place. Some folks are cut out for saving animals—they have compassion and mercy, and endless patience. I just felt sick and angry.

"I can't do it, Cody. Lookin' at that horse every day? I'll go nuts and want to punch someone over it."

He shook his head and gave a low, bitter laugh. "You and me both. But someone's got to. At least you'd know the horse was safe, and you have the facilities and the experience to handle a stud. It's better than asking someone else to take him who might get hurt."

I rubbed my jaw and kicked some mud with my boot. "Evan is going to kill me."

Cody nodded. "Probably."

Audrey

"Miss Livingstone? May I have a word with you?"

I stopped in my tracks and heaved a sigh. I'd hoped to pick Lizzy up from her after-school tutoring today without seeing anyone, talking to anyone, or even making eye contact. No such luck. I pasted on a smile and turned around. It wasn't her teacher this time... it was the principal.

"Oh, hello, Mrs. Delaney. So nice to see you!"

She wasn't smiling back. "Miss Livingstone, I'd like to speak with you in my office, please."

My stomach sank. This didn't sound good. "Of course. Shall I pick Lizzy up first, or..."

"She's already waiting in the office."

I blinked. "Oh."

What had that girl done this time? I didn't have the energy for this today! I blew out a sigh as I followed Mrs. Delaney into her office, praying it was nothing too serious. Maybe it was even something good. Didn't they have a Student of the Month program? And a crossing guard program for the sixth graders. Lizzy had mentioned an interest in that. It was probably—

"Miss Livingstone, we have to suspend Elizabeth for hitting."

That was what I was hoping not to hear.

I fumbled for the chair beside my niece, who was waiting for me with a none-too-repentant look on her face. "What happened?"

Mrs. Delaney arched her brows at Lizzy. "Would you care to explain?"

Lizzy swung her feet and looked down. "No."

I cleared my throat. Lizzy peered at me through the fringe of her bangs, a defiant twinkle in her eye. If I made her talk right then, she'd probably get herself in worse trouble.

"Mrs. Delaney, would you first tell me what happened from your perspective?" I suggested.

The principal scowled at the suggestion that her story could differ from my niece's. She puckered her lips, then leveled a hard stare at me. "Elizabeth struck a boy over the head with her math book this afternoon. *Hard.*"

I swung back to Lizzy with a horrified gasp. "You *what?*"

She stuck her lip out. "He was poking me."

"I don't care what he was doing! You don't hit someone with your math book!"

"But Aunt Audrey, he was poking me down *there*. You always said I shouldn't let anyone do that."

I squinted, my mouth probably hanging open. "I don't understand. He was touching you?" I glared back at the principal. "Is this true?"

Mrs. Delaney rolled her eyes. "Tommy Martin was sitting behind her in class. According to Elizabeth, he was poking her in the lower back."

"It was lower than that," Lizzy shot back. "He was poking me in my b—"

"I asked you not to speak like that," Mrs. Delaney reprimanded. "In my office, we do not use slang, Elizabeth Tracy."

I stood up, my fists clenching. "You're worried about rude words when that boy was touching her inappropriately? In any other school, that would be grounds for expulsion!"

Mrs. Delaney sighed and folded her hands on her desk. "Except the teacher did not see him doing this. Two children seated nearby claimed Tommy was innocent and that Elizabeth acted without provocation."

"They're his friends!" Lizzy cried. "And anyway, none of the kids like me." She crossed her arms.

Mrs. Delaney arched her brow and frowned. "Elizabeth, this is not the first time you have been in my office for acting out. You have exhibited a disturbing pattern of unpredictable and emotional outbursts, and you have not followed the rules of the classroom. You have disrupted the learning environment for the other students."

I was bristling. "Mrs. Delaney, I thought the rule was that a child was always to be believed if she claims another student is harassing her. Was I mistaken? This incident should be investigated, but you are choosing to blame Lizzy alone."

"Hardly without prior cause, Miss Livingstone. I am sorry, but Lizzy will be suspended for two weeks. You may see her teacher about her homework."

By this time, I was shaking and baring my teeth like a junkyard dog. "That will not be necessary. I am withdrawing her from this joke of a school, and you will be hearing from my lawyer." I snatched my niece's hand. "Come along, Lizzy."

"Except you do not have the authority to withdraw her because you are not Elizabeth's legal guardian," Mrs. Delaney called as we marched out.

I whirled on her. "We'll see about that," I hissed.

Lizzy's dejected face appeared over the edge of the kitchen island, her brown eyes round and haunted. I flicked off the hand mixer and sighed. "You're not in trouble, Lizzy."

Her fingers crept over the ledge, and she blinked. "Promise?"

"Can you promise that you were telling me the truth earlier?"

Her head bobbed forward. "Cross my heart, Aunt Audrey."

"And you will speak up for yourself in the future instead of hitting?"

"I'll try."

That was as good as I was going to get. "Then you won't hear another word about it from me. You don't have to hide behind the counter."

She blinked and slowly stood up. And that was when I noticed the tear streaks down her cheeks. "Oh, Lizzy. Have you been crying?"

She sniffed and swiped at her nose with the back of her hand. "No."

I tugged a paper towel from the dispenser and passed it to her. "You might want to take a look in the mirror."

Lizzy sagged against the counter and fumbled with the paper towel. "Did you really mean you'd pull me out of school?"

I rolled my neck and tried to stretch the tension kinks out of my shoulders. "Oh, I don't know. I need to talk to your mom when she wakes up. I would have a lawyer after that principal if it were up to me, but your mom probably won't agree. I don't know what other options we have if we take you out of school. I'm sure Kat will know what to do."

"No, she won't." Lizzy wadded the towel up without using it and threw it at the trash can. "She doesn't know anything."

I fisted a hand at my hip. "Elizabeth Marie Tracy! I'll not have you talking about your mother like that."

Her lip trembled, and her eyes started glistening again. "It's true, though. She's always sleeping. She doesn't..." She shook her head. "She just doesn't. Not anymore."

The kid had a point. I swallowed and picked up the hand mixer again. "Well... we'll see. I called your dad."

"He won't care. He says school is a waste of time, and he's right."

"Sure, if you don't mind flipping burgers for a living."

She set her teeth and stared me down. "What's wrong with flipping burgers?"

"Oh, Lizzy, please. I don't have the energy to argue right now. Why don't you help me finish dinner?"

"What are we having?" she asked suspiciously. Lizzy was not a vegetable enthusiast.

"Poison. Want to try? Close your eyes and put out your finger."

She giggled and, after a second's hesitation, did as I said. I dipped a spatula into the bowl and swiped it on her finger, and she stuck it in her mouth. And gasped. "Mashed potatoes?" Her eyes flew open. "Really? But you always say you don't have time to make those!"

I shrugged and smiled. "And I didn't, but I figured you deserved a treat after a rotten day. Here. Want to lick the beaters?" I popped them out of the mixer, and Lizzy grabbed them like they were covered in cookie dough. I hadn't figured out why she loved mashed potatoes so much, but they were one "treat" that didn't make her sick or hyper.

"When you're finished with those, rinse them off and put them in the dishwasher. And then set the table, please."

Lizzy was humming and pirouetting around the kitchen with her beaters, getting in my way more than anything, but at least she didn't look mortified and devastated like she did earlier. Give her a day, and she'd forget all about Tommy Martin and math books. But I couldn't.

What was I supposed to do with a kid who couldn't go back to school for at least two weeks? I had a business to run, and there wasn't exactly space in the waiting room for an extra kid. Not that it would be a good place for her, anyway. Lizzy would be bouncing off the walls in my office.

I couldn't leave her home. Kat's daytime caregiver was just that—medical respite help. She wouldn't want a bored twelve-year-old lurking around the house, and she certainly wouldn't want to try to oversee her schoolwork. So, homeschooling was out. And the nearest private school was an hour away and more than I could afford. Maybe

Morgan would have some ideas for me. She was pretty well connected with resources in the area. I'd call her later.

Lizzy and I ate our meal in the dining room, and I watched her mopping up the potatoes and gravy like candy. She put away her roast chicken with a fair appetite, but slowed down when she got to the peas. "I hate peas," she grumbled. "Can we have green beans instead?"

I pointed at her plate. "You can't always have your favorite things. Eat up."

"But they taste like dirt."

"Tell me that after you taste them." There was a shuffling sound from Kat's monitor, and I picked it up to check the video feed. "Okay, your mom's awake. I'm going to take her plate. Do you want to finish in there?"

Lizzy looked up, shook her head, and pushed her peas around the plate. I wasn't dumb. She'd scrape them into the garbage as soon as I left the room and try to cover it up. But I couldn't fight every battle, so today, I'd just let that one go. "Okay. Come on in when you finish and say goodnight."

She set her cheek on her fist and kept staring at her plate.

I slowly eased into Kat's bedroom to make sure she was still awake. Her eyes were closed, but she opened them with a weak smile. "Hi," she whispered hoarsely.

"Hey, there. Nice nap?"

Kat's eyes drifted closed in a ghost of a chuckle. "Nap. Hah. Slept all day."

I pulled out the bedside table we'd bought for her and set her plate on it. "Got your dinner. Mashed potatoes and diced chicken and peas. Yum!"

Her mouth twitched. "Lizzy talked you into potatoes?"

"Well, she kind of had a bad day." I waited, but Kat didn't seem to pick up that suggestion.

She drank some fresh air and pushed herself on her pillows to inspect the plate. "Oh, I can't eat this much."

There were hardly two mouthfuls of anything. I'd been bringing her smaller and smaller meals lately, and every day, I took half of it back to the kitchen. I swallowed. That little food couldn't possibly keep her alive. "Just eat what you like," I replied cheerfully. "I'll put the rest in the fridge for later."

Kat could still hold a fork and spoon, but eating was no longer a dignified process for her. She needed a lot of help, and by the time she finished, she'd be exhausted for the night. That was why I had started paying the caregiver extra to bathe Kat during the day—she didn't have the energy by evening.

She was between bites now, carefully scraping some peas and potatoes together with her spoon, and I took the opportunity to ask about her daughter. "So, uhm... Lizzy got in some trouble today."

Kat's shoulders lifted in a sigh, and she gave me a pained look. "What now?"

"It wasn't entirely her fault, I don't think. It sounds like she stood up for herself when no one else would, but... well, she hit a boy with her math book. She's, uh... suspended. Two weeks."

Kat's eyes closed, and she shook her head gently. "Can't you talk to the principal?"

"Tried that. The principal isn't interested in defending Lizzy."

"Lizzy has to learn," Kat insisted in a raspy voice. "She can't go around fighting with everyone."

I stiffened. "Look, I agree with you, but if what she says is true—and I believe it is—I wouldn't want her to let someone pick on her just to avoid a conflict. It's not fair to ask that of her."

Kat eased the spoon into her mouth and swallowed slowly. "I'll call Mrs. Delaney tomorrow," she said. "I'm sure we can sort this out."

"But Kat—"

She held up her hand, and right then, I saw something... break in her. "We don't have much choice, Aud."

Well... she was right about that. And Lizzy was *her* kid, after all. She would get a lot farther with Mrs. Delaney than I could. My head hung as I battled with my conscience, my anger at that principal, and the rotten situation walling us in. "Fine. Let me know what she says."

Chapter 4

Luke

"That's pitiful."

Cody crossed his arms and sucked in a breath. We were standing in the barn aisle outside the quarantine stall, staring in at a bedraggled mop of a horse. The stud was trying to pace his stall and occasionally sending up thin neighs to the mares he'd left behind in the trailer. "Yup. Have you ever seen feet like that?"

"Not in real life. I mean, his toes are curling, and he's practically walking on his pasterns! I don't even want to know how many diseases he has."

"Well, we'll find out. Doc Burns pulled some blood samples. You got the rehab feeding instructions, right?"

"Yeah, yeah. Little mouthfuls of alfalfa every four hours around the clock. Seems like a massive pain in the rear. Why can't I just keep the rack full and let him free feed?"

"Because his guts will just shut down. It's called Refeeding Syndrome, and it's bad. Patience is the only way to go, Luke. Seriously."

I sighed and kicked the shavings with my toe. "S'pose I'll have to come out here in the middle of the night."

"Like you won't be up all night checking calving cows anyway."

"Yeah, but I wouldn't have to go back and forth," I groused. "And washin' up every time I leave him like a surgeon in a hospital. Evan would *really* kill me if one of our horses got sick."

Cody shrugged. "I'm sorry to ask this of you, Luke. I really do appreciate it. We'll get him moved to White Pines as soon as we can. And besides, when Dusty and Jess get back, I'm sure they'll help take care of him. You just try keeping Jess away."

I grunted. "When can we get his feet done? How about worming? I can't stand lookin' at him like that."

"Morgan said he's getting a full checkup tomorrow, and the farrier will start on his feet if the vet deems him strong enough. He'll get hoof radiographs and maybe his first round of shots, and they'll check to see if he has any parasites."

"*If?* He's a gol-durned petri dish. At least let me give him a bath. He's stinkin' up the whole barn."

"Better not." He shook his head. "At least until Burns says the shock won't be too much for him. Remember, he just had an hour-long trailer ride and lost his mares in one afternoon. One day at a time, Luke. He's got food and water and shelter now, which is a lot more than he had this morning."

"Yeah. Well..."

"I know that look. Don't you go doing anything too elaborate. He's part of a legal seizure, don't forget that. We don't own him."

"Huh."

"I mean it, Luke."

"Sure, sure." I put my hands up. "I'll just feed him up and let Burns call the shots. Any idea when the case will go to court?"

"Nope. At least a couple of months."

"I hope the judge throws the book at them no-good rascals. They shouldn't be allowed to own a pet cricket. Heck, they should be in jail."

"I'm with you," Cody agreed, "but I gotta warn you, these things don't always turn out like they should. Morgan's seen too many repeat offenders. They just move to another state and do it all over again. Sometimes they even get their animals back."

"Naw. You're joking."

"Wish I was." Cody clapped me on the shoulder. "I'm going to head out. They'll have the first trailer unloaded by now, so I'll take these mares over. I assume you don't need your truck and trailer back tonight?"

My lip curled. "I don't *want* them back. Not till I've taken that trailer through the truck wash down at the freeway exit. Have you seen what those mares did to the inside?"

Cody chuckled. "Yeah, I saw. I'll get it washed tomorrow before I bring it back. Thanks, Luke."

"Uh-huh." I stuffed my hands in my pockets, staring at the black stud as Cody left. "Hey, wait up."

Cody stopped. "Yeah?"

"Whatcha doin' later?"

"Later? It's already after six. I'm going to go home and help my wife get nineteen rescue horses settled in before it gets dark."

"What about after that?"

He spread his hands. "I'm going to do my regular chores, just like you. And then, if I'm really lucky, I'm going to cuddle up with my wife on the couch for five minutes before crawling into bed to do it all over tomorrow."

"Oh." I shrugged. "Okay, then. See you tomorrow."

Cody narrowed his eyes. "Right. Night, Luke."

I blew out a sigh and leaned on the bars of the stall, gazing in at that stud. His ears were so erect they almost touched, and his eyes were ringed with white as he sniffed around his new home. "Bet you'd like to get out of here, huh?" I murmured. "Gonna get real boring in there till the vet says you can be turned out."

He swiveled his head at the sound of my voice and whinnied louder than before. He didn't come up for me to touch him, though. Just stood back warily, staring at me without blinking. He whinnied again.

"Hey, it's not my fault. Can't blame you, though. I don't like being bored, either."

The stud snorted, licked his lips, and cautiously sniffed over his hay. He tried to lip it up, then tossed his head and dropped half his food. He was acting like it hurt his mouth to eat. He'd need a full dental workup before he could start putting weight back on.

I rubbed my chin as I watched him. Speaking of dental work... it *had* been a while since I'd had a proper cleaning. A year, at least. Okay, maybe three or four. And hey, that new dentist in town seemed kind of interesting—way better than Dennis Watterson, the fat old guy who used to make my gums bleed when I was a kid. At least, I wouldn't mind having *her* leaning over me.

The more I thought about it, the more the notion stuck in my head. Wasn't Dusty always after me to take better care of myself? Maybe I'd do that tomorrow. Provided I could get away from the ranch.

"Well, my lad, you've had a rough time of it, haven't you?" Doc Burns switched on his headlamp and peered into the stallion's mouth. The black was already sedated, his head hanging on the swing we'd strung up to support him in the stocks. His eyes rolled back in his head and he looked ready to fall over.

"What do you see?" I asked.

Burns felt around the horse's mouth, spent a minute or two inspecting with his light, and asked for his dental tool. "He's got a bad wave to his molars and a couple of pretty sharp points causing him pain at the corners. Little wonder he couldn't eat. We'll get that cleaned up today."

"How old do you think he is?"

"Oh, I'd say eight or nine. It's hard to say because he's been so malnourished. He's no older than ten, I don't think."

"Really? I figured he'd be twenty if he was a day."

"It doesn't look like it. You know, he's got pretty straight legs, too. Good angle to his shoulder. Might have been a nice horse when he was younger. Wish we knew his story, huh?" Burns hit the switch on his tooth Dremel, and I didn't bother trying to talk over it.

The vet wasn't the only one asking those questions. I'd been eaten up with curiosity about the black stud in our barn. Who was he? Where did he come from? No one seemed to know, but I'd found either an old scar or a brand on his left hip when I...

Okay, I admit it. Cody told me I couldn't bathe him, but I did run a curry over him, just to get the biggest mud clumps off. That stuff had to hurt, and if he had any old injuries, wouldn't it be best to find them before the vet came? He was still a dirt ball, but at least he didn't have as many huge muddy knots dangling off his belly. I'd get Burns to clear him on the bath as soon as possible.

"Seems a little on the timid side, but pretty good manners for an unhandled stallion," Burns commented later when he was putting his tools away.

"He's undernourished and sedated. Of course, he has good manners."

Burns chuckled. "Right. At least his teeth aren't going to bother him now. He's not the thinnest horse from that herd, either. I'd put his body condition score at about a three, so he'll start to bounce back sooner than some of the others. Let's get some radiographs of his feet and see where we are on those before he starts to wake up."

I didn't hold out much hope for this part. The poor horse was walking on the backs of his heels because they were so far under-run, and I was sure he'd have laminitis. When there's that much pressure on the hoof wall, those sensitive live tissues start tearing deep inside the hoof, and you have all kinds of problems. Sometimes, there's not much you can do.

Burns and his assistant walked around, snapping the images they needed while I stood back out of the way. When he had all the angles he wanted, he pulled up the digital images on a portable monitor. He didn't say much—mostly grunts and nods as he clicked through each one.

"Well?" I asked.

"Well..." Burns pulled his glasses off. "It looks like he hasn't been trimmed in a long time, but he might be rehabilitated. I don't see any permanent damage to the coffin bones, and even the joints..." He went back to the monitor, clicked a couple of images, and shrugged. "He doesn't even have arthritis. I'm not sure how that's possible, but his joints are clean."

"You're pullin' my leg."

"No, really, he's not too bad. I think this one will pull through."

The way he said "this one" made me squint. "What about the others?"

Burns blew out a sigh. "I was just over at Cody and Morgan's place. We had to put a couple more down this morning. I haven't heard about some of the others. I'm not the only vet on the case, of course, but from what I hear, Morgan took some of the worst cases."

"She would."

Burns nodded. "Yeah. She would. Well, let's get this fellow's feet trimmed, and then he can truly start on the road to recovery. I bet we won't even recognize him in a month."

I nodded. "No, I bet not." I studied the horse for a few minutes. He was still drugged, his head drooping, but for a second, his eye rolled to me. And I swear, plain as the nose on my face, he asked straight up for my help.

My mind was made up. The poor thing deserved a fair shake. Maybe he'd be going out to White Pines soon to join the others, but for as long as he was in my care, he'd get all the pampering he'd missed out on. He might not have a fancy pedigree or a performance record like some of the valuable animals we raised at Walker Ranch, but as long as he was in our barn, he'd live like a king.

Audrey

"I called the school," Kat informed me when I opened the door with her breakfast tray.

I paused before setting her plate down. "And?"

She thinned her lips. "Lizzy can go back to school today, but she has to sit in detention afterward for the rest of the week."

I pulled out the bedside table and arranged her oatmeal and toast. "I'm not sure how I feel about that. Is the boy being punished, too? Will they make Lizzy sit near him again?"

"Audrey, it's..." Kat shook her head. "Let's just be happy they let her back in."

"But I'm not sure it's a good place for her. And that principal thinks Lizzy can do nothing right, so she'll always get the short end of the stick, no matter what happens."

She sighed and closed her eyes. "I know," she whispered. "It's not fair, but nothing is. I didn't have the strength to fight it."

I sat down and covered my sister's hand with mine. "I'm sorry, Kat. I know you did all you could. I didn't mean to sound like that."

"But you're right." She gazed at the wall, her eyes dull. Hopeless. I'd been seeing that look more and more lately. "I can't be what Lizzy needs anymore."

I tightened my grip on her hand. "You're her mother. You're exactly what she needs. Now come on, enough of this gloominess. Let's get your breakfast eaten, and I guess I'll drive Lizzy in today since she's missed the bus."

Kat's gaze wandered to my face. "You take such good care of me, Aud. You don't have to do all this." Was that a tear starting on her cheek?

I sniffed. "Nonsense. Mom would spin in her grave if she heard I wasn't helping my sister out when she was sick. Look, I put some cinnamon in the oatmeal today. You like cinnamon, right?"

Her cheek tugged sideways. "You always hated it."

"Well, it's not my breakfast. Orange juice? And a new bendy straw, too. I found some at the store again."

Kat sighed and picked at her breakfast, probably more for my benefit than her own. There was a knock on the door, and Mara, one of her caregivers, poked her head in.

"How are we doing today, Katherine?" she asked with her big perma-smile.

"I'm still here," was Kat's cheerful response. I'm sure she thought it sounded cheerful, anyway. To me, it smacked of gallows humor. I slapped my hands on my knees and leaned forward to kiss her cheek. "Okay, I'm off to work. I'll see you tonight, huh?"

Kat lifted her spoon in a little salute. "Thank you, Audrey. For everything."

I couldn't keep my eyes open at work. It was that after-lunch slump when business is slow, and it seemed like my most boring patients always scheduled their visits.

I was a one-doctor office, which wasn't unusual in a town this size. But one of the things it meant was that unless there was an emergency, most of the interesting cases went to the big city dentists to get their root canals and crowns. I'd been considered one of the top oral surgeons at the practice back in New York. Here, I just filled cavities.

Most of the time, there were three of us in the office—me, Kari, the receptionist, and Lucy, the hygienist. Barely enough staff to even call it a dental office. But today, Lucy had left at one because the school called that her son had broken his arm on the playground. Now, why did I fear at first that Lizzy had something to do with it?

But it wasn't her—he'd gotten hurt playing football, and our afternoon got even slower when we had to rearrange Lucy's appointments. I leaned on my desk and rubbed my eyes during one of my long breaks between patients.

"Audrey?" Kari knocked on the door frame. "What do I do about your two o'clock? He had a cleaning and a full checkup scheduled."

I pushed back from the desk. "How many other appointments do I have this afternoon?"

"Nothing until Mrs. Henshaw's filling at three. I already canceled Lucy's other appointments for the afternoon."

I swiveled to glance at the clock. "It's almost too late to cancel the two o'clock. I guess I could do the cleaning as well as the check-up, but it would be best if we wait. Maybe we can catch him if you call right now."

"Too late. He's already here. And trust me when I say you *don't* want to cancel this one." She winked.

"What?" I got up and straightened my scrub top. "Who is it?"

Kari shrugged with a sugar-sweet smile. "Oh, you'll see soon enough. I'd hate to spoil it for you. Shall I show him to the treatment room?"

I pulled my hair back into a fresh bun and stared at her with my best "boss" look. I wasn't very good at it. "Fine. Send him back."

Two minutes later, I walked into the exam room. The back of the chair faced the door so I couldn't see his face, but a cowboy hat perched on his knee, and thick, dark, wavy hair was leaning on the headrest. In a town full of cowboys, this wasn't an unusual sight. But this one looked all too familiar. Why did he have to pick today, of all days?

I cleared my throat, plucked his chart from the wall, and walked into the room. "Hello there, Mr. Walker. What are we doing for you today?"

Luke Walker craned his head up and turned on a mega-watt smile that didn't look like it needed any help from me. "Afternoon, Doc. You'll have to tell me what we're doing. Said I'd be here, remember?"

I remembered. I cocked an eyebrow and flipped over a page in his chart. The only way to handle this cowboy was to keep it all business. "I have you down for a cleaning and a full set of x-rays. How long since your last checkup?"

He shrugged. "Should be in the records somewhere. I used to come here when Doc Watterson owned the place."

I lowered the clipboard. "I purged all the records older than five years when I took over. And as you didn't come up in the system, I can only assume it means we've had at least two Presidential elections since you last brushed your teeth."

"Hey, sweet thing, I brush and floss and all that. Just figured might as well come in for a float."

I narrowed my eyes. "A... a what?"

"You know. Rasp my tushes down so I don't get so long in the tooth that I have to gum my oats."

My mouth dropped open behind my dental mask. "I have no idea what you're talking about, Mr. Walker."

"That's just Luke. Mr. Walker is my dad. So, how 'bout it? What do I do, just open wide?" He leaned back in the chair, linked his hands over his chest, closed his eyes, and opened his mouth.

He was like a little kid. I blew out a sigh and rolled my eyes. "Did the receptionist tell you that our hygienist is out this afternoon? She had a family emergency."

Luke closed his mouth and peered at me through one eye. "But I came to see *you*, doc. Can't you just take a look and give me a clean bill of health?"

I tapped my toes. I'd filled in for Lucy before when we were busy, and it made more sense for me to get patients taken care of myself. It felt unprofessional to me, but Luke Walker didn't seem like the kind of guy to care about that. Besides, the trouble with Luke was when he talked. He wouldn't be able to talk when I was cleaning his teeth.

"We'll start with your x-rays," I decided.

"How is this tooth not painful?" I poked the gum line of his second bicuspid with my cleaning pick, expecting him to flinch. Everyone did, even when they didn't think the tooth was problematic.

But Luke Walker just leaned back, rolling his eyes at the ceiling. "Waugh?"

"This tooth, right here!" I prodded it again, exploring anything that should have been sensitive. "How can you even drink coffee with this thing?"

"Haw ca oo tew I dwing caaghee?"

I pulled my fingers out of his mouth and reached for my rinse. "It's kind of obvious. You're a tobacco user, too."

"Not anymore. Cold turkey. Everyone kept raggin' on me, so I gave it up."

I stuck the rinsing attachment in his mouth. "I'm glad to hear it. Swirl and spit. Your x-rays show a cavity that's almost into the nerve. It's a root canal, for sure. How does it not hurt?"

He ran his tongue over his teeth, squinting in thought. "Never bothered me before. Don't you go tryin' to fix somethin' that ain't broke, now. It's fine."

"It's *not* fine. Left untreated, this kind of thing can turn into a blood infection."

His face was blank. "Uh-huh. So?"

"So? We have to fix it, or you'll be past tense."

"Aw, come on, doc. Little thing like that? It'll take more than a bad tooth to drop Luke Walker." He started to sit up in the chair, which was awkward because it was still leaning back with the feet elevated.

I pushed him back down with my finger. "Open up."

He laced his fingers on his stomach and grinned mutinously before slowly complying. I bit my lip and blinked at the ceiling. I didn't have time for flirty cowboys today! I should have made Kari send him home. But he was here now, and I was all scrubbed up. I might as well finish the job. I pulled my face shield down, grabbed a fresh pair of gloves, and picked up my cleaning tool.

Most people close their eyes when I work on their teeth. It's natural, I guess. We don't like having someone else right in our faces. But Luke Walker's eyes never left me. Even when I was focused on his molars, my cheeks were burning as his gaze seared into me.

"Don' 'urt yet," he said around my fingers.

"It's not supposed to. This is just a cleaning."

"Whan ya gohh figh it?"

"Not today. That will be a dedicated appointment. Hold your tongue still, please."

"You mean I gogha cong bach?"

I pulled back my cleaning tool and gave him a cup. "Rinse and spit. You know, this will go a lot easier if you stop trying to talk."

He did as ordered, his twinkling eyes still fixed on me. "My mama taught me to be polite to ladies. 'Specially pretty ones."

"I'm not a lady. I'm a dentist, and right now, I'm a busy dentist. Open, please."

He shrugged and lay back again. "Guess your niece didn't lose all her teeth yet?"

I lowered my tool. "What?"

"The chocolate. Didn't kill her, did it?"

"I would prefer not to discuss my niece, thank you. Will you please let me finish? You're turning what should have been a thirty-minute appointment into almost an hour."

"Sorry to be blunt, sugar, but you don't exactly have crowds busting in here to be next in line."

I ground my teeth. "Mr. Walker, I—"

"Luke. My name's Luke."

"Fine." I blew out a huff. "*Luke*, you are free to go find yourself another dentist, but from what I can see, it will be another decade before you make the effort. Now, if you would like to let me finish what I started, please open your mouth, and for the love of all that is holy, *stop talking*."

"Now, that don't sound all that professional. Did all those plaques on the wall really belong to you, or did you whip them up on the printer?"

I stepped back and propped the cleaning tool on its stand. "I think it best if we stop now, Mr. Walker. Clearly, you have no confidence in my abilities, and that is not conducive to a productive doctor/patient relationship."

He struggled to sit up again. "Aw, come on, don't be that way. Promise I'll stop talking. Scout's honor."

I studied him for a few seconds. It was more than the talking. It was the casual way he just assumed I wanted to be teased, the way he kept grinning whenever my hands weren't in his mouth. In another life, another time, I might have laughed and teased him right back. But I was *not* in the mood for this today.

However, I also didn't like the feeling of being beaten by a cocky cowboy whose ego was bigger than his brain. "Fine. I have ten minutes before I have to get ready for my next patient. No more interruptions, please." I grabbed the cleaning tool and gestured for him to lie back once more.

He slid back, his grin even wider than before. I straightened. "What now?"

"Oh, nothin'." He chuckled. "I was just thinkin' how that promise didn't mean much. I was never a boy scout."

Chapter 5

Luke

Dentists weren't supposed to look that good.

And they weren't supposed to blush like that when a guy smiled at them. I mean, how could I help it? I was stuck in that chair, staring up at her with nothing better to do, and she had her fingers in my mouth. It made my stomach all crawly, gazing up at those wisps of sleek brown hair peeking under her visor and those thick dark lashes flickering every time she accidentally met my eyes. The last time I was this close to a beautiful woman... let's just say she wasn't cleaning my teeth.

I didn't try to talk to her anymore. From the look in her eyes, I was ready to believe she'd actually make good that threat from the first day we met—grab the drill and go after me without any painkiller. What had I done so wrong that she seemed to hate me without even knowing me?

Was it the water truck thing at the wedding? Naw, that couldn't be it. Had to be more. That was why I'd asked about her niece, and I'd clearly struck a nerve, but she was irritated with me before I brought that up. I couldn't figure it out. I'm not sure why it mattered or why I cared, but it ate at me.

Finally, she switched off her tools and let me rinse my mouth out. "I've marked your chart, Mr. Walker. You may speak with the receptionist on the way out to schedule your root canal." She hung her face shield up, tossed her gloves, and started to slide out of her disposable smock.

"Wait, root canal?" I swung my legs over the edge of the chair. "You're serious?"

She pulled off her mask, and by golly, it was a good thing she'd been wearing that earlier, when she was so close to my face because her mouth was the stuff dreams are made of. I bet she tasted like chocolate chips and espresso. "I told you I was serious, Mr. Walker."

"Luke."

She bit her lip and rolled her neck, massaging it with her fingers. I hadn't noticed before that her nails were red. Interesting. "Luke, then. Yes, you need the root canal, and if I were you, I wouldn't wait."

I ran my tongue over that tooth. It didn't *feel* broken. "I don't hardly think it's an emergency, now, is it?"

She arched a brow and gave me a deadpan look. "The tooth? Probably not, but apparently, your memory is not to be relied upon. Kari will help you on your way out." She picked up my chart, marked something with her pen, and started for the door.

"Well, now, wait just a second," I said after her.

Her shoulders lifted in a sigh, and she turned around. "Yes?"

"Oh, I was just thinking... hey, you know, maybe I could schedule like a... a consultation. Something like that."

The corner of her mouth twitched. "This *was* your consultation. Unless you would like a second opinion? In that case, I can give you a referral."

"No, not that. I mean, yeah, I'm not too eager to have you start drillin' on me, but if you say so, it's gotta be done. But... well, now, are you sure?"

She rolled her eyes. "I've had five-year-olds who were less nervous about getting their teeth fixed. Honestly, Mr. Wa... *Luke*, this is a pretty standard procedure, and I've done it hundreds of times."

I blinked. "That's not that many!"

"Oh, for pity's sake. Schedule it or don't schedule it, I don't care. If you'll excuse me." She clutched my chart to her chest, and this time, she slipped out the door and closed it behind herself before I could say anything else.

Huh.

I rubbed my jaw. What made her so dad-gummed eager to get away? That never happened to me. It wasn't like I chased a *lot* of women, but I never had to try hard, either. This one was a puzzle. It wasn't like I was interested in her or anything crazy like that. I just couldn't stand that she didn't like me. It was a new experience.

I went to the front desk and paid my bill. It was a lot higher than I'd expected, and I had to check my account first before I broke out my card. How much was the root canal going to cost? Couldn't be more than a couple hundred, right?

"Doctor Livingstone said you would like to get on the calendar for the root canal," the receptionist chirped as I put my card away. "Would you like to schedule that for a week from Tuesday?"

"Sure. Uh, just out of curiosity, how much do those run?"

She squinted and clicked a few keys. "It looks like Doctor Livingstone quoted that for $1250, but it could vary up to $150 depending on how the procedure goes."

I gulped. "$1250!"

"That's industry standard pricing, Mr. Walker, but of course, if you have insurance, they will cover whatever your plan allows."

"No, I ain't got insurance! I just paid with my debit card, didn't I?"

The receptionist winced. "I hear this almost every day, Mr. Walker. We do understand that dental insurance is costly, and most ranchers do not carry it. We offer a payment plan if you might be interested."

I stuffed my wallet back in my pocket. "No way. I'm not breaking the bank on somethin' that don't hurt. You can tell that dentist to stick it."

She frowned and tapped a few more keys. "I'll keep your file in the system in case you change your mind, sir."

Hah. Fat chance of that. I just tipped my hat and shoved open the door. What a waste of a perfectly good afternoon.

My phone didn't even get through the first whistle from "*The Good, the Bad, and the Ugly*" when I swiped the screen up and put it to my ear. "Dusty? How's the honeymoon? What's the weather like in Fort Worth? You're not comin' back early, are you? Cause we're fine here. Cows are just doin' what cows do. Everything okay?"

He was laughing. "Hold off on the twenty questions! Everything's fine. Jess and I are having an amazing time, and it's actually sunny here."

"Uh-huh. I hate you now." I popped the door of my truck open and fiddled around in my pocket for my keys. Dusty always said I should keep it locked, but what for? Everyone in town knew my truck, and they knew better than to mess with it. "So, what's up? Why are you calling?"

"Yeah, hang on. Ran into a friend of yours, and he wanted to say hi." The phone got muffled for a few seconds. Then a new voice came on.

"Why, you dirty old windbag."

My grin probably split my face. "Joe Watson! I figured you'd be in jail somewhere!"

"Good behavior. Man, what's it been, five years?"

I blew my cheeks out in thought. "At least. What year was it when we ran into you in Tulsa?"

"Too long ago, whatever it was. Hey, how's the ranch treating you?"

"Oh, can't complain. We're short-handed now, since that old coot who handed you his phone up and got married. Who plans a wedding in the spring, right? How's the rough stock business?"

Joe laughed on the other end. He and his family were contractors for some of the rodeo circuits, and they had a few prize-winning bucking bulls that were worth a mint. "I was just telling Dusty here that Dad's trying to grow the business and looking to hire a few guys who know their stuff. You ever get tired of pullin' calves and fixin' fence, you give me a call."

"Hah. Yeah, I'll think about it."

"No, you won't, but it's nice to talk to you, anyway. You still got my number, don't you? Give me a holler sometime!"

"You too, Joe. Say hi to your dad for me."

"Will do, Luke! I'll give Dusty back his phone now. Boy, howdy, he's sure a lucky guy. Have you seen his new wife?"

I laughed, and I heard Dusty doing the same on the other end. "Yeah, I dated her first. Take care of yourself, Joe."

"Same to you, man."

Dusty came back on, telling Joe goodbye before picking up to talk to me. "Thought you'd like to say hi to Joe."

"Yeah, that was awesome. How'd you run into him?"

"Oh, Jess had some old friends from her rodeo queening days who wanted to meet us for dinner, and he came with them. Small world, you know."

"Sure is. What day are you coming back?"

"Wednesday. Cheapest day for flights. How are things holding up at home?"

I started the truck and waited until the Bluetooth stereo picked up the phone call. "Dude, you won't believe it. Cody and Morgan went and rescued a bunch of horses from like the worst place I've ever seen in my life."

"What? When did this happen?"

"Yesterday. I made the mistake of not looking busy enough, and Cody dragged me along to drive the second trailer. Then he talked me into taking a stud at our place until they can get a stall built for him out at their facility."

Dusty was silent for a second. "Evan's going to kill you."

"Yeah, well, Evan don't know yet. He's been riding herd almost nonstop. Last time I saw him was two in the afternoon yesterday when he got up from a thirty-minute shut-eye to go back out and saddle up again."

"Well, how's the horse? Is he going to recover?"

"Doc Burns thinks so, but it's like nothing you've ever seen, man."

"Wow. Sorry to miss it."

"Trust me, you're not sorry. You go have a good time, hear? Calves and horses will be here when you get back."

"Right."

We hung up, and I knotted my hands around the steering wheel. Gosh, it was good to hear Joe's voice. He and I rode a lot of bulls and roped a lot of steers together, back in the day. Then I broke my knee, he moved to Texas, and we didn't see each other except maybe when we hauled a bunch of show horses to Vegas or some big event.

He had the easy job, taking prize bulls from rodeo to rodeo. Getting sponsors and talking to the bigwigs. I'd have been good at that. I wasn't sorry for choosing ranching—it was sorta in my blood—but I sometimes thought if I hadn't been born a Walker, I might've found a gig like that.

I rubbed my left knee absently, just thinking about stuff. How two old buddies can go on completely different paths because of accidents or luck. Where might I have been if I hadn't taken that fall? I used to be one of the top guys, and I still had the buckles to prove it.

Well, no point in going all dewy-eyed about it. Life was different now. Instead of an eight-second thrill, I got to look forward to birthing cows, giving a muddy horse a bath, and getting my tooth drilled by a dentist who hated my guts.

Awesome.

Audrey

"The man is a perfect child. I told him he needed to get that root canal done."

Kari shrugged helplessly. "He said it cost too much, and it wasn't bothering him, so he wouldn't schedule it."

I set my hands on my lower back and heaved a sigh. "Well, I can't help what he does. Maybe he'll come crawling back when the tooth crumbles inside his mouth."

"I sure hope so. He's a dish, isn't he?"

I rolled my eyes. "Wow. Really? Aren't you married?"

"Married, not blind. Have you ever seen eyes like that on a man? And that Hollywood-star grin all those Walkers get. Whew!" She fanned herself. "My friends and I used to trade their names in notes like playing cards to see who got which 'boyfriend' for the week. Too bad none of us ever told them we were 'going out,' huh?"

I wrinkled my upper lip. "Each to her own, I guess. I'm going to pick up Lizzy from school."

"Oh, wait. There was a phone message for you." Kari ripped a sticky note from her stack and passed it to me.

It was just a name and a phone number with a 585 area code. But I didn't need any more information than that. My hand trembled, then I folded it quickly and shoved it in my pocket. "Thanks, Kari. See you tomorrow."

I hurried to my car, ducking from the rain and hitting the unlock button about fifty times before I heard the doors click. One of these days, I was going to get rid of this stupid thing. It was supposed to be a "luxury sports car," but the only luxurious things about it were the throaty engine and buttery leather seats. It was temperamental, terrible on icy roads, and it cost a fortune to fix whenever something went wrong with it. Which was pretty much every week.

But it was better than Kat's wheezing old minivan, and I didn't have the budget for a car payment when I was still trying to get the dental practice off the ground. It started on the first try this time, and I slammed my foot down on the clutch. Jess was right about my driving—I ground the gears, and I was never much good with the clutch. Why had I let Peter talk me into buying a manual? He said it was sportier, but I never cared about that. I just bought it because I thought he'd like riding in it better than the plush sedan I'd almost bought instead.

Peter. I eased my foot off the pedal and stiffened my leg out to dig that message from my pocket. I hadn't heard from him in three or four months. Why would he have called today? I stared at the number. He must have called from the office, which meant it probably wasn't a personal call. Of course, it wouldn't be. There was nothing personal between us anymore. Not since Kat...

I sniffed and wadded the paper up. I didn't need it to remember his work number. I used to work in the same office, after all. And besides, it was after 5:30 where he was, so it wouldn't matter if I called him now or tomorrow morning. I punched the clutch again, abused the transmission a little, and spun out onto the highway toward the middle school.

"How was your day?" I peered over the wheel and avoided looking at Lizzy while I drove. I'd learned pretty quickly that I could invite her to share more if I acted casual and let her take her time rather than challenging her with eye contact.

She was quiet for a few minutes. Then, "Why aren't we going out to the after-school program at White Pines today? We always go on Thursdays."

I cocked a sideways smile and slid my gaze to her. "You know why. You had detention."

Lizzy shifted in her seat and frowned at her hands. "Isn't detention supposed to make you a better student?"

"In a manner of speaking, yes."

"Well, I didn't learn anything in detention."

I chuckled. "And here I was hoping you would learn not to hit boys with math books. Words, not fists, Lizzy."

"Yeah, but I'd have learned that kind of stuff better out at the ranch. Can't you ask the principal if I can do volunteer work or something instead?"

"Oh, girl, you don't know how lucky you are that the principal let you back into school at all. I doubt she'll commute your sentence again."

"Hmmf." She folded her arms and pouted. "Doesn't feel like luck to me."

I drank in a breath and thinned my lips. It was hard to argue with her, given the string of bad breaks she'd caught lately. But it wasn't my job to be her buddy, and I wouldn't help her by telling her she was right to feel sorry for herself. I just patted her shoulder.

"It's not forever, sweetie. You're out of detention after Wednesday, and I told Morgan we'd be up at the ranch on Thursday of next week. Jess will be back by then, and it will be like it always is."

She kicked her feet on the floorboards and shrugged. "Okay."

I waited for her to say more, but she didn't. It wasn't until we passed our street and kept on driving through town that she got a suspicious look on her face and turned to me. "Where are we going?"

"Little surprise."

"I hate surprises."

I grinned wickedly. "I know you do, which is why I do it."

"Aunt Audrey, come on!"

I laughed. "Fine. We *are* going to White Pines, just not for the after-school program. They'll be almost done for the day by the time we get there, but when I talked to Morgan, she told me they'd rescued a bunch of horses that were in a bad situation. I thought you'd like to go see them."

She straightened, clasping the sides of her seat with her fists. "Really? Can I brush them? I bet Morgan will let me lead them around and stuff."

"I guess you'll have to ask Morgan, kiddo."

"*Merde,*" I breathed.

"Does that mean what I think it does?" Morgan asked.

I looked at her with a sheepish grin. "Sorry. Four years in a language-immersion high school. Sometimes it still leaks out. Uh... what... happened to them?"

She shook her head. "I'm not really at liberty to say. Not enough food, for starters. But they're here where we can help them now, right?"

"If you say so." The horses were lined up in brand-new, individual pipe corrals with modular shelters at the front end. Fresh sand and rubber mats had been laid down for footing, and every pen had a brimming bucket of clean water and a hay feeder. Each horse had room to move around, but they could also just rest inside their shelters if they wanted to. But nice as it all was for them, it almost didn't seem like it would be enough.

I swallowed and risked a glance at Lizzy, sticking her hand through the bars to pet any horse that wandered near. She didn't shrink at all from the pitiful forms in the corrals. Well, why would she? She was used to seeing her mother wasting away to skin and bones, and she still loved her. Why would some skinny horses bother her? "Should she be doing that?" I asked Morgan. "Are they sick or anything?"

"It's fine. Just don't let her touch any of the others here because these are being quarantined for now." She crossed her arms and frowned. "I probably shouldn't have had you guys come up yet, in hindsight. They're not exactly available for public viewing, and most people find it hard to see them like this. But when you said Lizzy was having a bad week…"

"This means the world to her. Really. Say the word, and she'll be out here every day hand-feeding them. She'd probably even find some way to talk me out of making her go to school."

She chuckled. "Well, we really could use the help. When she's through with detention, I'll put her to work every afternoon, if she wants."

I narrowed my eyes as I watched my niece, giggling as one horse tried to lip her fingers through the bars of its pen. She'd never get her homework done, and her grades would slip even further if she started working for Morgan. But it seemed like Lizzy needed something the books just couldn't give her. "I'll talk to Kat about it," I promised. "What do you have to do?"

"We're going through them all for health checks, hoof trims, managing any urgent things. There's one horse with a bad infection in his leg that—"

"No, I meant for Lizzy. What would she do?"

"Oh. Well, anything, really. Cleaning stalls, feeding. They need round-the-clock care right now." She gestured to a hose at the end of the row. "It's leg washing day. We don't want to chill them, but some of them are fighting fungal infections on their lower legs from all the mud they were standing in. The guys are getting ready to clean some of them up as much as we dare."

"Guys?" My eyes followed where she'd pointed, and I groaned. Cody was uncoiling the hose from the water faucet while another tall cowboy was bent over a portable water heating unit. I knew that hat. I didn't even have time to shield my face and walk away because Lizzy squealed and ran toward him.

"Luke!"

The cowboy hat jerked up, and a broad grin flashed. "Well, howdy there, Dead Eye!"

Lizzy was still running, and she produced a fist that I was just sure would turn into a solid right hook into Luke Walker's jaw. Not that I'd blame her, but before I could put a stop to it, Luke put up his own fist, and they pounded their knuckles together with a crack loud enough to be heard down the shed row.

"What're you doing here, scamp?" he laughed.

"Aunt Audrey brought me to see the horses."

The cowboy hat tipped my way, and I could see the muscles of his jaw clenching even from where I stood. "Oh, I see." His eyes cut away. "You been stayin' out of trouble?"

"Nope," Lizzy answered, with more than a hint of pride in her voice.

"Atta girl. Help me twist this hose onto the water heater, will you? These things always get me." He bent over again, fumbling with the threads of the hose. Cody stood at the faucet, shaking his head, and Morgan was giggling beside me.

"You're turning it the wrong way," Lizzy said. "Here, let me show you."

"Oh, is that what I'm doing?" Luke straightened and let her take over. "Funny, I never can get those things on right. Thanks, pal."

Lizzy twisted the hose on, wrenching it so hard I heard her grunt with the effort. "There. It will work this time. You have to go *this* way to tighten it and *that* way to loosen it."

"Got it. Think we can remember that, Cody?"

Cody was leaning on a fence rail, ducking his face so Lizzy wouldn't see him grinning. "Yep. I'll try to remember. Are you ready now?"

"If Lizzy says so. Turn the water on, and we'll see. Hey, kid, wanna help bathe some horses?"

She stiffened, then whirled toward me. "Can I, Aunt Audrey?"

I was already shaking my head. Kat's home nurse was supposed to leave at five, and we still had dinner to start and Kat's dialysis to run. But nobody needed to hear all our problems, and Lizzy didn't need me to remind her of our responsibilities at home. "Not today," was all I said.

At least she didn't whine about it like most kids would. No—it was worse because her broken look made me feel like the bad guy. She just froze, sagged a little in defeat, and I heard her sigh when she turned back to Luke Walker. "Guess not."

His gaze flashed to me, and his jaw set. "Waaallll," he drawled. "'Nother time, I s'pose."

"Yeah. See you."

"You too, kid." He tipped his hat to her, then flicked on the power to the portable water heater. And never looked back at me, even to say goodbye.

Chapter 6

Luke

I swung back up on my good ranch horse, Tucker, and coiled my rope. That was the second calf I'd had to help birth in the last four hours. Fortunately, it had been easy—mama cow might've done fine on her own, but she'd been starting to struggle a bit. I don't like to let cows get too stressed, so Danny and I gave her a little help.

I turned my wrist over to look at my watch and whistled. Eight A.M. already. "Hey, Danny! I gotta go back for a bit."

He just lifted a hand and continued on his circle. He'd keep an eye on this bunch until Brandon or Evan rode out to spell him. I clucked to my horse and headed up to the barn.

Emily had offered to help with feeding that stud when I was out working, but she had stuff to do, too. Besides, I wanted to do it myself. That way, I could make sure it got done right. And didn't it seem like it would be easier for the stud to relax and trust people again if he didn't have a dozen new people to get to know all at once?

I had some of our best small bales of alfalfa pulled down for him, and I'd started to get a good feel of how much he'd eat in four hours. Doc wanted me to keep him on small servings because too much all at once would jam up his digestive system. I couldn't have anyone else getting in there and making a fudge of it because they gave him too much or something.

Not that he didn't look like he needed more. I leaned on the stall door and tried to spot any improvement since he came three days ago. He was cleaner and didn't smell like an old swamp anymore. Better hydrated, so he looked a little less skinny because of that. And his feet were a lot better, though it would take a few months to really get them in shape. But he was still a rack of bones. Morgan said it would take a long time to put that weight on, if we did things right, but by golly, it hurt to take things so slow.

"Hey, Luke, I was looking for you."

My stomach crawled when I heard Evan's voice down the barn aisle. He still hadn't seen the stud, as far as I knew, but it was too late to hide him now. Evan was strolling my way—hands in his pockets, head down like always. I just leaned on the stall door, crossed my boots, and waited with a twig of alfalfa between my teeth.

"Dad wants us to take a load of steers to Blackfoot today. Caught wind that the market is..." Evan stopped and narrowed his eyes. "What's that?"

I pulled the alfalfa stem out of my mouth. "What's what?"

Evan pushed me aside to point at the quarantine stall. "*That*, right there."

I stuck the hay back between my teeth and shrugged. "It's a horse."

He gave me a sour look. "Where did it come from? We don't own anything that looks like that, and it doesn't look like something even *you* would buy."

"Nope. It sure don't."

Evan glanced between the stud and me. "I'm waiting."

I sighed and tossed the hay stem. "It's a rescue from White Pines. They got involved in a seizure case over in the next county."

Evan's jaw clenched. "The one I read about in the paper?"

"I don't know. Maybe. Cody knows all about it. You could ask him."

"I'm asking you. What I want to know—" Evan stabbed a finger at the stall—"is how that horse got here. We aren't a rescue, and we sure as heck can't afford to have it bringing contagion onto the property. We have over a thousand animals on this ranch, and—"

"Yeah, yeah, I know. I've got him quarantined, and Doc Burns checked him all over. Tests came back clear so far."

"The first tests, but what about incubation periods? He could have Strangles or Sleeping Sickness or even that new strain of Rhino that was dropping healthy horses like flies last year. You can't quarantine an airborne virus, Luke!"

I swallowed. "Come on, Evan, he's fine. The only thing wrong with this horse is a serious underexposure to food."

He dropped his hand in disgust. "I can't believe you. First, you drain your bank account buying a horse you can't even use, then you bring *this* onto the property? What's wrong with you?"

I stuffed my hands in my pockets and shrugged. "Cody and Morgan didn't have a place for a stud."

"And I suppose we're supposed to feed him and care for him? Wear out our ranch hands looking after a charity case, and expose our horses to whatever hitchhikers he may have brought along? He's riddled with lice, at the very least."

"No, he ain't. I checked him over, and he's fine. And I've been takin' care of him, so no one else has to."

Evan glared, his nostrils twitching. "I'm just going to say this one time. Get. Him. Out. Of. Here." He spun and stalked off. "And get the other stock trailer hooked up to haul some steers!" he called over his shoulder.

I rubbed my chin as I watched my older brother go. Well... he wasn't wrong. One bad virus going through the barn could set off a wildfire that would wipe out our stock, starting with our valuable show horses, then our good using horses and broodmares, and even our youngsters. There weren't too many things that could jump from horses to cows, but maybe the odd bacteria...

Naw, it wouldn't come to that. We'd already know if this horse had anything bad, wouldn't we? For one thing, he wasn't in good enough shape to fight off anything serious. He'd already be a goner if he was carrying anything to worry about. I stared at him for another minute, trying to decide if his breathing was any heavier than it had been yesterday. And that wasn't lethargy in his eyes, was it? Nothing more than before, anyway.

He'd be fine. Nothing wrong that a few months of good feed wouldn't put right. I went to wash up and ask Emily to take care of the next feeding. Guess I was heading to Blackfoot.

Audrey

Peter's phone rang a third time with no answer. I drummed my fingers on the reception desk at work. If it went through a fourth ring, I'd hang up and try again later.

I hadn't actually meant to call him back on his personal phone, but my memory came up with the wrong number, and I just crossed my fingers and let it go. But he'd called me on my office number instead of my cell, which was as clear a message as he could have possibly sent that this was a business call. Unless, maybe, he didn't have my new number.

No, I was pretty sure of it. He had to be calling about work—though what he could have wanted, I didn't know. I'd already told him I couldn't come back to my old job until things here were... were...

"Hello?" a woman's voice answered.

I blinked. "Uh... Hel... Hello. May I speak to Peter, please?"

"He's with a patient right now. May I take a message?"

My fist caught the pendant of my necklace and worked into a knot. Why did hearing a woman on his phone bother me? She was probably just his hygienist or something. "Just tell him Audrey returned his call."

"Audrey. Okay, I'll do..." In the background, I could hear Peter saying something. "Oh, wait a minute."

The phone went silent for a few seconds, and then his voice came on. "Audrey? Darling, is that really you?"

I smiled into the phone and tucked a lock of hair behind my ear. "Hi, Peter. It's been a while."

"I was starting to wonder if you were still alive. Your cell number doesn't work, and you had some mail show up here after being forwarded from your old apartment."

"Mail? That's weird. Anything important?"

"Oh, just junk mail. The odd jewelry catalog, a magazine or two. Did you change your cell number?"

I toyed with the phone cord. "Yeah, a few months ago. I get a lot of calls from Kat's doctors and Lizzy's school, and interstate long-distance charges are still a thing here."

"Get out. Where are you living, in a cave?"

I chuckled, smiling into the phone. It was good to hear his voice. "It's a small town. The nearest hospital is more like a band-aid center. It isn't much bigger than your dental office."

"And that right there is why I'm calling. Are you sitting down?"

I swiveled in Kari's desk chair and leaned back, crossing my ankles and propping them on a stool. "Alright, I'm as 'down' as I can possibly be. Hit me."

"I'm opening up a second office!"

A second office? Where, like upstate? Did that mean...?

"Audrey, are you there? Did you hear me?"

"Yeah, I did. So, what, this will be a satellite location?"

"Satellite?" He laughed. "No, Aud, this will be a state-of-the-art clinic, bigger than the original one and twice as nice. And if everything goes to plan, I'll be opening a third by the end of next year. What do you say?"

I tugged on the phone cord, trying to find the words. "Ah, I mean, it's amazing. Congratulations!"

"Thanks, but what do you say about the job? I need you, Aud."

I turned and put my feet down. "You didn't say this was a job offer."

"Well, what else would it be? I need the best of the best, and naturally, I'm starting with you. How about it? Like to have your picture at the top of the wall? Lead surgeon! You earned this, Audrey, and it's your turn now. You can name your salary, and I'd even consider a partnership in the near future."

My mouth ran dry. "Peter, this is... I don't know what to say."

"Say you'll be on the next flight home!" he laughed. "But I know you need a little time. I get it. How is your sister?"

I swallowed and leaned my forehead on my hand. "Not good."

"Oh, darling, I'm sorry. But you knew when you went back there that this was probably coming, didn't you?"

My teeth ground. Peter wouldn't mean to be insensitive—he wouldn't say that if he could see my face. He was right, though. I'd told him before I ever packed my car that my time in Idaho would be short. Because time was one thing Kat didn't have much of. It just stung to be reminded of it. "I don't know," I bit out. "It's just too soon to say."

He was quiet for a few seconds. "Well, I don't mean to rush you. I'm still signing contracts, but I wanted you to be the first to know."

Was that a tear burning the corner of my eye? I sniffed and cleared my throat. "Thanks for thinking of me. Congratulations, Peter. I'm so proud of you."

"Hey, gorgeous, I wouldn't be here if it weren't for you. You deserve to have your name on that wall more than anyone I know. You'll think about it?"

"I don't need to think about it. I'd really love to take you up on it tomorrow, but you know I can't just leave."

"I understand. I can't wait forever, but the job's yours if you want it, and I'll hold it for you until the very last second."

"Thanks." I sniffed again, then straightened when I saw Kari walking in from her car. "Peter, I need to go. It's been nice hearing from you."

"You too, darling. And hey, call me sometime so I have your cell number again."

I laughed. "I'll do that. Take care of yourself, Peter." I set the phone on the rest and folded my hands. I was still staring unseeingly at the desk when Kari's keys jingled in the door, and she blew in with a rainy gust of wind.

"Oh, Audrey! I didn't know you were already in. Sorry I'm late!"

I stood. "You're not. I came in early because I had some calls to make."

She glanced at the clock on her phone, sighed in relief, and set her purse down. "Anything I can help with?"

I smiled brightly and hung up my coat. "No. Everything's fine. Ready to start the day."

Kari shrugged. "Okay, boss."

Luke

It was late afternoon when I pulled into the driveway at home. Evan had taken another rig, and he'd stayed in Blackfoot to watch the Saturday auction and see if there were any pedigreed heifers worth buying. That gave me a whole day to figure out what to do about the mangy stud in the quarantine stall.

I stepped on the parking brake and sighed as I turned off the truck. Cody had dumped this problem on me. He could darn sure deal with it. I should just make him take that horse home with him and be done with it.

But something got under my skin when I thought about that. I couldn't really say what it was. Maybe it was just satisfying to give a critter food and shelter after he hadn't had them in far too long. Watch him start to come alive again. Sure, I could do the same thing if the horse was out at White Pines, but there was just something about knowing I'd been the one to make a difference. Like I was needed or something.

I grabbed my hat and stepped out of the truck, headed toward the barn. But I hadn't got very far when motion over at the bunkhouse caught my eye. The door was hanging open, and I just saw the tip of a dog's tail disappearing inside. Hard to even say which dog it was, but I had a good guess.

I walked over to the porch and whistled. "Daisy, get out of there! Come on, you old varmint! Get your muddy paws off the furniture."

I heard a couple of thumps, then Meryl Justice came to the door, a dusting rag in her hand. "What's that? Oh, hello, Luke." Daisy was peeking guiltily at me from behind her legs.

I backed away and held up a hand. "Sorry, Meryl. Thought Daisy pushed the door open. She's been nigh insufferable with Dusty gone."

"Oh, I know," she laughed. "I told her she could help me get the place ready for when he and Jess get home from their honeymoon. Care to see?"

I stuffed my hands in my pockets and shrugged. "Sure." What would there be to see? It was just the old bunkhouse, and no one expected it to be anything different. But Meryl was nice, and a good cook. You never offend a good cook, not if you know what's good for you. I followed her inside.

"Wow." I whistled. "What'd you do? The place looks all homey now."

"Oh, it was nothing. Jess's dad brought some of her things over yesterday, and Blake and I put out some of the wedding gifts. Silverware, plates, some towels, and things. Do you like the quilt?" She gestured to the back of the old wooden rocking chair.

I nodded. "Did you make that?"

"Me? No, that was one of your mom's. She had it tucked into her hope chest, made specially for Dusty. I found one with each of your names on them, except for Evan. Blake said she'd probably meant them to be wedding gifts for her boys, so I 'spect Evan already has his, and I gave Cody and Marshall theirs."

So that meant there was one of Mom's quilts still waiting for me? Huh. That would be just like my mom. She probably made a baby outfit for each of her future grandkids, too. Some part of me wanted to see that quilt she'd made for me, but if Mom kept it back till I found a bride... well, maybe I'd never see it. I let go of a slow breath. "That's... that's real nice, Meryl."

She nodded and sniffed lightly. "I figured Marci would want someone to remember. Well!" She set her hands on her hips. "It's real convenient that you showed up because I need someone to help me move something. Come on." She waved for me to follow her back to the little bedroom.

"What are we moving?"

Meryl opened the door and tackled the bare mattress. "This awful thing. It might have been good enough for Cody when he was a bachelor, but Dusty and Jess need something that doesn't have springs popping out of it."

I moved around and grabbed the other side for her. "It's not like they're going to be living here for long. They'll be breaking ground on their house this spring."

"And until they move in, they deserve something that won't put their backs out. Your dad and I bought them a new mattress. Didn't you see it out on the front porch?"

I hadn't paid much attention, but I just grunted and hefted the mattress. I could have wrestled the floppy old thing myself, but Meryl wanted to help, so I followed her out to the front porch with it. "Want me to haul it off?" I offered.

"Not until you help me get the new one inside. Come on!"

I put my shoulder into it and just carted the whole thing in myself, with Meryl holding doors out of my way as I went. I got it to the bedroom and she pointed which way she wanted me to turn it, then I flopped the new mattress onto the bed frame. "There." I smacked my hands together. "That'll do."

She framed her fists on her hips and nodded in satisfaction. "Thank you, Luke. I'll get this made up so they have something to come home to after their late-night flight. Thought I'd have some of that chuck stew waiting for them in the fridge in case they're hungry. And doesn't Dusty love cornbread?"

I studied her for a minute. "You know, you don't have to do all this, Meryl. Dusty and Jess are big kids."

She grinned and waved a hand. "Yes, they are, and I'm sure they'll want to set things up their way. They might end up changing everything, and if it were someone I didn't know as well, I wouldn't even try for fear of stepping on toes. But you know how modest Dusty and Jess are. They don't ask a thing for themselves, and sometimes it's those folks who really appreciate a little help the most. I hope they feel loved, that's all."

I scratched my eye and grunted. She was probably right about Dusty, but I wasn't one to stick around for mushy talk. "Well. I'm—I'm gonna go feed. You're good people, Meryl."

She caught my coat sleeve as I moved away, pulling me to a stop and staring up into my face. Then she patted my cheek, kinda like Mom used to do. "So are you, Luke. No matter how you try to hide it."

Audrey

I was scrolling through a message from Kat's doctor when Lizzy's brown eyes appeared over the top edge of my phone. "Is my dad coming?"

I blinked and flipped to the clock on my phone screen. It was hard not to scowl in front of her. James, Kat's ex, was scheduled to pick up his daughter on Fridays at six. But it was almost seven now, with no sign of him. He'd been known to show up at ten at night or not at all, and he wasn't good about calling. "He's supposed to be here anytime," was all I could say. "I'm sure he'll be here soon."

She didn't answer. Just turned away and plopped down into the chair beside the couch. I glanced at her a few times, but her eyes didn't leave the front window.

It wouldn't do any good for me to try to apologize for James Tracy. He'd let his daughter down plenty of times—at least once a month, he wouldn't show up, and he'd "forget" to call. The first time it happened after I'd moved in, I'd baked her a huge chocolate cake to try to make up for the disappointment. And I'd learned something that night—I couldn't fill the hole in her heart with cake, but I sure could give her a bellyache. So, I didn't give her chocolate anymore.

And I didn't make a big deal of him not showing up. I'd learned to let Lizzy handle it in her own way, and when she finally gave up looking for him for the evening, she usually ended up following me around the house. That was when I'd break out the puzzles or a movie or something. But that usually didn't happen for another hour or two.

I tried to finish cataloging Kat's medications so I could check back with her doctor, but Lizzy propped her elbows on the arm of the couch and just stared at me. I sent her a few sideways glances, but she hardly blinked. "Yes?" I asked at last.

She shrugged. "What?"

"I'm wondering what you want, that's what. You don't normally stare at me without wanting something."

"I don't want anything. I was just thinking."

I stretched back on the couch. "About?"

Lizzy pursed her lips. "Aunt Audrey, I've made up my mind. I'm going to drop out of school."

She said something like this about once a month, and I had my standard set of replies. "So, you've decided, have you? Well, that will make my life easier, not having to buy you school clothes or get you to the bus on time."

She narrowed her eyes. "I mean it. I'm dropping out on Monday."

"Okay." I shrugged. "And what do you plan to do instead?"

"I'll be a cowgirl, of course. I'll go work for a ranch."

"Oh, of course. I should have guessed. And... ah, how do you plan to get there?"

Lizzy lifted her chin off her arms. "Well, you'll drop me off. Then I can stay there all the time. All the big ranches have places for their workers to stay."

"But they don't cook for them. What about your meals?"

Her eyes clouded for the first time. "I'll figure something out."

"I'm sure you will. What ranch do you think you will work for?"

She grinned. "Luke Walker would hire me. I know he would. He said I swept his barn cleaner than he's ever seen it. And when I'm not working for him, I could volunteer with Morgan. She can't hire any more people for money—she already told me that—but she always needs volunteers, so I'd work for Luke in the morning and Morgan in the afternoon."

Luke Walker, again. Why in the world would Lizzy have taken a liking to that hare-brained cowboy? I was trying to think of what to say to that when a pair of headlights swept across the front window. I sighed in relief and just blurted whatever came to mind.

"Fine, Lizzy. You go apply for that job if you want, but it'll have to wait a few days. Your dad just pulled in. Go get your bag, okay?"

"Yes!" She hopped up and bounded to her room, and I closed my eyes to count to three again. She was only twelve. Stubborn and adventurous, and absolutely fearless. In a few more years, it was going to be impossible to argue with her when she came up with these schemes of hers. And that terrified me because unless something changed drastically, I'd be the only voice of reason to talk some sense into her.

James was still sitting in his car, not even coming to the door. I glared at him through the window, but he wasn't looking up. He actually had the nerve to honk when Lizzy took a few extra seconds to appear. Oh, I'd love to give him a piece of my mind! But then he'd call Kat and complain about me again, and she didn't need that.

"Bye, Aunt Audrey!" Lizzy called as she raced through the house. I jumped when the door slammed. And then everything was still. Not a sound echoed through the house but the ticking of the clock from Kat's bedroom.

Chapter 7

Luke

"How's he looking?" I asked.

Doc Burns pulled the stethoscope out of his ears and stood back from the black stud. "About the same as yesterday, Luke. His lungs are clear, temperature normal, no nasal discharge. Has he been coughing? Not cleaning up his food? Why did you need me to rush back out to look at him?"

I shrugged. "Evan's all hot under the collar about him being here. Says he'll make every horse in the barn sick."

Doc patted the stallion's bony wither. "Have you been following the quarantine protocols?"

"Yeah. I'm not dumb. But Evan's all worried about something airborne, like strangles or influenza. He doesn't have anything like that, does he?"

The vet chuckled and started to put away his equipment. "I don't see much risk of that. The horses from that place had lots wrong with them, but I haven't seen or heard of anything infectious showing up. They weren't exposed to anything but each other for who knows how long. If any of them were sick, odds are we'd have started seeing something by now. You can tell Evan I said that."

I rubbed my jaw. "Okay. Well, what about his weight? He's looking better, isn't he?"

Doc Burns stood back and tilted his head. "Too soon to say, but his eyes are a little brighter."

"See, that's what I mean! He's already improving, right?"

The vet laughed. "Sure, Luke. This one's probably going to make it. You can start doubling his hay per feeding for a couple of days, and if he still does fine with that, you can keep food in front of him twenty-four-seven. In about another ten days or so, we can talk about introducing some grain. But I imagine Morgan will have a place for him by then, right?"

"Morgan? Oh. Right. I'm supposed to help Cody build that pen later today."

Doc nodded. "Then he'll be out of your hair, and Evan won't have to worry. See you in a week or so, Luke."

I grunted and slid the stall door shut as Burns headed out for his truck, then tossed another flake of hay through the feed window. "Hear that, old man?" I asked the stud. "Doc says you get a bigger lunch today. You slick that up now, and you can have some more in a few hours."

I don't know why I bothered talking to the horse. He usually stood warily in the back of the stall whenever I was around, the whites of his eyes showing like he thought I was going to beat him or something. What in blazes had happened to this horse? The more I thought about it, the more I wanted some answers.

I stared at him through the bars for another minute, then sighed and stepped my boots into the bleach bath outside the stall. I still had to shower and change before I went back out to the herds. Even if

Doc said the stud was probably fine, no one was going to accuse me of cutting corners on the two-week quarantine.

"You had the vet out again?" Cody asked. "What for?"

I drove the post-hole digger into the hole again, cleaning up the edges left by the tractor auger. "Just makin' sure everything's okay. What's the matter with that?"

"It's Saturday. Vets charge extra for after-hours and weekend calls, and if it wasn't an actual emergency—"

"I got it. I paid him myself, so the rescue doesn't have to worry about it."

He squinted. "Luke, you remember this horse is part of a legal seizure, right? He's basically a ward of the state. You couldn't buy him even if you wanted to. Are you sure you aren't getting too attached?"

"Me? I'm not attached to no horse."

"Uh-huh. And whenever I catch you loving on Duchess..."

"She's pretty and sweet," I said as I scraped another load of dirt out of the hole. "And she's Dusty's horse, so I just pamper her for him while he's gone."

"Oh, right."

"Yeah, that's right. There, do you think this will work?"

Cody leaned over the hole and nodded. "Good enough. Help me with the post."

We each grabbed an end of the six-by-six post to heft it toward the hole. Cody dropped his end down into it, and I lifted mine until the post was propped crookedly upright. This was the last of the four tall posts that would support the stud's new shelter at White Pines. Today we were setting these in concrete, and then we'd have the framing and the sheet metal done over the next couple of days. After that, the fence rails could go up, and the stud would no longer be my problem. Not that I minded that much anymore, but... well, this was probably the best place for him.

We got the job done for the day, and we were putting the tools in the back of the farm pickup when Cody's phone went off. He grinned as he answered with the speaker on. "Hello, my love! Don't say anything bad about Luke because he's listening."

Morgan was laughing. "Then you can tell Luke that dinner's ready, and I made extra. Want to join us, Luke?"

Cody grimaced and made a slashing motion across his throat. Morgan's cooking was the butt of a lot of jokes, but I'd had her food, and it wasn't half bad. I pulled off my gloves and stuffed them in my coat pocket. "If you're offering, I'll eat."

"You sure about that?" Cody asked.

"I can hear you, you know," Morgan teased.

Cody laughed. "Just kidding, love. We'll be up in a few."

Audrey

One of the most uncomfortable things I did these days was balancing Kat's checkbook. I didn't mind helping her bathe and dress and all the other personal things she needed help with. I wasn't bothered by the cooking and the cleaning and the getting Lizzy to and from school. But trying to make sense of the wreck of my sister's financial life just broke my heart.

It wasn't just the medical bills. The problems started years earlier, back when James emptied her checking account when he left her. She tried to stay afloat, and for years, I'd thought she was doing okay. But when I found out her health had been struggling even then, and she kept getting fired from her jobs for being sick too often... well, it made sense now that she'd never been able to catch up again. Disability checks only went so far.

And her ex-husband was no help. He sent his child support when he felt like it, which wasn't too often, and he always had some iron-clad excuse. Even if Kat wanted to take him to court for back payments, it wasn't like there was anything to get. And she didn't want to rob Lizzy of her father. The whole thing was a snowballing nightmare. If it weren't for me paying most of the bills, Kat and Lizzy would have been homeless by last year.

I sighed as I closed the lid on the laptop. Another month's bills paid, and just in time for Kat's dialysis machine to beep. She was in the living room with me this evening, watching television. At least, the TV was on. I leaned over her chair and discovered she'd fallen asleep. "Kat," I whispered. "Time's up."

She blinked and drank in a sigh, then sleepily offered her arm for me to unhook the tubes. "Can you take me to bed early? Tired."

"Sure. Let's just get this... and up we go. Can you walk?"

Kat put an arm around my neck, but she was so thin and weak that I could have carried her easier. How long would it be before her muscles simply... quit? I didn't like thinking about that.

"Can you have Lizzy come in?" Kat slurred as I helped her into the bed.

"Darling, she's at her dad's house tonight. She'll be home tomorrow." I stroked the hair from my sister's head and searched her eyes for understanding. Recognition. Something.

"Oh," she sighed. And then she was asleep.

I thinned my lips. Well... no one ever said this would be easy. But watching what was left of my sister's life implode around her and not being able to do anything about any of it was like a black cloud on my heart.

Half an hour later, I was in the kitchen, chopping vegetables for tomorrow's soup, when my phone rang. It was Lizzy.

I wiped my hands on a towel and answered. "Hello?"

"Aunt Audrey? Can you come pick me up?"

"Not really. You're supposed to be with your dad all weekend."

"Yeah, but he's not here. I don't like being in the house by myself."

The hair on the back of my neck prickled. "You're alone? Where did he go?"

"I dunno. Some girl called him, and he left."

My lip curled, and I was already walking to the hall for my coat. "He left you home alone, and he's out with some girl? And he didn't say where? When will he be back?"

Lizzy was quiet for a few seconds. "Last time, he was out all night."

"*Last* time? This has happened before? I'm on my way."

I thought I heard a faint sniff, but I couldn't be sure. "Okay."

Luke

"That was, hands-down, the worst stew I've ever had." I raised my spoon to Morgan in salute. "Got any more?"

Morgan chuckled as she passed me the ladle. "I feel honored. I've heard the legends about yours... what was it? Cabbage stew?"

"With sausage. And carrots and celery and onions. And I like to add a little jalapeno to mine. Warm ya right to your toes."

"In all the wrong ways," Cody said with a wink at his wife. "Ever have your dinner eat a hole clean through your stomach lining?"

"Guess only the real men can handle it," I answered as I dug into my second bowl. "But this one's pretty edible, too. Except for these green things. What *is* that stuff?"

Morgan grinned and shook her head. "That's asparagus, Luke. It's good for you."

I wrinkled my nose. "It ain't good for you if you can't choke it down."

Morgan leaned her head toward Cody, who had slipped his arm behind her. "Should I be offended?"

"Nah. He's just jealous that your cooking is getting better because his never will. I thought it was delicious, baby." He kissed her then, sliding his hand up to cup her cheek and twine in her hair. She giggled and kissed him back.

And I just stared. I think my mouth was even hanging open for a few seconds.

"What's the matter with him?" Morgan whispered.

"Like I said. He's jealous." Cody pulled his wife closer for a little more.

I swallowed. "I ain't jealous. Come on, man, we're eating! You know what? I got better stuff to do than sitting here watching you two." I stood up and grabbed my hat.

"See you tomorrow, then?" Cody asked.

I fumbled with the brim, looking down at my hands. "Yeah, sure. Tomorrow." I glanced up just briefly, at the way Cody's arm still draped intimately around Morgan's shoulders. At the way she leaned into him, the secret smiles they shared. It made my skin feel all hot and prickly.

I cleared my throat. "Anyway, uh, thanks for dinner. 'Night."

"Good night, Luke!" Morgan called as the door slapped closed behind me.

I jumped in my truck and just sat there for a minute before turning over the ignition. My whole body was crawling, and I felt like a pup after the first time it got stung by the electric fence. Lord almighty, what was wrong with me? It wasn't like I hadn't seen my brothers and friends kissing their wives. And I wasn't jealous... exactly. Morgan was a great gal, but I'd never figured her for my type.

But something I'd seen between her and Cody from day one had been eating at me, and it was starting to boil over. It was the same when I was around Marshall and Kelli, and even Dusty and Jess. What was it? They just... well, they *fit*. Like a top cowboy and his best horse, like two halves of the same whole.

Like that something in your life that you don't even know is missing until it comes up and smacks you in the face.

What would it be like to have that with someone? A girl who'd call me her own; someone tough and sassy enough to put me in my place when I deserved it, and someone just tender enough that I could be the hero for her when she needed it. But women like that don't grow on trees. I know because I've looked.

I blew out a sigh and started my truck to head for home.

Audrey

Sometimes, all you can do is scream. Beat something with your fists and sob and scream again.

I was doing all of that, and it wasn't working. My car was a groaning scrap pile on the side of the road, and nothing I could do would budge it. Oh, and to make it even better, I was in a dead zone for cell towers. No service, so I couldn't even call for a tow.

"I *hate* you, you stupid car!" I yelled. "Why don't you just *start?*" Like an idiot, I kicked the tire with the point of my shoe and—big shocker—earned myself a bruised toe. I hopped and let out a string of words I wouldn't dream of using in front of my niece, and then I kicked the door. Because I'll never learn, apparently.

"Augh!" I grabbed my sore foot and spun around to sit in the driver's seat. "Come on. Please work!" But the starter gave a cough and a wheeze, then clicked silent.

"You've got to be kidding me." I slammed my forehead on the steering wheel and didn't even try to stop the frustrated tears. "I should've taken Kat's stupid van. At least it would *drive!*" I shouted at my car. Oddly enough, it didn't answer.

I just had to wait. Someone would be along eventually, and I could only hope it wouldn't be a carjacker or a murderer. Why in heaven's name had Kat followed that loser James out to the middle of this God-forsaken nowhere? If I were back in New York, I'd have had a tow truck at my fingertips and a friend to pick me up in just a few minutes. And now I couldn't even get to my niece when she needed me!

James lived about five miles west of town in the dump of a mobile home that he'd grown up in. It was a wonder Lizzy didn't come home with fleas every week; the place was so run-down. But my problem right now was that there wasn't a lot of traffic on this highway at night, and what traffic there was could be... suspect. I had zero protection if the wrong person came along.

I growled as I flipped on the hazard lights to flag down some help, then leaned my head back on the headrest. I could be here all night. Maybe I should think about walking.

I'd been sitting there long enough to doze a little when a pair of headlights flashed in my rearview mirror. It looked like a lifted truck, something big. Maybe big enough to even give me a tow. I watched the mirror for a few seconds to see if the driver would stop. The lights swayed a little, then dipped to the right, pulling in behind me.

"Please, God," I prayed, "don't let it be a drunken axe-murderer."

A door opened, and I heard boots hitting the pavement. "Hey!" a voice called. "Do you need help?"

My heart bubbled in my throat. That sounded an awful lot like...

Luke Walker bent to look into my car window, and his eyebrows shot up in surprise. "Well, I'll be," he drawled. "Car trouble, doc?"

I closed my eyes and swallowed. *It could be worse*, I assured myself. It could be an axe murderer. I jerked the door open and pushed it, so Luke had to step back.

"I don't know what's wrong with it," I said, gesturing at my car in frustration. "It just chugged to a stop, and I can't get it to go."

"Pop the hood, and lemme take a look." Luke bent over the front of my car and waited for me to release the catch. When I did, he lifted the hood and poked around. "Your mechanic's light isn't working."

I shrugged. "Is it supposed to? I'm so used to things on this car breaking that I can't keep track."

"Uh-huh." Luke stepped back and stuck his hands in his pockets. "I know what your problem is. It's an import."

"Nothing gets by you, does it?"

He winked and tapped his forehead. "I'm good at this stuff. Naw, actually, it's probably your alternator. You've got no power."

"So... you can jump it, right?"

"Sure, but it would just strand you again in a few minutes. 'Fraid it's dead till you can get the new part in there."

I turned over my wrist to look at my watch and hissed in exasperation. Lizzy had called me an hour ago, and I still wasn't there. "Does your phone work so I can call a tow truck?"

"Shoot, naw. Nothin' works till we get over the hill. S'pose you'll have to hitch a ride."

I crossed my arms. "With you?"

He grinned. "Unless you want to wait for a better offer. Where you headin'?"

"Home, I guess."

He squinted back at my car, then looked up the road. "But you're pointing west."

"That's right. And now I have to go back to town."

He turned to the east, then swiveled around to face west again. "But you were going that-a-way. Where to?"

I rolled my neck and stared up at the dark sky. At the fresh pricks of spring snowflakes just starting to fall. Whatever I was going to do, I needed to do it soon because the weather report said we were in for another storm. "Not that it's really your business, but I was going to pick Lizzy up from her dad's house."

"What, that old mobile home on the other side of the hill?"

"That's right, but now I can't, so I need to home and get Kat's van."

"Well, why didn't you say so in the first place?" He walked back to his truck and popped open the passenger door. "Hop up, sister."

I was reaching for my purse, and I straightened, arching a brow at him. "'Sister?'"

"I could call you 'darlin',' but I don't know you that well yet. Come on, did you want to stay here?" He patted the truck seat. "Look, I've even got a seat belt, and the heater works."

I bit my lip and closed my eyes. "Fine." I walked up to his truck, but the seat was almost as high as my head. "How do I...?" I threw my purse on the floorboards and backed up to it so I could put my elbows on the seat and my feet on the running boards. I strained, and my shoes slipped on the gravel. "That won't work. Is there a handle somewhere?"

"Yeah, but you probably can't reach it. Here."

Without warning, Luke grabbed me around the thighs and picked me up, my stomach pressed against his chest, and my... well, I could feel his five o'clock shadow scratching on my sweater. I yelped and beat on his shoulders, instinctively twisting away, but in seconds, he had tossed me up into the seat and was closing the door. I glared at him as he walked around the front of the truck and got into the driver's seat.

"What was that all about?" I snapped. "You don't just grab someone like that!"

He buckled his seat belt and started the truck. "Just fixin' a problem. You couldn't get in without help, I was tired of standing out in the cold, so I fixed it."

I gritted my teeth and pointed at him. "Don't *ever* do that again!"

Luke rested his arm on the console between us and leaned over with a wicked grin. "Does that mean you want another ride in my truck sometime? We could arrange that."

I stiffened and turned straight forward. "Just drive."

He shrugged and put his foot on the gas. "Fine by me."

Chapter 8

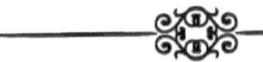

Luke

"I thought you were dropping me at home," Audrey said, twisting in the seat to look backward. Her back was rigid, her hand clenched on the armrest, and her voice was tight. "Where are we going?"

I glanced sideways at her. "You have some serious trust issues, don't you?"

She huffed a nervous denial. "You offered to take me home. I just can't help but notice we're going the wrong way."

"That's right. You said you needed to pick up the kid, didn't you? Might as well swing by and grab her first, right?"

Her shoulders relaxed slightly. "That's even more out of your way. Are you sure?"

"Ah, I got nothin' better to do."

I risked another glance at her and found her watching me suspiciously. "I'm sure you do, but..." She swallowed.

"What is it? How come you gotta go out and pick her up at..." I glanced at my clock. "Ten-thirty on a Saturday night?"

Audrey chewed her lip, then swung to look me in the face. "Her dad left her home alone, and I guess it's not the first time."

"So? She's, what, twelve? That's old enough to be home for a little while."

"All night?"

I twisted my hands on the steering wheel. "That might be pushin' it. I mean, me and Marshall and Cody, we'd go camping and hunting up in the hills at that age, but we knew how to take care of ourselves."

"And you had each other. Lizzy doesn't even have a neighbor close—at least, no one I'd trust for her to call."

I scowled and squinted through the windshield. "Kid needs a dog."

Audrey laughed. "Right, and I need another mouth to feed, another thing to look after. No, thank you."

"Nah, really. Do her good. Be good company and give her some protection, and it might even keep her out of a lot of trouble."

She shook her head. "Out of the question. She already wants to drop out of school. I don't need to give her another thing to distract her from her homework."

"How come?" I asked.

Audrey had dropped her hands in her lap, and she looked over at me with a soft arch to her brows. Dad gum, did she know how pretty she looked when she let her guard down? "What?" she asked.

I had to clear my throat. "Uh. Lizzy. How come she wants to drop out?"

"Oh." She shook her head. "She says she wants to be a rancher. Kids, you know."

"What's wrong with that?"

"Well… I mean, she can't be serious. You don't know Lizzy—next week, she'll want to be a circus performer, and the week after that, she'll decide to be a lemonade tycoon down on Main Street."

"Yeah, so what? I hear lemonade tycoons are raking it in. Think I'm in the wrong line of work."

Audrey slowly turned her head toward me, her brows pinched and something that looked suspiciously like a smile forming on her lips. "I can't decide whether you sound like a really supportive guy or a terrible influence."

I shrugged as I turned onto the gravel driveway where James Tracy lived. "Probably the second one."

Audrey

Lizzy had hardly gotten the door open when she barreled into me, head down and arms around my waist. I stiffened, my hand reflexively stroking her back. "Lizzy? Hey. What's wrong?"

She pulled away almost immediately and shrugged. "Nothing. I'm fine. What took you so long? I thought something bad happened." Then, her eyes lit on Luke, standing just behind me on the porch. "Hey, were you guys out on a date?"

I sucked in a gasp and backed away from Luke, my hands up. He was doing the same thing, his eyes wide and his head shaking. "No, no, no! Nothing like that. My car broke down, and he stopped to help me."

"Oh." She shrugged. "I guess that makes more sense. Are we going to the ranch?"

I closed my eyes and pinched the bridge of my nose. "Lizzy, it's almost eleven o'clock. Please don't be rude."

"But I wasn't rude! Can we go, Luke? Please?"

Luke chuckled and patted the top of her head. "Some other time, squirt. You got all your stuff?" He peered through the door, the muscles of his jaw clenching warily. "Your dad around?"

"Nope!" She sounded almost pleased with herself when she said that. "It's just me, and I got my bag already." She beamed up at him like he was some kind of a comic book hero, then, almost as an afterthought, smiled at me.

"Are you okay, Lizzy? You're acting a little weird." I said. The way she'd flung herself out the door at me, then casually brushed it off, had my senses tingling.

"Sure, I am. Why wouldn't I be? Are we going, or what?"

Luke's eyes met mine—just for an instant, but there was something there. A faint squint that said he'd seen something odd, too. But then he just laughed and grabbed Lizzy's backpack from her. "Yep. All aboard, kid."

"Can I ride in the back of the truck?"

"Maybe when it's not snowing." He bent down and whispered—loudly—"And when your aunt ain't lookin'." He followed this with a grin and a wink at me, and I couldn't decide if he was teasing or if he really meant it. Given that it was Luke Walker, anything was possible.

I thumbed out two tens from my wallet and offered them to Luke. "Thanks for the lift."

His brow creased, and he looked at my money like it was going to bite him. "What's that for?"

I pressed the money closer. "For gas."

"It's a diesel."

I sighed. "Fine. For your time, because you went out of your way twice. It's the least I could do. I know it's not much with fuel prices, but I can get more cash on Monday."

His cheek flinched. "Shoot, I don't want your money. Keep it."

My hand started to drop. "I need to repay you somehow."

"How do you figure?"

"Well, you didn't have to stop."

A slow grin appeared, and I remembered what everyone said about those Walker brothers. They could make a girl forget her own name with a smile like that, and from what I could see, Luke was fully aware of that fact. "Naw," he said, "I didn't have to. But my daddy'd have my head on a platter if I didn't."

"What's that supposed to mean?"

"Aw, you know. Citified car like that stuck on the side of the road? Gotta be a pretty girl inside."

I stiffened and stuffed my money back in my purse. "If you're looking for some other kind of reimbursement, I'm afraid I'll have to disappoint you."

"What?" He squinted, then his eyes widened. "Hang on, that's not what I said! I just figured you couldn't have any other help comin', and it was gettin' late."

I started breathing a little easier. "Oh."

"And besides, a guy oughta help out when he can. That's all I meant."

"I see." I narrowed my eyes and tilted my head. "Did you just say I was pretty?"

He cleared his throat and rubbed the back of his neck as his feet scuffled on the porch. "Uh. Well, I mean, you ain't Myrtle at the diner."

"Who's Myrtle?"

"You don't know her? Stop by sometime and ask her for a cup of coffee. She's the one wearing dentures and a wig."

I laughed. "I guess that's a compliment, then?"

"Sure." Luke shrugged. "Night, doc."

I couldn't help following him out to the porch as he turned and walked back to his truck. "Good night, Luke. And thanks again."

He stopped. Shuffled his feet a couple of times. Then he turned with a funny look on his face. "Say, I could use some help tomorrow. Think the kid would like a job for the afternoon? I'll pay her."

I didn't like the sound of that. Could I trust this guy with my niece? Everyone around town said the Walkers were all good people, but why would a grown man take an interest in a twelve-year-old girl?

"You can stay, too, if it makes you feel better," Luke offered, as if he could read my thoughts.

I drank in a breath. "I'll talk to her mother in the morning."

The cowboy hat nodded with a jerk. "Sounds good. 'Bout two o'clock, if you wanna come. Gate'll be open if you decide to head out."

I leaned against the porch railing and watched him climb into his truck, my mind spinning. Of all the people in town I might have expected to come to my rescue, Luke Walker was last on the list. But he'd been a gentleman—a rough one, but kind, nonetheless—and he had a way with Lizzy.

I'd be stupid to start thinking about that cowboy. He wasn't my type... like, at *all*. But as I said goodnight to my niece and finally collapsed into bed, it was hard to think about much else.

Luke

"There you are. I've been looking for you all day." Marshall walked up the barn aisle, jingling his keys. "Where's the flatbed? I was going to haul a couple of tons of hay over to White Pines."

I threw the saddle over my afternoon horse and snuggled up the cinch, avoiding looking up. "Uh. In the shop. Hooked to my truck."

"In the shop? Why? Flat tire?"

I cleared my throat and fetched my bridle. "Got a dead car on it. At least, it used to be dead. Maybe still is."

"Meryl's car? What's wrong with it?"

I shook my head and kept my gaze fixed on my gelding as I eased the bit into his mouth and the headstall over his ears.

Marshall leaned over my saddle and stared at me till I looked him in the eye. "What car? Or maybe I should ask *whose* car?"

I shrugged. "The dentist chick."

"Audrey?"

"That's the one. Came up on her last night on my way home. Bad alternator, so she was stranded."

"And she asked you to fix it? I thought she was great friends with Jess. Why wouldn't she just have it towed to the shop?"

"Jess won't be back till Wednesday. She can't be without her car till then."

Marshall squinted, then stuck a gloved finger at me. "She doesn't even know you have it."

"I was figurin' on tellin' her."

"When? After she reports it stolen?"

"Naw. I was going to drop it off after I make my circle. Danny just called, got a cow down and needs help."

Marshall raised an eyebrow. "Maybe you'd better call Audrey before she starts to worry about her car."

"How's she even going to know it's been moved? Besides, I don't have her number."

"Well, Kelli does."

I scoffed. "No way. You get her number for me, then I have to call her, and it gets all weird."

Marshall fisted his hands at his belt. "Just what's so weird about calling a woman to tell her you fixed her car for her?"

"Well, she ain't exactly my type. I call her, then I have to talk to her, and then I have to say something nice but not *too* nice, and... I'd rather just drop the car off without buggin' her. Don't want her gettin' ideas, you know."

Marshall shook his head. "You're not making sense."

"Yeah, well, I didn't say it made sense to me either." I dropped the stirrup off my saddle horn and gathered my reins to lead the horse out of the barn. "I'll get that trailer unloaded soon as I'm back from helping Danny."

"No. *I'll* go help Danny. You get that car back to Audrey so I can use the flatbed."

I blew out a sigh and scowled at my brother. "I wasn't going to be gone long. I might've had..."

"What? You might've had what?" Marshall stepped up close to stare me in the face.

"Hello?"

We both turned at the sound of a feminine voice and from the corner of my eye, I saw Marshall taking off his hat. "Oh, hello, Audrey," he said with a cheesy grin. "Fancy seeing you this afternoon."

I shot him a glare. She was at least an hour earlier than I'd figured, so how much had she overheard? But Marshall just kept grinning and even gestured with his hat to remind me of my manners. I cleared my throat and pulled off my hat.

Audrey walked slowly up the barn aisle, her dark eyes sweeping the wash rack and the tack room, and the stalls until they came to rest on us. "Sorry to interrupt, but Lizzy overheard me talking to her mother about your offer, and she's talked of nothing else since. Is that... still on? Are we early?" Her gaze flicked over Marshall and the horse I was still holding. "I made her wait in the car, just in case. If you have other work, I don't want to intrude."

"You're not intruding." Marshall pulled the reins out of my hand. "Luke was just saddling a horse for me."

My head snapped around. "What?"

"Yeah, didn't you have that thing to do?"

I gave him a blank look.

"You know, the thing?" He was smirking, the creep.

"Right. Ahem. Uh..." I put my hat back on and gave Marshall a dangerous look. If he started crowing about me and Audrey, making up ideas and blabbing them to his wife, I'd hog tie him and toss him in the iciest water trough I could find. He led the horse away, whistling his most annoying little tune and never looking back.

Audrey was watching me with a suspicious look. "Did I interrupt something?"

I shook my head. "Not really. But… I guess I'd better walk you up to the shop."

Audrey

"I don't understand. You went and picked up my car? Why would you do that?"

Luke was busy letting Lizzy twist his hand into a thumb-war, and laughing whenever she pinned his fingers. Obviously, he was allowing her to win because his thumb was half again as long as hers, but she didn't seem to care. It gave them both an excuse to avoid listening to me.

"Luke. Seriously, why did you pick up my car? What if I'd been able to get a tow truck up there and it was gone?"

He cleared his throat and looked a little embarrassed as he pulled his hand away from Lizzy. "Ah, well, I figured I'd have it back to you before old Roy down at the towing yard even returned your call."

I narrowed my eyes. "What, does that mean you planned fix it, too? How did you even intend get into it? I had the keys!"

"Yeah, but you didn't lock it. Noticed you don't lock your house door, either."

"I never had a problem before. Do I now?"

"Nah. See, I thought you'd ask Jess to fix it for you, but she and Dusty won't be back for a couple more days. And, I was going to town this morning anyhow, so..."

"What were you going to town for?" I asked. It wasn't my business, but I had my suspicions.

He rubbed the back of his neck and squinted at me. "Auto parts store."

"You bought an alternator for my car," I stated, crossing my arms.

"I might've. But I don't know if it works 'cause you took your keys with you."

Lizzy was grinning. "See, Aunt Audrey? Told you Luke's cool."

I closed my eyes and made myself take a few slow breaths. "Well... thank you, but really, I'd wish you hadn't done that. It's a finicky car, and if you mess one thing up..."

"Is that your way of saying it's a lemon?"

"I..." I sighed and rolled my eyes. "Okay, yes, it's a piece of junk, but it's all I have besides Kat's van, which barely got us here today. And right now, I really don't need things to get worse, so..."

Luke interrupted me by putting out his hand, palm up. I stared at it. "What?"

"Keys, doc."

I thinned my lips and fished them out of my coat pocket. Luke took them and hopped up on the flatbed to climb into the driver's seat of my car. "I had the battery on the charger this morning, so it oughta start," he said as he plugged the key into the ignition. "Question is how long will it keep running."

My car purred to life, and I realized that I'd been holding my breath. I really didn't even expect it to click for him, but there it was, idling as well as it ever had.

"Well?" he asked, grinning at me from the front seat.

I put my hands on my hips and smiled back with a sweet challenge. "How long before we know if it's fixed?"

He shrugged and hopped down. "You tell me. It's your car. You can hop inside and babysit it while Lizzy and I go get to work. You ready, kid?"

"Yesss!" Lizzy skipped off after him, pumping her fists in the air and whooping like a crazy thing. She really was a different person when she was out at one of these ranches. Eager and engaged and just a touch wild. But...

"What, you're just going to leave me here with the car?" I called after them.

"Unless you want to help muck some stalls," Luke said over his shoulder. "Better roll up that big door so you don't get gassed out, doc."

I just stood there, my face frozen in wonder as they walked out.

Chapter 9

Luke

"So, how long has your aunt been living with you guys?"

Lizzy leaned on her pitchfork and counted on her fingers. "Nineteen months and... four days."

I chuckled as I pushed the wheelbarrow out of the stall. "Is it that awful that you're counting the days?"

"She came the day after my eleventh birthday, so that's how I remember."

"Oh, I see." I grabbed my pitchfork and went into the next stall, and Lizzy followed. "So, what, she came to take care of your mom and stuff?"

Lizzy went quiet, working with her eyes down. "Yeah, I guess."

"Where'd she come from? I mean, where did she live before?"

She shrugged. "New York, somewhere. She says it was 'upstate.' But she used to live in Michigan, like my mom."

I stopped working. "Your mom was from Michigan? How'd she end up here?"

"I dunno. Aunt Audrey says my..." Her forehead wrinkled, and she squinted up at the ceiling in thought. "My no-account, loser dad duped her into following him out here, and he took all her money and ruined her life." She dropped her eyes back to mine, lifted her shoulders, and got back to work.

"Gee, I wonder how she really feels. Is that what you think, too?"

Lizzy tossed a forkful of bedding into the wheelbarrow, then stared at the floor. "I guess. I mean, Dad's not great at lots of stuff. But he's still... he's okay."

I lowered my own fork. "I probably shouldn't'a asked. Sorry."

She shook her head as she attacked the soiled shavings. "It's alright."

I watched her for a few seconds, but she didn't seem like she wanted to say any more. We worked for a little while in silence until at last, I frowned and stood back. "Well, I s'pose that's about it. This was the last stall in this aisle. I'll dump the wheelbarrow while you spread that fresh load of shavings, and we're done."

She was finished when I came back with the empty wheelbarrow, and I set it down to pull some cash out of my wallet. "There you go. Six stalls at six bucks apiece, that's... forty-five, right?"

"Are you that bad at math?" Lizzy giggled. "Even I know that's not right."

"Oh, well, you just count that out and tell me if I messed up." I handed her a wad of bills. "Reckon we oughta go find your aunt? I figured she'd have hunted us down by now."

"Okay, but what about that stall over there?"

I looked where she was pointing. "Oh. That's the quarantine stall. I wasn't going to have you do that one."

"Why not? There's a horse in it."

"Yeah," I grunted as I shoved my wallet back in my pocket. "He's a problem, that's what. I'll take care of his stall when I clean him up this afternoon."

Her eyes brightened. "Can I help brush him?"

"No. Your aunt really would have my head. Come on, let's go." I started for the door, but she raced around to crouch in front of me, her hands folded.

"Please, Luke? I'll be smart, and I won't do anything wild or noisy!"

"It ain't that, kid. That horse is a stud, and what's more, he's a neglect case. Don't know what's happened to him or what sorts of things might set him off."

"Okay, how about this? You handle him, and I'll stay out of the way and clean the stall. Please?"

I laughed and shook my head. "Never saw a kid so eager to muck out horse dung. What's the deal?"

"She doesn't want to go home and do her homework, would be my guess." Audrey appeared at the end of the barn aisle, her hands in her coat pocket and a wry little smile for her niece turning up those cherry lips.

I straightened and tugged at my collar. When she smiled like that, it did funny things to my stomach and it got hard to breathe. "Uh. Yeah. Car still running?"

Her gaze shifted to me, and one eyebrow raised. "It was until I turned it off. Wasn't there a faster way to test that part to see if it would work?"

"Sure, there was. I have a volt meter, but you never asked about that."

Those thick lashes flickered, and she got a dangerous look in her eye. "You mean, you could have answered the question in mere seconds, but instead, you let me sit there for forty-five minutes?"

I shrugged. "Inside of your car's warmer than the barn. Figured you were doing okay, and you knew where we were."

Her teeth flashed, and I saw her fists clench. "Uh-oh. She's counting again," Lizzy whispered.

I made the mistake of snickering.

"I am *trying* not to say something I'll regret," Audrey retorted, her eyes blazing. "Is everything a joke to you, Luke Walker?"

"Me?" I pointed at my chest. "I thought I was bein' nice. What did I do wrong?"

"You can't just make assumptions for other people!" She flicked a lock of dark hair off her face and put up her hands. "You know what? Never mind. You won't listen to me, anyway. So, *thank you* for fixing my car, but it's time for us to go."

"But, Aunt!" Lizzy complained. "Luke just said I could help him with the last horse. He's a rescue, and he needs special care."

"I didn't say you could help," I protested.

"You were about to. Please, Aunt Audrey? I'll help with dinner later and do all my homework super fast!"

And right then, I saw something melt inside that brunette's eyes. Maybe she wasn't all ice and steel after all. She took a breath, frowned sadly at her niece, then shook her head. "I don't know why I let you talk me into these things, Lizzy."

"So, I can stay? Yippee!" Lizzy dashed for the wheelbarrow and trotted down the aisle with it. "Are you gonna catch him for me, Luke?" she chirped over her shoulder.

My jaw dropped. Hornswoggled by a middle-schooler! I had a lot of words, but none of them would get out of my mouth. I just had my finger in the air, and I was trying to spit out all the reasons why it was a bad idea to let her help me with the stud. But I couldn't make so much as a squeak.

Audrey was just grinning—that sassy little smile I'd seen the night before, when I dropped her on her porch. "She got you, too, didn't she?"

I closed my mouth. "She did not. I meant to ask her to stay."

"Of course, you did. And that look on your face, like a fish gasping for air?"

"Just thinkin,' that's all."

"About?"

I coughed as I walked away. "How I'm gonna get out of this one."

Audrey

"There. See how tender his skin is there? You gotta be careful brushing that, so's you don't hurt him."

I leaned against the stall door, bundled into an extra work coat that Luke had found hanging in the tack room, watching the two of them grooming that skinny black horse. Lizzy was, for once, awed into near silence, hanging on every one of Luke's words like they were gospel.

"How'd he get that?" she asked him in a hushed voice. "Was it a fight with another horse?"

"Nah." Luke took the brush from Lizzy's hand. "It's called a bed sore. Basically, he was so bony that when he laid down, there was no padding, and he wore clean through the hair. Here, let me swab that part with some medicine."

The pair of them were working with painstaking care, going bit by bit over the ragged-looking animal to brush him and dress his sores. I'd been watching them for so long that my feet had turned numb, but it was too fascinating to look away. I knew next to nothing about horses, but it didn't take an expert to see what rough shape this poor creature was in. And Luke Walker, the craziest, most impetuous cowboy in the whole county, was nursing that scrawny creature like it was his child.

"Okay, here," he said to Lizzy at last. "Take that bucket over and fill it about halfway with warm water. Too soon for a full bath, but we'll swish his tail around in it and see if we can't get some more of the mud out of his hair." Even as he said this, he walked over to a shelf outside the stall and grabbed a pair of electric clippers.

"What are those for?" I asked.

Luke looked up like he'd forgotten I was there. "Oh, hi. I guess we'll see. Don't know if he's ever been clipped before, but it'd sure be nice to clean up some of the long hair off his lower legs. He was standing in mud when we found him, so he might have some fungus to treat. That stuff can turn foul pretty quick."

"You mean, like athlete's foot?"

"Sure, if athlete's foot can make your whole leg swell up and even spread through your system."

"It can spread and get worse? That sounds more like what a cavity can do." I crossed my arms and shot him a smirk.

He shook a finger at me. "That was a cheap shot, doc."

"And yet, I'm not at all ashamed."

"Huh. Yeah." He scratched his ear, then turned away and flicked on the clippers, his eyes on the horse. The stallion was watching him with an ear half-cocked and his muscles tense, but he didn't startle from the noise. "Well, that didn't bother him too much."

"Does that mean he's been clipped before?"

"Maybe. He might've been a pampered show horse as a youngster, and he's used to this stuff. Or it could be he's just shut down with fear. Hard to say what this fellow's history was. See his eyes? He still hasn't decided if he can trust me."

I nodded and just watched as Luke rested a hand on the horse's neck and gently brought the body of the clippers to lay against his shoulder. A muscle twitched, but the horse didn't seem to be any more afraid than he'd been before. Luke carefully moved the clippers down the horse's leg, talking to the horse the whole time. Pretty soon, he was buzzing off the long hair above his hooves. It only took a few minutes per leg, and before long, Luke was done.

"There," he said, patting the horse in satisfaction. "He's got a few scabs on his skin, but we'll be able to treat them faster now."

Lizzy was ready with the bucket, and she marched up with it. "Can I do this part?"

I didn't miss Luke's furtive glance at me. If I hadn't been there, I know without a doubt that he'd have let my niece splash a bucket of water up a strange horse's behind. I wondered how many times he'd been kicked in the head as a kid. Too many, apparently.

He cleared his throat and thrust up the sleeves of his Carhartt. "Better let me, squirt. Here we go. Just a quick rinse, get some of the clumps out. I got most of them out the other day, but this will help. When it gets a little warmer, we'll give him a proper bath with soap and everything." We watched as he dipped the lower half of the sad-looking tail in his bucket and swirled it around for a few minutes. When he handed the bucket back to Lizzy, the water was nearly black.

"There. That ought to be good for today," he announced. "We keep this up, kid, this horse'll look like a show pony in no time."

"You know," I mused, "it's too bad you don't know his name."

Luke shook his head. "Naw, it don't matter. He's going over to White Pines, just as soon as Cody and I can get that shelter finished."

I squinted and studied the tall cowboy before me. "So, first you talk about how good he's going to look after you get him healthy, then you say he won't be here for you to help. Which is it?"

He rubbed his jaw and looked up at me with a bashful smile. "Guess you caught me, doc. Truth is, I don't know what'll happen to him."

"Well, I think you should name him," I said. "Even if it's not going to stick very long. You can't just keep calling him 'horse.'"

Luke shrugged and looked at Lizzy. "What do you think, kid?"

"You definitely need to name him," she agreed emphatically. "How about Thunder?"

"Eh." His face wrinkled. "Not bad, but no self-respecting cowboy is gonna call a horse 'Thunder.' No offense, but my brothers would never let me live it down. Lemme see." He stood back, cupping his chin in his hand and frowning.

"You know, my old buddy Joe Watson used to have this black stud back in our rodeo days. It was his calf-roping horse, won tons of money for Joe and lots of other folks. Gotta be twenty years old or more by now, but I'll never forget that horse. Blacker than coal, except for these two little white spots on his left rear pastern. Joe used to call him Two Bits."

I looked down at the horse's freshly clipped legs. Not a white hair to be seen, except... I tilted my head and walked closer to the horse's flank. "Is that the same marking?" I asked, pointing at the horse's left hind leg.

"Naw. Well, not exactly. Two Bits's mark was bigger and more to the front, but this horse does have a couple little freckles of white hair down there by his hoof. Whaddaya say, Lizzy? Shall we call him Two Bits, after my buddy's horse?"

"Two Bits," she repeated in a flat voice. "Sounds dumb."

"Lizzy!"

She rolled her eyes and sighed. "Fine. Two Bits it is. Can we feed him now?"

"Sure. And then I'd better haul your car home, or Marshall will roll it off the flatbed himself."

Chapter 10

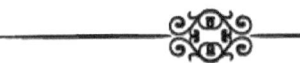

Luke

Audrey hadn't been joking about her sister's minivan. The thing was a rust bucket from the early nineties, with peeling paint, black smoke gasping out of the tail pipe, and a bad alignment problem. I made sure to stay well back as I was following her in my pickup, because I was afraid the thing would give out right there in the middle of the road. Turns out, that was the least of the problems.

The woman was the craziest driver I'd ever seen, and that was saying something. She'd launch away from a stop sign like she was trying to beat Dale Earnhardt, and passing people on the highway was like a game of Chicken, trying to see who would jerk the wheel first. When she screeched the tires to a halt in front of the house, I pulled up behind her white as a ghost.

She got out of the car, pushing her over-sized sunglasses up into her hair, and pointed to the next-door neighbor's driveway. "The Andrews are out of town, so I don't think they'll mind if you have to pull in there to turn your trailer around," she called.

I rolled down the window, my fingers still trembling on the buttons. "What are you, nuts? You almost got yourself killed about five times back there!"

She tilted her head. "When?"

"When! The whole gol-durned way from the ranch to here! How many laws did you break?"

"Technically, I don't think I broke any."

I snorted and threw my pickup into reverse to park the trailer somewhere. "Well, sweet thing, that's not how we drive around here. You're lucky no one's run you off the road."

She shook her head and just waved her hand. "You should try driving in New York. You wouldn't get two miles."

"And that's why I don't live in New York." I checked my mirrors, turned the wheel a bit, and then nosed forward into the neighbor's driveway, with the back of the trailer pointed toward Audrey's house. That would work. I hopped out and walked back to the flatbed to pull out the ramps, then rolled the car down to stop in front of her.

I handed her the keys when I got out, and she looked down at them instead of meeting my gaze. "I suppose I should thank you again for bringing my car back home." She rolled her eyes and bit her lip, like it hurt her to say it. "And for going to get it... and for fixing it."

I tipped my hat. "You're welcome. See, I'm not such a bad guy."

"I never said you were a bad guy."

"But you thought it."

"No, I..." She blew the hair off her eyebrows with a huff. "Look, you sort of caught me at a bad time during the wedding. I didn't mean to sound irritable. There's... just been a lot going on."

I shrugged. "That's okay. Not like I was trying to impress you or anything. I bet you don't even like cowboys."

"Not especially."

My mouth dropped. "I was joking."

She smiled. "And I *might* have been joking."

Oh, man. It was sure a good thing she didn't smile very often, because a look like that could get me into a mess of trouble. My heart hammered in my ears and I had to tug on my shirt collar so I could breathe proper. And I started to wonder something. Could I make her smile again? Might be worth trying. I've never been able to resist playing with fire.

"So, uh..." I doffed my hat and held it over my chest. "You know, I may not be a real mechanic like Jess, but I'm pretty good at tinkering with cars if you ever need a hand. I noticed your coolant was leaking, and you have some kind of electrical bug in the stereo system."

She blinked and caught her breath as if hesitating to answer. "That's really nice, but I don't think I'd be comfortable asking that of you."

"I offered. It's no bother."

Her lips pressed into a thoughtful pout, and she looked at the ground. "Thanks, but I'd rather not."

I swallowed. "Oh. Well, then..." I put my hat back on. "Guess this is good afternoon, then." I turned to go, but she put her hand out.

"Wait. Why did you ask Lizzy to come out to the ranch today?"

"I don't know. She's a good kid. I like her."

"But there are lots of good kids around. She told me what you paid her, and it was outrageous."

"I don't cheat kids, ma'am."

"But you paid her almost $50 for cleaning a few stalls. Stalls that you were helping with!"

I stuffed my hands in my pocket. "Yeah? It's my money. I can give it to her if I want to."

"That's not the point," she huffed in exasperation. "I just need to know if I can trust you, Luke Walker."

My forehead crunched. "Trust me? Of course, you can. What do you think I was trying to do?"

"It's just... Lizzy doesn't need anybody manipulating her. She's got things hard enough as it is."

I pulled my hands out of my pockets and held them up defensively. "Geez, is that what you think? Like I'd try to hurt her?"

"If I truly thought that, we would not have gone to the ranch. I guess I'm just checking. Does that make sense to you? I don't really know you at all, but Lizzy thinks the world of you. I just don't want her to get hurt."

I was scowling, irritated that anybody could think something like that, but when she asked me again, I looked up and met her eyes. "I mean, I guess that makes sense. I was hoping to ask her to come up and work for me again, but wouldn't want to freak you out."

"I'm not freaking out. Lizzy just doesn't have anybody else to look out for her, so maybe I take things a little too far."

"Oh." I rubbed my jaw. "That sorta makes sense."

She released a long sigh. "Thanks for understanding."

"Sure, yeah. So, what do you think?"

Audrey tilted her head. "I think... I think she has a lot on her plate right now."

"Is that a no?"

She held her breath, and her eyes dropped. "That's a maybe. I'll think about it."

"Oh."

"Anyway, I really do appreciate everything you've done. Thank you again." She put her hand out to shake mine, and I took it. Her hands felt stronger than I'd expected. Slim and petite, but she had a grip of iron. Interesting.

I couldn't stop staring at her, but she pulled her hand from mine and looked back at the house. That seemed to be the end of the conversation. I frowned and tipped my hat, like I'd do for any lady, but it didn't seem like Audrey was paying attention or that she understood the gesture. So, I just got back in my truck and left.

Audrey

"Did Lizzy have fun at the ranch today?" Kat asked when I brought her dinner in.

"Hmm? Oh..." I looked away as I started arranging the silverware beside her plate. "Yes, I think she did. She hasn't stopped talking about horses since we left."

Kat lay her head back on her pillow and smiled. "That was real nice of the Walkers to let her come up. She sure likes being around the animals. I never have figured it out, but they've always held something special for her."

I sat down and folded my hands in my lap. "I suppose so. How are you feeling this evening?"

"Oh, I'm so boring. Let's not talk about me." Kat waved dismissively. "What did you guys do at the ranch?"

I snorted. "I didn't do much of anything, except watch over my stupid car."

Kat lifted her head a little. "What was wrong with your car?"

I buttered a roll for my sister and set it back on her plate. "Whew, that's a long story. I'll just sum it up by saying that the alternator was bad, and Luke fixed it for me."

Kat tried to sit all the way up. "He did? So?"

I narrowed my eyes. "So?"

"Well, you thanked him, right?"

"Come on." I rolled my eyes. "Do you honestly think my manners got so bad in New York that I forgot how to say 'thank you'?"

"Yes."

I laughed and play-jabbed at her ribs, like we used to when we were kids. "Seriously!"

"I am being serious. You could do a lot worse than being friendly to Luke Walker, Aud."

"Oh, please. You act like I should start dating him now. He just fixed my car for me, like a nice neighbor." I frowned. "And then he let me sit in it for forty-five minutes to see if it was going to stay running when he could've just used his tester on it."

Kat laughed. "It sounds like he was teasing you, Audrey."

"No, he was mocking me. And I didn't appreciate it."

"Aw, Luke's a good guy. At least, I always heard he was, and whenever I saw him in town, he seemed like it." Her brow dimpled. "I doubt he'd remember this, but about a year after I first moved to town—Lizzy was just a newborn—I was at the store one day, and I'd forgotten my wallet."

"You forgot it? Or James 'misplaced it'?"

Kat shrugged and smiled weakly. "My memory fails. Anyway, I was trying to buy some formula for Lizzy, and I got to the checkout stand before I realized I didn't have any money with me. Luke just happened to be behind me with Dusty, and the two of them pulled out some cash to pay for my formula. I never even asked, they just did it. I tried to follow them out to the parking lot to offer to pay them back, but they said they wouldn't hear of it."

"Luke didn't know who you were?"

"I don't think so. Called me ma'am, just as if he'd never seen me before. I don't think he knew I was James's wife. But James sure knew who Luke was."

"Why do you say that?"

"Oh!" She tried to laugh, but it sounded more like a cough. "Because when I got home that evening and told him all about it, James got angry and told me never to have anything to do with the Walkers again."

"Really?" I frowned. "That sounds odd."

Kat lifted a shoulder on the pillow. "Yeah. I thought so at the time, too. Just one of the many red flags I overlooked." She sighed, and her gaze became blank. And then, a tear slipped down her cheek.

"Hey, Kat..." I brushed some hair off her face. "Can I get you something?"

"No." She shook her head. "I'm okay. Just wish there were some things that I could do over, you know?"

I smiled and twisted that stray lock of hair behind her ear. "Yeah."

Kat caught my hand, her eyes searching hungrily for mine. "You'll let her go back out to the ranch again, won't you?"

I lifted my shoulders. "I mean, she had a lot of fun, but I'm not so sure it's a good idea for her to be spending all her time out there. She can't get her homework done as it is. She wants to volunteer at White Pines, and Luke Walker says he wants to hire her, but she can't even get through a week in the classroom without having some kind of an incident that sends her to the principal's office."

"Don't you think this is exactly what she needs? Listen, Audrey, Lizzy needs good people in her life more than she needs books right now."

I tilted my head and narrowed my eyes. "And why are you so sure that Luke is good? Paying for your groceries a long time ago doesn't prove his character."

"No, but it's more than most people have done."

"Well…" I shook my head. "I guess you're right there. Here, let's get your dinner eaten before it gets colder.

Kat studied her plate with a longing look on her face, then pushed it away. "I'm not hungry tonight."

A drop of fear shivered through me. *Please, no.* "Come on," I begged. "You need to eat something. We need to get your blood sugar up."

Kat rolled her head to the side and gingerly picked up a cherry tomato from her salad. She took one nibble, pushed it around in her mouth for a few seconds, and swallowed it like it was sawdust. She dropped the rest of it. "I can't, Aud. Just let me sleep."

I gulped and just stared. Kat's doctor had told me this was coming, but I wouldn't believe it. And now, here it was, right in my face. My sister really was giving up. "Right. Uhm… Okay. I'll just… put this in the fridge."

I watched for a little longer as my sister's eyes drifted closed. And there wasn't much else to do but pick up the plate and take it back to the kitchen.

Chapter 11

Luke

There's an old Ian Tyson song that gets stuck in my head on these crystal-skied days of early spring. *"Made it through another on the northern range."* It's about the new thing coming after a long, hard winter. The hope and relief of baby calves dotting the hillsides, a breath of warm life after all that cold; the hard work of just surviving every year to see it all again.

That song was playing in my mind a lot today as I looked out over the fields, green with fresh grass and alive with baby calves playing beside their mamas. The weatherman said no more snow, at least for the next week, and today was one of those balmy days that makes the grass grow. It seemed like we were into spring for good. About bloody time.

I settled my hat a little lower on my forehead and leaned on my saddle horn, just smiling out at all that open range. God's country, it was. Dusty could've said it better, but today I felt like even I could string together a few pretty words in my head about the paradise we called home. There was just no place like it on earth. Why would anyone want to be anywhere else?

I had just finished a round with Marshall, doing a morning check of our younger heifers. We'd still be seeing calves for a couple more weeks, but most of them were healthy and on the ground, and the few stragglers that were left would be landing on warm new grass instead of snow. Now, it was time for the broodmares to start dropping their foals, and that was when spring really took hold for me. Baby calves are cute, but there's nothing to a newborn foal taking its first steps.

"Reckon Evan will be back from the Lower Eighty about now," Marshall said as we turned back for the barns.

I snugged my hat down a little tighter. "Yeah. Reckon he will."

"Is he talking to you yet?"

"He asked me for some bacon this morning. Guess that's an im-provement."

Marshall chuckled. "He's still hot under the collar about that horse you brought here, isn't he?"

"Eh. I'm not sure that's actually it. He had a talk with Doc Burns and that made him feel better about the stud being here. I think there's something else bugging him."

"Isn't there always? It wouldn't be Evan if there wasn't something eating him."

"That's about right," I grunted.

"Well, I'm ready for some lunch. Come on, race you up to the corrals."

That sounded dandy to me. I put heel to my mount and whooped along with Marshall as our horses busted it for the barn. There's nothing like a good run to sweep the cobwebs out of a guy's head, and on a sunny day with the air smelling like growing grass and pine trees? Doesn't get any better than a nice long run on your best horse.

And also, Dusty should be out and about by now. He and Jess had rolled in at the bunkhouse at about two in the morning, and they hadn't been up yet when I came by at six. I was itching to know how their time in Texas went.

I mean... I didn't need to know *everything*. But it sounded like they'd seen a bunch of friends of mine, and Dusty had told me they were going to go out skydiving one day. I still didn't believe him about that, so I was eager to get the whole story. He probably lost a bet.

When Marshall and I trotted into the yard, there were a bunch of cars headed up the driveway to the house. Marshall and I traded glances as we swung down from our horses. "Do you know what's going on?" he asked.

"Nope. Open house of some kind? Cody got some more sponsors coming to sniff him out? I ran into one of them yesterday."

Marshall started loosening his cinch. "A sponsor?"

"Yeah. Wanted Cody to try our show horses on some fancy new gut supplement. Supposed to prevent ulcers or something in performance horses. I said I'd try a horse on it, too."

"Which horse?"

I chewed the inside of my cheek. I'd probably catch it from Cody or Doc Burns for this, but I'd figured that if that fancy supplement was supposed to help keep performance horses' stomachs healthy, it couldn't hurt a starving horse. "Oh," I fibbed, "just my rope horse."

"Huh. Well with all those cars headed up the hill, it doesn't look like sponsors. Wonder what the fuss is."

"No clue." We led our horses into the barn, expecting to solve the mystery, but we didn't see anybody in there. That was when my phone buzzed. It was from my dad.

Unsaddle quick and come up to the house. We're waiting for you.

I squinted and showed my phone to Marshall, but he'd just gotten the same message. "What in blazes is going on?" he asked.

"I don't know, but if everybody's waiting for us at the house, I bet there's food."

"Good call," he said, and stripped the saddle off his horse. When we got up to the house, Kelli ran straight for Marshall and dragged him away, whispering something into his ear. I didn't stick around to see what they were talking about, because I spotted Dusty over in the dining room.

"Hey there, little brother!" I greeted him with a high five.

Dusty laughed and clasped my hand, then pulled me in for a bear hug. "Hiya, big brother. I see you survived around here without me."

"Barely. I had to keep that rotten dog of yours out of trouble. Hey, I want the full report about Texas later. But what's going on here?"

Dusty pointed across the room. "You made it just in time. Dad and Meryl are eloping. Well... does it count as eloping if you don't go anywhere?"

"What? They're getting married right now?"

"I guess so."

Dad was over by the fireplace waving at us, and he bellowed across the room. "Luke! Marshall! You finally made it. All right, Pastor, everybody's here."

I pushed my way over to my dad, which wasn't easy because I think all his old cronies were drinking coffee, eating donuts, and standing in the way. "You're getting married right now? How come? I thought you guys were going to go on a destination wedding to the Caribbean or something."

Dad shrugged, and Meryl lay her head on his shoulder, hugging his arm. "We figured we might as well just get it done. Couldn't find any cruise dates that didn't mess with calving or branding, and we thought what's the point of waiting any longer? So we decided as soon as Dusty and Jess got back from their honeymoon, we'd have ourselves a little ceremony and make it official. Hey, why don't you give the bride away?"

I blinked. "Huh?"

"You're just standing there, looking like you don't have anything to do. I'd ask Evan, but he's stuck talking to Bill Randall. No saving him anytime soon."

I laughed and shook my head. "All right. Let's go, Meryl." I held my elbow out for her to take, but then I stopped. "Wait. Where are we going? Is there an aisle or something?"

"Uh…" Meryl glanced around. Dad and the pastor were both doing the same thing, but there was barely room to stand in our living room. Forget making an aisle for the bride to walk down.

Finally, Dad put his fingers in his mouth and let out a loud whistle. "Folks! Simmer down, and we'll get started."

The chatter in the room quieted a little, and the pastor cleared his throat and held up his Bible. "Well, here goes. Dearly beloved, we are gathered here today…"

I felt like I was standing in the way, with everyone staring at me and wondering what I was doing up there. My ears started burning, but pretty quick, the pastor got to the part about "Who gives this woman."

I looked around, wondering if I should say anything, and Meryl nudged me. Not sure what else to do, I just gave her hand back to my dad. "Is that all? Am I supposed to make a speech or something?"

Everyone started laughing. "Down in front, Luke!" someone shouted. "Always good for a joke," someone else said. I glanced around and caught a couple of other people shaking their heads and clapping, like I was some kind of sideshow.

That stung just a mite. Because, for once, I hadn't been trying to get a laugh, but apparently, that was what folks thought about me. I sniffed, ducked my head, and went to stand behind Dusty and Jess.

Audrey

"Doctor Livingstone? You have a phone call."

I was just reviewing the treatment plan with a patient when Kari poked her head in the door. I couldn't remember the last time she'd interrupted me for a phone call when I was with a patient, so I immediately excused myself and followed her.

"I'm sorry," she apologized as she handed the phone to me. "It's an attorney's office. He said it was urgent."

That couldn't be good. I sighed, bracing myself, then punched the hold button and put on my most professional tone. "This is Doctor Livingstone. May I help you?"

"Yes, I'm calling for James Tracy about the custody arrangement my client has with Kat Tracy. The weekend visitation agreement was violated, and I'm seeking restitution. Right now."

I pinched the bridge of my nose and sighed. "James, I know it's you. Drop the bull crap."

He was quiet for a few seconds. "I have my rights, you know. I could call the cops on you for picking my daughter up early."

"And I could report *you* for leaving your minor child unattended overnight! How long before you noticed she was gone?"

"That's none of your business. *You* broke the custody agreement. I could take you and your stupid sister to court. Do you think they'd leave Lizzy with you two after they review all Kat's medical records? No judge in their right mind would—"

"Listen, James," I hissed. "I'm going to say this once, so you'd better pay attention. You keep away from Kat! If I find out you're trying to cause trouble for her and Lizzy, I'm going to make your life even more miserable than it already is. Your truck? I'll tell the repo man where to find it next time he comes knocking on Kat's door. And you can forget about "borrowing" her SNAP benefits. I know you applied for the program under her name, and I know you're not buying food for Lizzy with it."

"Now, just a minute—"

"I'm not finished!" I interrupted. "Kat won't turn you in for not paying your child support, but I will. If you so much as think about making things harder for her, *I'll* be taking *you* to court! Got that?" I slammed the phone down before he could get another weasely word out, seething and panting in rage.

That was when I realized that Kari, Lucy, and two patients were staring at me with their mouths hanging open.

I straightened, swept a hand down the front of my scrubs, and faked a smile. "Telemarketers. Ah, Kari, will you please help Mrs. Hatfield schedule her follow-up appointment?"

I rushed back to the break room, away from prying eyes, and shut the door as fast as I could. That creep! To think he'd actually threaten *me* for getting his daughter out of the bad situation he'd left her in! I *knew* I should have called someone—the police, or Kat's social worker, or something! Now *I* looked like the bad guy.

Lizzy still hadn't opened up to me about why she seemed so fearful when we first got to the house, but I hadn't been able to get it out of my mind. I'd never trusted James Tracy, but Lizzy claimed to love her dad. Even Kat swore that while he'd been a lousy husband, he'd never harm a hair on his daughter's head. Just because I didn't like him and he set off all my alarm bells didn't give me a right to keep him away from his daughter, but this was just about the last straw for me.

I'd tell Kat. That was what I'd do. I'd tell her it was time to push for a different custody agreement since he was so far behind on his child support payments. Maybe I'd even talk Kat into leaving town since part of their original agreement was that she'd stay close enough for Lizzy to see her dad.

I threw myself into a chair and punched up Kat's number. But then my thumb stilled on the screen, and I lowered my hand. Something stopped me from pressing Send.

Kat didn't need me calling her in the middle of her normal nap time to vent about her worthless ex. There were better ways to approach that with her. But I could really use a sounding board just now—someone to talk me down before I blew my top. I blinked, released a breath, and scrolled down one name in my phone book. *Kelli*. There was a girl who wouldn't put up with being pushed around.

She picked up on the first ring, her voice bright and cheerful. "Hey, stranger! Your ears must've been burning because we were just talking about you. Hang on. I'm going to put you on speaker."

"Oh, no, Kelli, that's okay," I started to object. I wasn't in the mood for a conference call right now.

"Say hello to our newlywed!" Kelli said. "Jess got back last night, and I finally cornered her. You should see the tan on this girl! She hasn't stopped grinning yet, so ask her if she had a good time. Spoiler—it's a yes."

Despite myself, I couldn't help a smile. Jess was one of my favorite people in the world, and if anyone could offer a sympathetic ear just now, it was her. "Hey, girl. Did you guys have a good time?"

Jess was laughing, probably at something Kelli was doing on the other end. "We did. I married the sweetest man this side of anywhere, did you know that?"

"Yeah," I said with a chuckle. "I knew that."

"I'm so glad you rang because I was going to call you this afternoon anyway. How's Kat?"

I blew out a sigh. "Oh, you know. About the same." *Lie.*

"And Lizzy? I heard she was up here over the weekend cleaning stalls for Luke. That's a great way to keep her busy!"

"Yes, it is." I drummed my fingers on the table. That felt like a lie, too.

"Hey, Morgan is here, and we're just about to head up to White Pines together. She said Lizzy wanted to start doing some volunteering. Are you guys coming up after she gets out of school?"

"Not today." I bit my lip and tried to change the subject. "What do you mean 'here'? Are you all up at the Walker's ranch right now?"

"We are. Oh, boy, you missed it," Kelli put in. "Blake and Meryl decided to get married today."

"What? I thought I heard they were going to go on a cruise or something."

"Well, they changed their minds. None of us knew what was going on, either. He just sent us all a text asking us to show up for brunch if we could. Man, I thought Marshall was going to faint when he walked in the door!"

"Marshall?" Jess asked. "Luke was the one who turned green. Poor guy, he looked so nervous when they asked him to give the bride away."

Kelli scoffed. "You're imagining things, Jess. Luke doesn't get nervous. So, anyway, Audrey, is there any chance you can get away sometime soon? I've informed this girl that just because she's married now doesn't mean she gets to bail on us for pizza and nacho nights."

"I don't know, Kelli. The fact is, things are kind of overwhelming right now. That's sort of why I was calling."

"What do you need?" was her blunt response. "We'll make dinner, clean the house, pick Lizzy up—"

"No," I laughed quietly. "Nothing like that. It's..." I slumped in my chair and gazed up at the old-fashioned cork ceiling tiles. "It's just good to hear a friendly voice once in a while. Someone I don't have to fight and someone who doesn't need something from me."

There was silence for a few seconds. Then, "Tacos," Kelli said. "We are bringing over tacos. Tonight. Be hungry."

Chapter 12

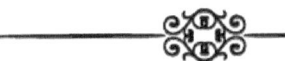

Luke

If there's one thing I don't mind staying up all night for, it's waiting for broodmares to foal. I'll take that over calving cows any day, because for one, the horses are halter broke. It's a whole lot easier to handle our nice mares than a half-wild mama cow when she needs a hand. And for another thing, we'd bring the mares into a big heated foaling stall when they got close to their time. There were always clean towels, hot water, and fresh coffee nearby.

Tonight, we were waiting on Evan's favorite mare, Goldie. She was a sweetheart of a horse; a big-hipped palomino with a baby-doll head and the softest brown eyes you ever saw. She was a half-sister to Morgan's horse Biz, and she was carrying a foal by Five Iron. With any luck, the baby might become one of our top horses someday, but first, we had to make sure it arrived safely. I didn't mind that one bit.

"We should just take to raising horses and forget the cows," I grunted as I blew the steam off my cup. "This is a little bit of alright."

Dusty laughed as he squatted on the straw bale beside me. "No complaints, except I'd rather be in my own bed right now."

I snorted. "I bet you would, but your wife ain't there anyway. Where'd she go?"

Dusty shrugged. "Something about going over to Audrey's house this evening. Kelli and Morgan went, too." He glanced at his watch. "I'm surprised they're not back yet."

I straightened. "Audrey's house? What for?"

"Jess didn't really know much, except it sounded like Audrey had kind of a bad day. She's got a lot on her plate, you know."

I shrugged, but my eyes were on the mare in the stall. "Who doesn't?"

I felt Dusty staring at me, but I refused to look at him. "Are you serious? Do you know what she juggles every day?"

I felt my insides crawling. Yeah, I knew. I'd thought a lot about it, more than Dusty had, for dang sure. "She's got stuff," was all I said.

"Boy, does she. Hey, what's this I hear about you fixing her car for her?"

I glanced over at my brother. "What's the matter with that? Y'all act like it's weird. It's no different from Evan plowing people's driveways or Marshall donating hay or you doing..." I waved my hand. "All the stuff you do."

"Hmm." He shrugged. "Okay, sure. You couldn't have helped anyone who needed it more, I don't think. She's a nice girl. I really like her."

I glanced sharply at him.

"Hey, I'm just saying!" He held up his hands. "Sheesh. Stop being so defensive."

"I'm not being defensive. Just don't you go gettin' any ideas about me and Audrey."

Dusty snorted. "As if I could. She strikes me as the kind of girl who likes *nice* guys."

"Oh, and what, I don't qualify?" I asked testily. "I'm a nice guy!"

Dusty was grinning, but his face fell. "Sorry, Luke. I was just teasing."

I hunched a little deeper inside my coat and fixed my eyes on the mare in the foaling stall. "It's alright."

I was hoping he'd let it drop, but no such luck. Dusty was just staring at me. Ever since we were young, my kid brother was always able to just look at me and peel me open like an onion. I never figured out how he did it, when Dad and Evan, and Marshall never had a clue. Dusty could pry into my head as well as Mom could.

"You like her, don't you?" he asked suddenly.

I sipped my coffee and wouldn't look at him. "So what if I do? Ain't like anything could come of it. She's a city girl. Don't think she'd take up with a guy like me."

Dusty shrugged. "Stranger things have happened."

Huh. Yeah. Because a classy girl like Audrey Livingstone—smart, successful, and knock-out gorgeous—wanting to hang around a musty old cowboy with a broken knee and a lot of shattered dreams... yeah, that would be pretty strange. I sighed and stared down into my empty coffee cup.

"Oh!" Dusty nudged me. "Hey, look at our girl here."

I glanced up at Goldie. The mare's flanks had broken out in a sweat and she had left off her restless pacing to paw and try to lay down. I checked my watch. "Dang. Only ten-thirty. We may have a foal before midnight this time."

"Looks like it," Dusty agreed. "Should we call Evan on this one? He practically worships this mare."

I watched as the mare lowered herself clumsily to the ground and thrashed her head in the straw. She wallowed a bit, trying to get comfortable, then put her front hooves out and lurched to her feet. As she stood up, her water broke.

"Yeah," I said. "Better call him."

Audrey

"I wish I knew enough to give you some advice," Morgan said. She tucked her stockinged feet up on the couch and sipped the herbal tea Kelli had just made in the kitchen. "Custody cases aren't really my specialty. I know a few social workers I could ask, though."

I leaned my forehead on my hand and sighed. "Thanks, but I really can't do anything without Kat's approval, and she's not interested in making a fuss right now."

"Well, I'll do it," Kelli announced as she dropped into a chair beside me. "I'll call and leave an anonymous tip about a little child abandonment, that's what I'll do."

"I don't think that's actually going to help," Morgan pointed out.

"Sure, it would! Enough tips, they have to investigate. They'll check things out and find out what a loser he is."

"And that Lizzy's mother, who is already known to be terminal, is coming close to the end." I gulped my tea and fought the waver in my voice. "Custody arrangements change pretty quickly when the primary parent can no longer provide care."

Everyone fell silent. Morgan was fiddling with her cup, Kelli was sticking her lip out and frowning at the carpet, and Jess scooted closer to me to put her hand on mine.

"Has Kat made arrangements in her will?" she asked softly.

I shrugged. "Yes. She's named me as her desired guardian, and she even talked James into signing off on it for now. But nothing's binding until..." I cleared my throat. "I don't have legal guardianship now because Lizzy still has two custodial parents. And I know the reason Kat's afraid to rock the boat is that she doesn't want James to challenge her will. He can ask for full custody, and since he's Lizzy's father, the judge would award it."

"Then we keep records," Kelli decided. "Phone calls, texts, whatever you have to show in court what a deadbeat James is."

"Oh, I've been doing that since the beginning," I said. "I just can't guarantee it'll do any good."

"What about Lizzy?" Morgan asked. "She's old enough to tell the judge where she wants to live."

I scoffed. "Right, like she'd pick her stuffy, strict, overprotective aunt over the dad who lets her do whatever she wants."

Jess squeezed my hand. "You might be surprised."

I studied her face—Jess's clear, honest eyes, the hopeful smile she offered, and I forced a little smile in return. "Maybe. I mean, I keep food in the fridge. She likes that."

"See?" Kelli encouraged. "Lizzy'd choose you in a heartbeat."

"I don't know." I swallowed more of my tea and let my gaze drift to the floor. "I just feel like there's so much I can't offer her."

"Like what? Name one thing old James can offer his daughter that you can't."

I lifted my shoulders. "A father."

"That's... not really a good argument," Morgan said carefully.

"Dang right," Kelli agreed. "She needs a mother figure, too, doesn't she? And if you ask me, you're a whole lot more likely to marry someone nice down the road than James is."

My cheeks felt hot, and I squirmed deeper into the loveseat. "Not exactly what I meant."

"I'm serious, though! It's actually something you have to think about. What happens if…" Kelli bit her lip and glanced at Jess and Morgan. "I'm not trying to sound cruel, you understand, right? But when things… change, what happens? You'll have a life to resume, and that would look a lot different if you have a teenager to raise. What would you do?"

I shook my head and finished my tea. "I have a job offer back in New York. It's exactly what I always wanted, so I don't know how I could turn it down. If it's still there, of course."

Jess sucked in a long breath. "How would Lizzy do in New York?"

"I don't know." I pushed myself out of the couch and started collecting everyone's mugs. "I guess I'll cross that bridge if and when I come to it."

Kelli slumped, her chin in her hand. "Pity we couldn't tempt you to stick around here. Maybe if you met someone? I know lots of handsome, single cowboys between the ages of twenty-four and twenty-nine-and-a-half."

"No, you don't. The only one I know of is Luke, and he's…" Jess glanced at me apologetically. "Probably not your type."

A prickle raced down my neck, and I forced a tight smile. "No, he's not." Luke might be a lot of things, and I hadn't figured most of them out yet, but Jess was right about one thing. He wasn't the kind of guy for me, no matter how cute he was when he smiled.

"Too bad. He's actually a good guy—once you get to know him, of course." Kelli stood and took the cups from my hand. "Let me wash up."

I hesitated before letting her take them. It didn't feel right, letting someone wash my dishes, just like it didn't feel right that they'd bought groceries and cooked dinner. I was used to being the one who came to other people's rescue, yet once again, someone was stepping in and taking on what I should have done. Just like Luke, fixing my car for me without even asking. Making my life just a little easier for the moment, when I couldn't do anything in return.

"Thank you," I finally murmured as Kelli bustled off to the kitchen. Jess got up to help her, but Morgan didn't follow because her phone was ringing. "It's Cody," she said as she answered. "Hang on. Hello?"

I looked away and tried not to listen as Morgan talked to her husband, but it wasn't a long conversation. He said something on the other end, and while he was still talking, Morgan jumped up and shot to the door to pull her boots on. "Okay, I'm on my way," she told him. Love you." She hung up and sighed.

"Sorry to run, Audrey. Rescue emergency."

I waved her off. "Don't worry about it. Thanks for coming over."

Morgan smiled and reached to pull me into a hug. "We're all here for you, girl."

I patted her back awkwardly just before she pulled away. I wasn't even sure how to process all this... help. Warmth. Community. I just sniffed and my voice went raspy. "Thanks, Morgan."

Luke

"I always had a soft spot for a palomino," Evan murmured. He was squatting in the straw, his eyes full of the spindly-legged colt suckling his mama. "Look at the hip on that little guy already! And those shoulders. Just perfect."

I grunted. "Yup. Oughta be a good one."

Evan nodded slowly. "Think I'll plan on keeping this one around. He might be something special."

"Uh-huh." I was putting away the foaling supplies and checking my phone. It was morning, and just as we'd figured, the foal had come before midnight. I'd even managed to get a few hours of sleep, but when I came back down to the barn this morning, I'd found Evan still sitting in the foaling stall, right where I'd left him. If he'd slept at all, it was there in the straw. "Hey, you want some coffee?" I called as I shuffled stuff to the medicine room.

"Already had some." Evan finally got to his feet and came out, sliding the stall door closed behind him. "When is Doc Burns coming to check him?"

"He said about nine. I guess he was out on an emergency foaling all night." I tossed the soiled towels in the barn hamper and put the medical gloves back on the shelf. We were pretty well set up for this kind of thing—in fact, we could handle most emergencies ourselves, but we still liked to have the vet come to give our colts a once-over and check their antibodies and so on.

We heard tires crunching the gravel outside, so I popped my head out of the medicine room, wondering if it was Doc Burns already.

But it was just Cody, ambling in with his head drooping and his eyes blood-shot.

"What the heck happened to you?" Evan asked.

Cody scrubbed his face. "I married a horse rescuer, that's what happened."

Evan and I glanced at each other with "this ought to be good" expressions. "So?" I asked.

Cody sank down onto the straw bale that Dusty and I had been using for a chair last night. "We had an emergency intake. Morgan was over at Audrey's still, but I got a call from another one of the places fostering those horses from the big seizure case. They had a few pregnant mares, too, but they didn't have a way to keep them all separate. Anyway, one of them got aggressive—started savaging the other mares and almost killed a one-day-old foal, so they had to get her out. We drove over to Idaho Falls last night to get her."

"Dang," I said. "Where'd you put her?"

He lifted the brim of his hat and squinted. "Uh... in the run we built for the stud."

Evan rolled his eyes at me. I could see it, plain as day—he wasn't the littlest bit thrilled to be boarding one of the rescue horses indefinitely, but he was also tickled pink about that new colt that had landed last night. I'd caught him in a good mood. I just grinned and waited for him to say it.

"Fine," he growled. "The stud can stay. Just don't let him cause a problem." And he walked off.

Cody was smiling tiredly, and he shot me a wink. "Looks like you get to keep him. For now, anyway."

"Huh. Yeah, for now."

Audrey

A week doesn't seem like a long time. Seven short days—just enough for the end of March to roll away and April to waltz in the door. Five work days with a couple of book ends, that was all. But when you're caregiving, a week can feel like both an eternity and the blink of an eye.

There was just so much to be done, from doctor's appointments to social worker calls to the regular business of keeping my job and staying on top of Lizzy's schoolwork. I scarcely had ten seconds to breathe, but the days just dragged on forever. By the time my head hit the pillow at night, the morning seemed like a long-ago memory.

I peeked at my watch one afternoon as I pulled off my mask and gloves at work. That was my last appointment for the day, and I'd finished ten minutes earlier than I'd expected to. Ten minutes! Why, that was enough time to sit down and take a five-minute power nap in the treatment chair, and still have time to tidy up before Kari caught me sleeping. Or I could scroll on social media, catch up on what everyone I knew was doing with their lives, out there in the normal world.

Better yet, I'd use those ten minutes to stop by Beaufort's steak-house and pick up a big tub of their smoked brisket chili and a to-go box of fresh honeyed cornbread. Kelli had picked Lizzy up from school today to take her to White Pines for me because I was supposed to interview a new home health nurse for Kat at five. Then I'd need to pick up Lizzy at six, start Kat's dialysis as soon as I got home... It would be a busy evening, and chili was comfort-food treat that I wouldn't have to cook. I punched up the phone number and made my order, then pulled my sweater on and grabbed my keys.

"Good night, Kari," I said as I passed her desk.

"Wait, I have a message for you." She ripped off a sticky note and passed it to me. "And I hate to ask, but you said something last month about... maybe talking about a raise?" She winced and grinned nervously. "My car insurance went up."

"Oh. Right." I glanced at the sticky note—at that 585 area code—and stuffed it into my pocket. I'd have to call Peter later when my brain was working. "What kind of raise did we talk about?"

"A dollar an hour."

Whew. That would bite into my operating budget, which was already slim. But Kari did deserve a raise, and she deserved a lot more than she was asking for. I released a sigh and chewed my lip. "You got it. Remind me tomorrow, will you?" I jingled my keys and opened the door before she could ask for something else. "Good night!"

When I got to the steakhouse, there was a line ahead of me. What were the odds of that? There were like, what fifty people in this whole town? I huffed and looked at my watch. Okay, maybe that was an exaggeration, but since when did the steakhouse have a line at four-forty-five in the afternoon on a Thursday? I stood on my toes to look around, and that was when I realized it was some sort of a party. Just my luck.

"What's going on?" I asked the lady in front of me.

She shrugged. "It was like this when I got here twenty minutes ago. Did you see the buses outside?"

"I didn't," I admitted. I hadn't really been paying attention to anything, because I'd been trying to figure out what I was going to tell

Peter when I called him back. He probably wanted a decision about the job in New York, and I couldn't give him one yet.

"I think they're part of a guided tour going over the mountains," the lady said. "They've all got cameras and some of them aren't speaking English. I don't think they were expected either, because there aren't enough waiters for all the tables."

"You said you've been here twenty minutes already?"

She nodded. "They told me it might be a while for my to-go order."

Great. I should just leave and go home, but I'd already paid for my order over the phone. The thought of fifteen dollars' worth of yummy chili just going to waste almost made me cry. What should I do? Maybe I'd find the owner, a bent old guy who called himself Cowboy Bill, and ask him to just hold my order when it came up. I'd try to make time to stop by again after my interview.

I turned around, looking for Bill, but instead, I bumped into a different cowboy. He was tall, and he smelled like leather and hay, and he was standing about six inches behind me. And he caught my hands in his when I slammed into him.

"Howdy there, Doc," Luke Walker said with a grin. "Nice to see you, too."

My heart turned a flip, and I pushed away from him and beat my hand on my own chest. "Holy Moses! You scared me. What are you doing breathing down my neck?"

"No room." He jerked his head toward the door, where a line was forming behind him. "We might have to share a table, huh?"

"I'm not staying. I came to pick up my to-go order, but I don't have time for this."

"Aw, that's too bad. Surf and turf is on special tonight, all you can eat. They're famous for it, from Treasure Valley to the Big Sky. That's why I'm here."

"And that's probably why everyone else is here, too." I cast another glance around.

"Not everyone."

I squinted at him in confusion. "What?"

"You know, the kid. Where's Lizzy?"

"Oh." I shook my head. "Up at White Pines. I have to go get her later. What time is it?" I snatched another look at my watch. "Shoot, I can't wait any longer. Excuse me."

I pushed past him—not in a rude way, but there really wasn't another way to get by. And I'd be lying if I said it was a punishment to brush against that firm chest, but it did make me jump when I felt his arm slide behind me.

"What are you..." I twisted around and found my nose just centimeters from his chin. "Why are you hugging me?"

"Easy, doc. Just tryin' to make a hole for you. Outta the lady's way, people!" he said, raising his voice above the din. He grabbed my hand and pulled me through the opening. He had to step out of his place in line to do it, and he even opened the door for me when we got there.

I turned and stared at him as my feet hit the sidewalk outside. "Um... Thanks?"

He didn't say another word. Just tipped his hat and disappeared back inside the restaurant. I walked away feeling more flustered than I had in... well, far too long.

When was the last time my whole body felt tingly and dizzy just because a guy touched my hand? And what was wrong with me that I had that reaction to Luke Walker, of all people? Okay, sure, he *was* cute.

I slid behind the wheel of my car, my lip caught between my teeth as I cringed at myself. Because I had to admit, Luke was a lot more than cute. I used to think Marshall was the most handsome of the

Walkers, but when I actually looked at Luke, with that boyish twinkle in his blue eyes, that little curl of brown hair that sometimes peeked out from under his hat, and that care-free crooked grin, it was hard to remember what his brothers even looked like. What *any* other man looked like, for that matter.

Peter was handsome. Peter should have been a model or a movie star, with his square jaw and Mediterranean complexion, and salon-perfect hair. But right now, when I tried to remember his face, I kept envisioning a cowboy hat and laughing blue eyes. I grabbed the steering wheel and banged my forehead on it.

"Stressed. You're just stressed," I lectured myself. "And hungry. Don't think about men on an empty stomach." My stomach growled in reply as I started my car and turned for home.

Chapter 13

Luke

I didn't get it. Why did that pretty dentist always act like she couldn't get away from me fast enough? I glanced self-consciously down at my shirt. Was I wearing hay crumbs on my flannel? Fragrant mud on my boots? I sniffed at myself, but I only earned an offended look from the lady in front of me in line. She probably thought I was sniffing her.

It couldn't be anything wrong with me. Audrey took everything too seriously. That was what it was. She didn't giggle and tease like other girls, so maybe she didn't know how to take a joke.

On the other hand, she didn't treat me like *I* was a joke, either. I frowned as I shuffled another place ahead in line.

Audrey Livingstone seemed like a girl with pretty high standards. The kind of girl who wasn't just out for a few laughs. She wouldn't goof around, hang on a guy's arm until he lost his heart, then dump him for someone who was "marriage material."

Not that anyone had ever done that to me, of course. I mean, no one important. It was hard to get serious about any of the women I knew when they all seemed to think I was just a wild, ex-bull-rider who'd never fully left the rodeo behind.

But that wasn't true at all. Maybe it took me longer to come around, but I wanted what my brothers had found. A girl who would be the missing half of a greater whole—someone to lie out under the stars and dream with, and someone who would wait up with the porch light on when I was out working. The kind of girl who could sink her teeth into a challenge and make me want to be a better man than I was.

I gave my bum knee a little twist to stretch it out as I was standing there. It ached at the end of the day, a little more now than it used to. I probably ought to get it looked at, but I didn't want to be told that I needed surgery. So, I just limped along, smiling, and pretending everything was okay. But one day, "okay" wasn't going to be good enough anymore.

The line moved ahead again, and I scuffed my boots on the worn wood planks, my eyes on the floor. I'd been doing the same old thing, trying to relive the same old dream for years now, and I was always frustrated that nothing changed. The more I thought about it, the more it made sense. It was time to do something different.

I was going to change Audrey Livingstone's mind about me.

"To-go order for Audrey!" someone called from the kitchen. That snapped me back to attention. She hadn't been able to take her food with her. Was she coming back for it? Couldn't be. She was rushed for time, she'd said.

It didn't take me more than a second to decide what to do. Surf and turf could wait till next week. I stepped forward and claimed Audrey's dinner. Then I asked for some napkins and took it out to my truck.

Audrey

"I'm sorry you weren't able to speak with Katherine this evening. She should be awake tomorrow." I stood and offered my hand to the home health nurse and led her to the door. She wasn't half as experienced as we really needed her to be, but she was also the only person who'd applied. Kat's regular nurse had given her notice, and frankly, I didn't have much choice.

"You said you're available to start in the morning?" I asked. "I can make arrangements with the agency."

She nodded, said she'd be there at eight-thirty, and I showed her out. I closed the door with a sigh of relief. There was one problem solved for the evening. I slipped back to the bedroom to check on Kat before I did anything else.

She was still asleep. The blankets hardly stirred, her breathing was so shallow. And was it my imagination, or did she look grayer than she had this morning? I swallowed and rested my forehead against the doorframe. "Oh, Kat," I breathed. "It wasn't supposed to be like this."

She didn't answer, of course. I sniffed and wiped my eyes on the backs of my hands, then went to the kitchen for my purse. I hadn't had time to make anything more for dinner than a piece of toast for Kat and a leftover hard-boiled egg for me. It didn't do much to fill the void, but I had to go pick up Lizzy. I slipped my purse over my shoulder and was headed for the front door when the knock came.

Who could that be? I slipped quietly to the door and looked through the peephole. Holy smokes, it was Luke.

The bubbled lens made his nose look enormous while his chin almost disappeared into his collar, but I'd know those blue eyes anywhere. What was he doing here? I gulped and brushed my fingers frantically through my hair. I was probably a mess!

"Hey, doc, are you home?" he called through the door. "It's Luke Walker."

I blew out a huff and set my purse down, then thought better of it and hung it on the hook by the door. In case I needed it. Then I smoothed down the front of my blouse and jerked the door open. "Luke? Hi! What a s-surprise." I cleared my throat. "Can I help you?"

He was standing the porch, half-smiling and holding a white paper takeout bag. "You left your dinner."

I blinked and stared at the bag. He brought my chili? How could he know? And he had to have skipped his surf and turf to do it. That was... well, it was incredibly sweet. Maybe a little crazy, too—I don't know. All I could think was how hungry I was and how good that would taste right now. My stomach rumbled in agreement. Loudly.

Luke grinned, took of his hat, and lifted the bag for me to take. "Figured you'd be hungry. Guess I was right."

I laughed in embarrassment. "Yeah. This is amazing, Luke. Thank you, but I was just on my way out the door to get Lizzy. I'll have to eat it when I get back."

He held up his phone. "No need. I made a call. Kelli's going to bring her by. They're already on their way."

I narrowed my eyes. "You asked Kelli to bring Lizzy home? But she had already picked her up from school. I wouldn't want to ask—"

"She was happy to do it. She only lives a couple of blocks away, so it's not like it was a big deal. Said she tried to tell you the same thing earlier, but you wouldn't let her help any more. So, we outvoted you."

"Luke, that's... well, that's thoughtful, but maybe I had a reason for wanting to pick her up myself."

He shrugged. "Maybe. And maybe you need to let someone else shoulder some stuff for you." He lifted the bag again. "Are you gonna take it?"

I crossed my arms. "No, I don't think I will."

Luke's smile faded. "Really? You won't take it because I called Kelli for you?"

"No. I won't take it because I'm inviting you to bring it in yourself." I pulled the door open a little farther and stood back. "Come in?"

That sideways grin reappeared, and Luke glanced between me and the door. "Well, now, I can hardly refuse that kind of invitation." He stepped inside and hung his hat on the hook beside my purse. And then, he did something that made my mouth run dry and made me question everything.

He stopped in the entryway and toed his boots off with a sheepish look on his face. "You can make fun of my red socks if you want, but it's better than tracking mud and germs inside, right? Mind if I wash my hands somewhere?"

I just gaped at him, no words coming. It wasn't that I thought his wooly red socks were funny. But one of my biggest challenges was keeping a clean environment for Kat. No one ever thought to take their shoes off when they came in—not even the nurses. And to watch Luke Walker, the cowboy with the wild streak and that heart-stopping swoony smile of his, carefully pulling his boots and scrubbing his hands all the way up to his elbows, made me realize that he was thinking about a lot more than I'd ever guessed. What other secrets was this guy hiding?

While I was busy staring, Luke found some clean plates and forks still in the dish drainer from earlier and set them on the table. Then, he pulled out a chair and smiled at me. "Hungry, Audrey?"

My gaze shifted from the chair to his face. "So, it's Audrey now, instead of 'Doc'?"

His smile widened. "If you don't mind."

I hesitated only a second, then moved to slip into the chair he was holding for me. His hands were warm at my shoulders as he helped slide me up to the table, and I could feel his breath feathering through my hair. Something shivered down deep in my stomach—a veil pulled back that I'd tried so hard to hide behind. I caught his hand as he started to step away. "I don't mind," I whispered.

Luke

"So." Audrey set her glass down and leaned back in her chair, challenging me with a little smile. "I have a question that's been on my mind for some time."

I swallowed my mouthful of chili. "Okay. Shoot."

"Why Lizzy?"

I frowned. "What do you mean? Why did I take a shine to her?"

"Yes. There were a dozen kids at the wedding that day. Why was she the one you put on top of that water truck and hired to work for you?"

"Oh." I shrugged and scraped the bottom of my bowl while I thought about an answer. "I guess because she had grit. Couldn't stay outta trouble and was dyin' for a little fun, but she ain't really bad." I looked up. "Did she tell you what happened?"

Audrey shook her head, her soft chocolate hair piling around her shoulders. I could spend all evening just running my fingers through hair like that. I had to blink and look back down at my bowl to keep from staring.

"She shot me in the butt with a nerf dart. After she shot Dustin."

Audrey tried to hide a smirk behind her napkin, but it wasn't working. She broke into a snicker. "I feel like there's more of a story there."

I shrugged. "Not really. I lost my temper a little, but then I saw she was starting to cry. Really bad kids don't break like that when they realize they've screwed up. So, I put her to work sweeping, and we had some fun with the water truck. That's all."

She studied me for a few seconds, then shook her head. "That's not all."

My ears got hot. Did she still not trust me? "What do you mean? Sure, it is."

"No, because if that was all, you wouldn't still be looking out for her, and she wouldn't think you hung the moon."

I leaned forward in my chair. "I don't follow you."

"Lizzy doesn't get attached to people like most kids her age. I guess having a terminal mother with caregivers coming through a revolving door and an emotionally unavailable father figure will mess up the way a person forms relationships. But there's something about you that resonates with her. It's more than you joking around with her and giving her a job with animals. So, what's the connection?"

I picked up my water glass and drank about half of it before I answered. "Probably that I used to get into trouble all the time, too. And I never meant any harm by it, either, but there was just this... I don't know, this energy crawling around inside that had to bust out once in a while. Evan was always so perfect no matter what he did, and Marshall was such a rule-follower. Guess I just had to be different, so I'd be seen."

"Ah, yes. I've heard about shooting out the stadium lights and opening fire hydrants to flood the parking lot."

I smothered a proud grin. "Anyone ever tell you about the time I repainted a billboard?"

Her expression went blank. "Missed that one."

I chuckled and shrugged as I finished my water glass. "Only reason I didn't get in trouble that time is because I painted Evan and Anne's names all over it with a bunch of pink hearts. He was too shy to ask her out to the prom, so I did it for him. He was so tickled when she said yes that he took the fall for the vandalized billboard."

Audrey laughed and shook her head. "And the bull riding?"

"Aw, sweetheart, that's just a bit of thrill-seeking. Laughing at danger in the face, that kind of thing."

She arched a brow. "Normal people don't do that."

"Sure, they do. What do you call your driving?"

Audrey puckered her lips in thought. "Efficiency."

I pointed my spoon at her. "More people die in car accidents than on a bull."

"That's because most people ride in cars, but only a select few are crazy enough to strap themselves to a ton of angry hamburger," she shot back with a teasing smile.

I couldn't help that warm feeling swimming around in my chest. She was too sweet and pretty and just too delicious when she was poking at me like that. It wasn't like with everyone else, who just chalked me up as crazy Luke. With Audrey, it felt like she was actually trying to understand me, but she wasn't above having a little fun with me along the way. I pulled my chair around the table a little to get closer to her.

"See, on a bull, it's like this. You're trying to outsmart him. He could be jumping to the right, you're in your rhythm and everything, and it's just the two of you in this kind of dance. But then he can duck off to the left and just spin right out from under you, so you gotta be ready for anything."

"Or he could throw you and then attack you," Audrey added softly. Her gaze dropped. "I heard you got hurt."

I framed my hands around my left knee. "Never been quite the same," I admitted.

"What happened?"

I huffed and shook my head. "It was stupid. I was in the running for the championship that year—high school rodeo, nothing big like PBR yet, but that's where I was headed. My friend Joe and I were neck and neck all season, and it was our last go of the finals."

"And?"

I shrugged. "And I never even got out of the gate. Bull started slamming around in the chute as soon as they brought him in, but rather than waiting till he settled before I got on, I decided to just jump in there."

"Showing off?"

I shook my head. "Nah, that wasn't really it. I just thought I'd get away with it. Never figured he'd pin me against the side and actually try to kill me."

She dropped her eyes. "So, that was the end of your bull-riding dream."

"If you could call it a dream." I leaned forward, waiting for her to look me in the eye. "I s'pose what I really wanted was... something big. See, my family has this name—everyone knows my dad and my brothers. 'The Walkers.' It's like we're all the same person. I guess I wanted something that would be just mine, no one else's."

"Ah," she breathed. "And you're still looking for that, aren't you?"

I shifted my jaw and gazed at her—so unique and different from everyone else I'd ever known. Beautiful and kind and strong in ways I was only beginning to discover. And smart enough to see right through me.

"Yeah. Maybe I am."

Audrey

"Aunt Audrey, you'll never guess what I did!"

We heard Lizzy's voice even before she got the door all the way open. I pulled my gaze away from Luke and waited for her to flounce into the kitchen, braids bouncing and tracking muddy footprints all over the floor. She raced in with flushed cheeks and stopped dead when she saw Luke at the table. Her mouth fell open.

"Did you leave some chili for me?"

"Lizzy! Manners!" I chided her.

Luke just laughed and showed her the takeout container, still half-full. "Plenty left, kiddo. Grab yourself a bowl."

She did, and raced back to the table to start filling it. "Guess what!" she cried around a mouthful of chili. "Morgan let me play with a baby horse that was just born last night. Did you know that baby horses are born with pads on their hooves? They fall off like right away, but Morgan found one and showed it to me. And they have a special smell, too. They don't stink, honest. It's like a new car smell. I got to touch him and brush his mom, and you know what? I think Two Bits must have been his dad because he's black like Two Bits, and he has a little white mark on his leg like—"

"Please, Lizzy, slow down," I begged. "Take a breath before you choke on your dinner."

She took a big gulp, swallowing her chili, then tore off a hunk of cornbread with her bare hands. "Luke, can I come up to the ranch this weekend? I want to see if the baby really looks like Two Bits."

"If your aunt says it's okay."

They both stared at me, and I sighed and nodded. "Sure, I guess." What else was I supposed to say?

Luke smiled—but that smile wasn't for Lizzy. It was for me. And I think I smiled back.

"Tell you what," he said, looking back at her. "Quarantine is up now, so I'll be turning Two Bits out in a little field of his own this weekend. He gets all the hay he wants, and he can even start having a little fresh grass. Doc says we can officially give him a real bath now, too. You wanna help?"

Her eyes rounded, and she nodded.

"Good deal." He pushed back his chair and dropped his napkin on his plate. "Well, guess that means it's time for me to head out. See you around, kid."

I stood up with him. "Thank you again for picking up our dinner. Really, it was nice."

He stopped and turned slightly, looking down at me with a softness in his voice and in his eyes that nearly made my heart seize. I almost expected him to slip his arm around me and nuzzle my hair—that was the kind of look he was giving me. But he didn't touch me, and I couldn't decide why that felt disappointing. It wasn't like I'd ever go for a cowboy.

But I kind of liked Luke. A lot more than I'd expected to.

"Hey," he said, "I really mean it when I say folks are willing to help you. It's not wrong to let them."

I tipped up my chin. "By 'them' do you mean 'you'?"

One side of his mouth tugged into a boyish grin. "You caught me."

"That's too bad," I sighed. "I can't possibly ask for your help when I need something."

Luke's brow furrowed. "Sure, you can. Anytime. All you gotta do is call."

"I suppose I could, if I had your number."

Luke's smile widened, then he dipped his head and broke into a bashful chuckle. "I guess that helps." He pulled out his phone and handed it to me. "Send yourself a text, and then I'll have your number, too."

My cheeks felt hot as I typed my number into Luke's phone. I knew Lizzy was watching, and I could only guess what she was thinking. I bit my lip and met his eyes when I passed his phone back. I couldn't say it in words, so I could only plead with a look—*Don't hurt her. Don't hurt us.*

And there it was again. That faint twitch of his cheek, the little squint that said he'd understood... something. But I didn't dare let myself imagine he really got it. There was no way he could.

"Well," I said, stuffing my hands in the pockets of my jeans before I could do something crazy, like hug him. "I need to start Kat's dialysis. We have to keep her schedule pretty strict, so..."

He sniffed and looked down. "Got it. Night, then."

I followed him to the door so I could lock it after he left. "Good night, Luke."

Luke paused on the porch and smiled one last time. "I think you have more company. I must've scared her off." He stuck a thumb over his shoulder at Kelli, still parked in the driveway. It looked like she was texting someone—or just looking at her phone so we didn't see her watching us. Luke chuckled and held up his fist, like he did with Lizzy.

I shrugged. Sure, why not fist-bump the guy? I wasn't planning to kiss him, but it felt a little cold just to stand back and wave. I thumped his knuckles with mine, and his smile lit up the whole porch. "Good night, Audrey."

When Luke passed by her car on his way out, he knocked on the window, and I saw Kelli wave at him before she opened the door. I waited for her in the doorway with my arms folded. "Spying on a girl?" I teased.

"Lordy, no! I would never." She crossed her chest with her fingers. "Okay, maybe I spied a *little*. Just enough to see that I shouldn't interrupt... whatever you two had going on in there."

I rolled my eyes. "We didn't have anything 'going on.' He was just being a friend."

"Oh, is that what that was? Huh. Because the first time Marshall looked at me like that, it didn't end with a friendly fist bump."

"Did you need something?" I asked impatiently.

Kelli thinned her lips and looked over my shoulder, then gestured for me to follow her out onto the porch. "Close the door."

I shivered and wrapped my arms around myself as I stepped outside. "Okay. What's up?"

"It's just something strange I saw with Lizzy. It's probably nothing, but I thought I should tell you."

I shook my head. "Well?"

"So, we're up there taking care of all those rescue horses, right? Morgan's there, a few other volunteers are helping, and Lizzy's happy as a clam. But about five, she starts getting super anxious and asking what time it is, over and over again. I think she was looking for you."

I scoffed. "Me? I'm the last thing she wants. She had horses to play with, and she practically worships Morgan."

"Yeah, and that was all fine until it was about time to go home. She stopped talking to anyone and just hung out by the driveway, watching for cars. I thought she was going to lose it when Luke called me and said I should bring her home."

"Really?" I squinted in thought. "That doesn't make any sense. She bounced in the house all excited to tell us about her day."

"Because you were there. I'm telling you, Audrey, she was freaking out when she expected to see you, and you *weren't* there. She'd never admit it, mind you."

"Well, what does 'freaking out' look like? Was she getting into trouble? Hitting kids again? Yelling, what?"

"No, she just shut down. Biting her nails and staring at the ground without blinking. Anyway, she seems fine now, but I just thought you should know that happened."

I frowned. "Yeah. Thank you for telling me. And, really, thank you for bringing her home. It was a huge help tonight."

"No problem, girl. I got your back, remember?" She hugged me, then smacked my shoulder and pointed. "Oh, and watch out for Luke. He'll break your heart."

I laughed as I opened the door. "I'm sure he will. But there *is* a good way to have your heart broken, you know."

Chapter 14

Luke

"Would you look at that?" Dusty said as he hopped down off Duchess and came to stand beside me. "That skinny nag can actually run."

"'Course he can." I glanced at my brother as he leaned on the fence post beside me to watch. I'd turned Two Bits out in the field for the first time today—Doc said he could start with twenty minutes on green grass—and he'd spent the whole time trotting up and down the fence and calling to the broodmares.

"Yeah, he can run just fine. It's gettin' him to stop that's the problem." I picked up a stem of hay to chew on and crossed my arms over the gate, waiting for the stud to run out of steam.

"He has zero muscle," Dusty observed. "How's he even moving in a straight line?"

"Yeah, well, you just wait till he gets his weight back on. He's put together right, got all the parts where they're supposed to be. See those shoulder and hip angles? And look at how long his strides are! Betcha when he's all muscled up again, he'll look and run every bit as good as Duchess."

Dusty huffed. "That didn't take long."

I turned to look at him. "What didn't?"

"You, that's what. You're already figuring on keeping him."

I scowled. "No, I'm not. I'm just saying he's too nice of a horse to be thrown away."

"They all are, Luke. That's kind of the point. They all deserve a chance."

I shook my head. "This one is different. Somebody somewhere knows about this horse. He's no mutt. Shame nobody got his papers."

"If you say so." Dusty turned to Duchess to tug his cinch loose, and then paused. "Hey, it looks like you have company."

I looked where he was pointing and felt a big grin growing on my face. Audrey was just closing the door of her car, and Lizzy was already halfway to where we were standing, running as fast as her feet would carry her. "Right on time," I said.

Dusty cocked his head and put his hand up. "Hey, wait. Are you..." He cleared his throat. "You know. Being you?"

"I haven't the foggiest idea what you mean."

"You would if you'd think about it for half a second. You're not... toying with them, are you?"

I glared at him in horror. "Good gravy, what would make you think that? I just hired the kid to do some work around here."

"Yeah, and her aunt is single, good-looking, and kind of lonely. I'm just saying—"

"You've said it," I interrupted. "Go on, now. I got stuff to do."

Dusty shrugged. "Catch you later, I guess."

"So, do we start on his face?" Lizzy asked.

I took the hose from her. "Do you like getting squirted in the face? Here, let's find out."

"Ew, no!" She squealed and put her hands up. "I'm telling!"

"I haven't even turned the water on. Go get that shampoo bottle, will you?" I uncoiled the hose and stretched it across the wash stall, flopping it around Two Bits' legs to make sure it didn't scare him. And, of course, it didn't. Hoses, clippers, cars, ropes—pretty much everything he'd seen wasn't a problem. Someone, somewhere, had put some time into teaching this horse right.

It was a pity someone else had taught him not to trust people.

He'd settled in okay in the last few weeks. Just about everyone in the barn had fed him at some point or another, and he'd lost most of that wary look when they approached. But he didn't like for just anyone to touch him. I was the only one to really spend time trying to pet him and make friends.

He was okay with me now, but he still rolled the whites of his eyes at a few others if they got too close. He really didn't like Danny for some reason, and the best we could figure was that Danny was the only one of us who always wore a baseball cap instead of a cowboy hat. Could be it triggered some bad memories.

I turned the water on, pointing the warm spray at my feet as I adjusted the temperature. Lizzy was standing by with the shampoo bottle. "Okay," I told her. "Here's how we're going to do this. He's pretty okay with me brushing him, so I'm going to use this scrubber here, and you're going to stand there and keep me loaded with shampoo when I need more. Sound good?"

She nodded smartly and tossed a salute. "Yessir."

A faint noise from Audrey brought my attention up. She was smothering a chuckle, but she waved me off and didn't say anything when I raised my eyebrows in question. Too bad. I liked it when she talked to me, and talking about Lizzy was one of the surest ways to get her started.

"You wanna help?" I asked her.

"Oh, no. Horses scare me."

I turned to face her all the way. "But you volunteer up at White Pines all the time."

"Yes, and I make Jess or Kelli handle the horses. I'm strictly crowd control."

"Aw, come on. This poor guy isn't even strong enough to hurt a fly."

"I saw him running," she retorted. "He is most definitely still stronger than I am."

I reached for her hand. "Trust me?"

She shook her head "no," but a playful little twist was turning her mouth. I grabbed her hand, and she let me tug her close.

"See?" I moved her fingers over Two Bits' neck and down his angular shoulder, and he stood rock still. His ear was cocked toward us, but he wasn't snorting, wasn't trembling. He just froze, his eye following her movements.

"Hey, he kinda likes you."

She swallowed hard. "Is that a compliment?"

"From him it is. You should try riding one sometime. I've got a nice gentle old gelding you'd like."

"Haha." She shivered. "I don't think so."

"You sure? Because week after next, we'll be pushing cows out to summer pastures, and I'm telling you, there's just nothing like watching the sun rise over the mountains from the back of a horse. Tin cup of coffee and dinner around the campfire? Best place on earth, I promise."

She lifted her eyes to mine. "I'd have to see that to believe it."

"Invitation's open."

"Oh, I couldn't do anything like that. Even if I knew how to ride, my life is…" She sniffed and blinked, then let her fingers spread beneath mine, sinking into Two Bits' shaggy hair. "He's so warm."

"Didn't you expect him to be?"

She shook her head and wetted her lips. "I guess I was thinking of… of Kat," she whispered, close to my ear so Lizzy couldn't hear. "She's so thin she can't stay warm anymore. He's thin, but he feels so…" She shivered. "Alive."

I held her gaze, and I wasn't thinking about horses anymore. Just having her so close, her hand beneath mine, her breath whispering against my cheek there, had set off an explosion of terrible ideas in my brain. And the trouble was, the longer I chewed on them, the less terrible they sounded.

Was she thinking the same things I was all of a sudden? Her eyes had grown black, and I was sure she was holding her breath. What would she do if I made up some excuse to send Lizzy outside the barn for a second, and then pulled her into my arms and kissed her dizzy?

She'd probably slap me.

I sucked in some fresh air and released her hand. "Well," I said in a louder voice, "Lizzy, shall we get started on this? We don't have all day. Let's go with that shampoo."

The work cleared my head a little. It was actually pretty satisfying, watching all that deep-down dirt work loose from his skin, scrubbing away old scabs and dead hair to reveal the good stuff beneath. I was sure glad of the distraction because that tall brunette watching from six feet away was about to make me leap out of my boots.

I scrubbed around the horse's front end, and finally, I made my way to his left hip. I'd been wondering about this spot since I first saw that mark on him, so maybe after a bath, I'd be able to make it out enough to decide if it was a proper brand or just an old scar. The water rinsed down his hair, and as I squinted, I saw clear as a bell, two straight lines, and a curve.

"Aha. That *is* a brand."

I passed the hose and scrubber to Lizzy and traced the lines with my fingers. An H? No... a sideways J. Or was that an R? He still had too much winter hair to be sure.

"Hey." I gestured to Audrey. "Reach over there and pass me those clippers, please."

Audrey and Lizzy were peering over my shoulders as I towel-dried the hair and flipped on the clippers. "Well? What does it say?"

"Don't know yet. Probably just my imagination, but this looked a little familiar. You know there are hundreds of brands, and every state has its own records, so the chances of me recognizing it are next to nothin'." I smoothed my hand over the stud's hip, then buzzed off about a four-inch square patch of hair.

And when I saw that Rocking J brand underneath, I dropped the clippers.

"What is it?" Audrey asked.

I sucked in a breath and pointed. "That there looks like my friend Joe's brand." I turned to Audrey. "I think I know who this horse is."

Audrey

"Oh, come on. What are the odds of that?" Luke had dragged Dusty into the barn to stare at the brand he'd discovered on the black horse's hip. Jess had come with him, and the five of us were gathered around the dripping horse, trying to verify what we were seeing.

"Can't be one of Joe's horses," Dusty decided. "That would mean this horse came out of Oklahoma."

"So? Trailers go back and forth to Oklahoma," Luke argued. "Joe's been raising good rope horses for fifteen years, and his program's nationally recognized. Lots of his horses have made their way across the country. And Cody did say the folks who had this horse were trying to get some kind of breeding operation going. Stands to reason they might've tried to get a nice stud to start with. Ten bucks say this horse really is a son of Joe's old stud Two Bits."

Dusty shook his head and gazed at Luke with a patient smile of disbelief. "Fine. I guess there's one way to test your theory."

"Yep." Luke pulled his phone out and tapped up a phone number. "Are you taking the bet?"

"Oh, why not?" Dusty waved and walked off. "Tell me what he says."

I leaned over to Jess while Luke waited for the phone to ring. "What would it mean if he's right?"

Jess rolled her eyes and chuckled. "Just that maybe the horse's pedigree and history could be traced. That would make it easier to find someone to adopt him, if and when the time comes. But I think Luke's already forgotten all the things that have to happen for that to be possible."

"Like?"

"Well, for one, even if you can prove who the horse is, it's doubtful you'll ever be able to get registration papers on him because the old owner will probably refuse to sign off."

"What do papers do?"

"I guess you could say they're like a horse's resume. Especially if he's a performance or a breeding horse, you really want them. Lots of good horses aren't registered—I've owned some, myself—but I still say it's better for a horse's prospects down the road if he has them."

"Like a college degree. That makes sense, I guess."

Jess pointed at the tall cowboy who was pacing and fast-talking on the phone. "And if I know Luke, he's already scheming a way to rehabilitate this stud and build a rope horse breeding program around him, but if he's legally adopted as a rescue, he'll have to be gelded. But all that doesn't even matter because I talked to Morgan the other day, and she says the people are trying to work out a deal where they get their animals back. She thinks they'll succeed."

My mouth fell open. "How? Has no one looked at these animals? I'm no expert, but even I can see this was horrible neglect and abuse!"

"Yeah." Jess lifted her shoulders, and her jaw clenched in anger. "It just doesn't seem right. Doc Burns and a few others are set to testify about the case, but it's in the hands of the lawyers now. Anyway," she sighed, "it probably doesn't matter too much whether Luke is able to identify the horse. It doesn't change anything."

I felt sick. Was it possible that this horse had been rescued, cared for—even loved, because you couldn't call the attention Luke was giving him anything less than that—all for him to go right back to the people who'd nearly killed him? And now I understood the sad, pitying looks everyone shared when they talked about Luke and Two Bits because anyone could see how invested he was in this horse. I folded my arms and watched him as he was talking to his friend on the phone, and his expression said it all.

"Dusty, you owe me ten bucks!" he crowed as he hung up. "Joe's digging up his records, but he remembers this horse. Man, he was ticked when he heard what sort of shape he's in. Better not send him any pictures yet until I get some meat on his bones."

He stared at his phone and tapped a message when it came up. Then he gave a low whistle. "Dusty, check this out. Joe just sent me his pedigree. Boy, howdy, he's bred in the purple. I told you!"

Dusty tugged a ten out of his wallet without saying a word. He and Jess exchanged a look, and then he walked over to peer at Luke's phone. "Wow," he agreed. "Very nice."

"See? Look back here..."

I didn't understand much of what they were saying from there on. Something about this line or that foundation or one horse's lifetime earnings. I was relieved when Jess touched my elbow and whispered, "Come on, I'll make you some tea in the bunkhouse."

I followed her out of the barn, still glancing over my shoulder several times. Lizzy was staying behind to clean stalls, but she wasn't the one I couldn't take my eyes off of.

Cowboys weren't supposed to steal your breath and make your knees turn to jelly. They weren't supposed to be able to flip your heart inside out just by touching your hand, or make you dream about the kind of life you could never have when they gazed down into your eyes. But Luke was doing all that, and I didn't know how to make him stop.

Or if I wanted him to.

"Herbal tea or black?" Jess asked as she put on the kettle and opened her cupboards.

"Black, please. Something stout, if you have it." I glanced around the tiny bunkhouse that Jess and her new husband had made their temporary home—the cozy quilts and throw pillows, the earthy smells of old leather, and outdated wood paneling. It spoke of a different world than I'd ever known—a simple life, a comfortable life full of hard work and quiet pleasures. A place where the crisp, modern glitz and grace of my life in New York seemed pretentious and over-stated.

I sank onto her couch and just filled my senses with the place. It was nothing special. Just an old mobile home that would probably fall apart if they ever tried to move it, but it was clean and it was dry, and it had a wood stove for the cold evenings. And a view like no other, because with the curtains open, I could see past the rolling fields near the barns and up into the mountains.

My apartment in New York looked out into a back alley at another building. It had cost me nearly three thousand dollars a month, with neighbors who made noise next door but wouldn't make eye contact in the elevator. It had felt isolated, cold, and unwelcoming compared to the home-spun charm of the ranch bunkhouse.

"Here you go," Jess said as she carried a cup and saucer to me. "I hope English Breakfast is okay. I used to keep more varieties, but I don't have room here to store all the boxes."

"This is fine. Thank you." I blew the steam off the cup and reveled in the bitter aroma. This was what I needed—something familiar to remind me of who I was. The last thing I wanted right now was some small-town romantic idea stealing my common sense and making me forget about all the goals I'd worked so hard for back home.

"So..." Jess plopped down beside me. "What's up with you and Luke?"

I choked on my first sip of tea. "Wow. Blunt much?"

"I guess I am. But you know me, right? I'm not trying to be nosy just to have something to gossip about."

I shook my head and pulled the tea bag out of my cup. "That's one thing I do know. You're not a gossip."

"Right. And maybe it's not my business, but you're both my friends, and I care about you guys. I just hope..."

I chuckled ruefully. "That we won't do something stupid?"

"Not exactly what I meant to say."

I shook my head. "You don't have to warn me about Luke. Kelli already did, and I've heard enough about him... no. It's not happening, Jess."

"Actually, I wasn't going to warn you. Kind of the opposite."

I squinted at her in astonishment. "You're not serious. You think I should date Luke?"

"Well, technically, I didn't say that, either. I was just going to..." Jess puckered her lips and stared at the ceiling in thought. "Observe. That's the right word. I was going to *observe* that Luke's been different lately. Less flirtatious, more serious. He used to tease every pretty girl who walked by him, but he hasn't been doing that."

"That doesn't mean anything."

She laughed. "With Luke, it does! Seriously, what would you say if he asked you out?"

"Oh, dear, I hardly know." I sipped some tea and savored it for a minute. "I admit, he's... He's..." I couldn't even say it. I just shrugged and laughed.

"He's adorable, isn't he? You just can't not like Luke."

"Something like that. But I can't get involved with him! For one thing, there's Kat and Lizzy."

"So?"

"So, I'm too busy for a relationship! And it would be a relationship that can't go anywhere because it doesn't make any sense for me to put down roots here."

Her expression sobered, and she sipped some of her tea. "I keep forgetting that you plan to move back to New York someday."

"There wouldn't be much reason for me to stay here. Even if Lizzy comes with me, I can provide her with a much better life there. Better schools, I can save more for her college. It's just a no-brainer."

"Mmm." Jess sighed. "Okay, what about experiences?"

"Come again?"

She uncrossed her knees and leaned toward me, her eyes alight. "You've done nothing but care for Kat and Lizzy since you came here. You can't go back to New York after living here for two years or better and say you never... I don't know, kissed a cowboy. Rode a horse. Went on a camp-out. What if you just tasted what real life here is like before you went back?"

I raised a brow. "You've been eavesdropping, haven't you?"

"No, why?"

"Because Luke practically dared me to go on a cattle drive with him. Me! I've never been on a horse in my life, but he was talking like he could just toss me on some gelding he had and hit the trail!"

"Ah, you could do that." Jess waved a hand. "Easy. There won't be any fancy riding or theatrics. It's just pushing fat old mama cows and their babies onto green pasture, so they have to go slow. And Luke might act like a wild child, but he's dead serious about his horses. If he says it's gentle, it is. You'd just have some pretty sore muscles when it was all over."

"But what about Kat? You know I can't leave for an overnight camping trip in the mountains."

Jess frowned and swirled what was left in her cup. "You know, Dusty and I aren't going on this trip. They don't need everyone, and they decided that Dusty and Cody would stay home and keep things running on the ranch for a few days. Plus, I actually do still have a job when I can get to it."

"What are you saying, Jess?"

She shrugged. "Just that I could fill in for you on the night shift. Pick Lizzy up from school, help with Kat, get the meals on the table. You'd have to show me what to do, but I know how to start an IV."

"You wouldn't have to start an IV. She has a fistula."

"See, there you go. What would you say?"

I scoffed. "I say it's crazy! I can't just..."

"Yes," Jess interrupted. "You can, and you deserve a break. But only if you want to."

I swallowed and fisted my hand at my mouth. "It would only be one night?"

"You'd leave Thursday morning at daybreak and be home sometime Friday evening. They've got all the bedrolls and camp setup, so you won't have to worry about anything. Just show up."

"But work—"

"You're the boss. Reschedule so it's just dental cleanings and no fillings those days."

I stared at her as a wild, reckless thrill started to tremble through me. "I'm really doing this, aren't I?"

Jess grinned and gave me a thumbs-up. "Yes, girl, you're really doing this! The cattle drive part, at least. The kissing the cowboy part, I guess you'll have to decide on later."

Chapter 15

Luke

"Are you sure this is a good idea?"

I yanked the straps of my pack horse's load and adjusted my hat to look at Evan. "What's a good idea?"

He tipped his head to the side. "You know what. Audrey's never even ridden before, and you're just going to bring her along on a cattle drive?"

"She's ridden. Jess and Morgan put her on Biz a couple of times this week, showin' her the ropes. Then I had her sit on Gambit yesterday to find a saddle that fits her."

Evan scowled. "Be serious, Luke."

"I am being serious. She's a doctor, so she knows how to look out for herself."

"She's a dentist, and it's not her riding the horse that concerns me."

I pointed at my chest. "You're worried *I'll* be the problem?"

"There's enough history to justify that, yes."

I shook my head and grabbed my pack horse's lead rope to stalk off. "Awesome, thanks. What a brother." I jerked to a stop, bristling and annoyed. "What makes you think I'd do anything to hurt her?"

Evan looked down and shoved his hands in his pockets. "Just seems like you're throwing her in the deep end. You barely know each other, and she's never done anything like this. You sure she knows what she's getting into?"

"I didn't twist her arm. Matter of fact, I never expected her to say yes."

"And now that she has?"

I shrugged. "I'm gonna show her a good time. And if she's still walkin' and talkin' to me when it's over, I might ask her out on a real date." I grabbed an extra rain slicker off the hook and threw it over my shoulder, then tugged my pack horse out of the barn into the pre-dawn darkness. "Are we gonna get this show on the road, or what?"

"Are you warm enough?"

Audrey's teeth were clenched, and it looked like she was shivering, but when I got close enough to peek at her big brown eyes under the rim of her hat, I could see what it really was. She was trembling and white as a ghost.

"F-fine. I'll be alright." She sucked in a breath and clenched her eyes. "Tell me again why I'm doing this?"

"'Cause it'll be fun. You'll see." I pulled the collar of her coat so it would stand up and fluffed her scarf up around her throat a little better.

"Right." She made a pair of fists like she was psyching herself up. "Saddle sores and pit stops behind a bush. Can't wait."

"That's the spirit. Here, I brought you a slicker. Keep you a lot drier than that short coat you have."

"Is it supposed to rain?"

I chuckled as I tied the slicker to the back of her saddle. "Darlin', it's April in the Rockies. We'll probably get hail and snow, and if we're lucky, maybe even some lightning."

Her lips parted, and she just blinked at me. "And this is your idea of fun?"

"No. Fun is when you saddle a cold-backed colt first thing in the morning after a long rainy ride the day before." I flashed her a grin. "Always good for a little excitement."

"Please tell me my horse isn't... what did you say?"

"Cold-backed? Nah. Gambit's as steady as they come. He'll take good care of you. Ready? Evan wanted to get rolling before daylight if we can." I checked her cinch and patted the saddle seat.

She sucked in a deep breath. "No. Help me on before I chicken out."

I came close and flicked the brim of the hat she'd borrowed from Jess so I could see her face better. "You're going to be fine, Audrey. I won't let anything happen to you."

Her throat bobbed. "Promise?"

"Cross my heart."

Her shoulders lifted, and her eyes fluttered closed. "Okay. Let's go, cowboy."

Audrey

Luke was right about one thing. Watching the sun rise over foggy mountains, shattering the jagged hills into breaks of blue and green below, was a sight I won't forget as long as I live.

He told me to stay right beside his horse until it was full daylight, but I think that was more to give me confidence than to keep me safe. I learned pretty quickly that Gambit could see what I couldn't, and really, all I had to do was let go and let the horse do his job. But letting go proved to be harder than I thought.

"Are you breathing?" Luke asked.

"Mostly."

He reached over and grabbed the hand I was holding the reins with. "You've got a death grip. You're gonna give yourself arthritis before the end of the day. Here, loosen up."

He pried my fingers apart, twisting his between mine and breaking my fist into something softer. We were both wearing thick gloves, but it was easy to forget I was holding the horse's reins when Luke's hand was tangled with mine. He massaged the center of my palm with his thumb. "Better?"

I just looked over at him—a hat and a strong chin and broad shoulders silhouetted by a pink morning sky. And right there, I finally understood why so many women can't resist a cowboy. "Y-yes."

"Just close your eyes for a second. I like to do that sometimes. Hear the birds wakin' up, the cows mooing as they walk, the saddle squeakin'. Feel your horse rockin' and that solid ground under you. This is what it's all about."

I closed my eyes like he said, and it was like a new landscape slipped in beneath my feet. There was so much that I could hear and feel when I wasn't just trusting my eyes and what I was used to. His hand slid out of mine, and at first, I tensed up again. But his voice got me through, reminding me to breathe and trust and just *be*.

When I opened my eyes again, the sun had fully pierced through a break in the mountains beyond. Daylight blossomed around us almost immediately, and I swept my gaze over the clearing with new appreciation.

I could see Blake out in front, giving the herd something to follow. Off to his left, about a hundred feet away rode Meryl, and Evan was over to the right. Luke and I were pushing the left flank of the bunch, with Marshall and Kelli and the two pack horses closing in the massive circle. And in the midst of it all was the cows—a hundred or more mothers snatching bites of grass as they ambled along, their babies scampering and colliding with each other.

I tipped back my head and let the morning light bathe my face and felt my lower back loosening to roll with my horse's stride instead of resisting it. And I remembered to breathe. "You know?" I said to Luke. "This is much prettier than my usual morning commute."

He laughed. "Knew you'd like it."

"I don't even think I care if it rains later." I waited for him to look my way, and I gave him the biggest, most honest smile I'd ever managed. "Thank you for inviting me."

Luke

"Just so you know, it doesn't always rain *all* day."

Audrey was hunched inside her slicker, her hat running rivers of water down the back of it, and she clenched her teeth as her eyes rolled over to me. "Just most of it?"

I checked my watch and earned a trickle of rainwater down inside my sleeve. "Don't worry about it. We'll get to the campsite in about another hour, and you can warm up by the fire. We're making pretty good time."

"What time is it?"

"Almost seven. Last year we had a washout at the creek. Took us extra time to cross, and we didn't get to camp till the middle of the night. So, this is a good year."

"Remind me not to go with you on a bad year."

I trotted my horse a little closer to her. "Hey, wait a second. Does that mean you'd come again sometime?"

Her mouth dropped into a little round, surprised gasp. "Oh, well, I was joking. I mean, I guess..." She looked away, scanning the line of cows beside us, then glanced down at her saddle horn. "Sure. Yeah, I'd maybe come again sometime. But I might change my mind when I get off and have to try walking."

"You get used to it. See, your legs will just sort of bend so they fit the saddle better. You'll be walking like a bow-legged bronc rider in no time."

She giggled. "That's got to be made up."

"Nah. Watch my dad walk sometime. You'll wonder how he even gets around on the ground. Hang on a second." I turned my horse to check out a cow that had been making an all-fired ruckus for a couple of minutes. I could see her, but she was frantically turning around and bellowing every few seconds.

Audrey stopped. "What's the matter?"

"Sounds like she's lost her calf." I cupped my hands around my mouth. "Hey, Marshall! What's up with this one?"

He shook his head and pointed. "I didn't see her calf wander off," he shouted back. "She just started that. I think she forgot the little feller when we stopped for water."

I groaned. That was half an hour ago. Someone would have to ride back and try to find him. "Well?" I called.

"I got the last stray. Your turn."

I slumped in my saddle with a growl. Yeah, it was my turn. Having Audrey along had meant that I'd taken the easier points, ridden a little slower, and stayed with the main group all day. I guess I couldn't have it like that the whole time. I rounded my horse and walked over to her.

"I'll have to backtrack and fetch that calf. Now, you'll be fine. You just go ride beside Kelli over there or stay about where you're at. Nice and easy, you've got the hang of this now."

"Do I have to stay here? I mean, can they get along fine without a rider where I am?"

I lifted my hat a little. "Well, sure. They'll spread out a little to cover the hole. It's what we do."

"Then, I'd like to come with you, if you don't mind. It's part of the whole experience, right? Going after a stray?"

I rested my arm on the horn of my saddle and grinned, shaking my head. "For the girl who didn't really even want to do this, you're cowgirlin' right up. You sure?"

She nodded vigorously enough that drips of rainwater splashed off the brim of her hat. "If I won't be in your way."

"Nope. I'll be glad of the company. Come on, then. If we hurry, we'll get back in time for some of Meryl's camp stew."

Audrey

I hadn't felt my toes in a couple of hours, but I was pretty sure they'd be shriveled like raisins when I pulled my boots off. Luke had outfitted me with the slicker and a pair of thick leather leggings to keep me warm, but nobody had boots my size, so I'd had to make do with the cheap western boots I'd bought for Morgan's wedding last year. More for looks than for using, they pinched my toes and did nothing to keep out the water when we splashed through the creek. I'd already sworn they were going in the garbage when I got home.

"Let's check the other side," Luke said. "He might've gotten stuck in the brush down by the bank."

I nodded wordlessly and steered my horse to follow his. This part wasn't so hard. The horse just plodded along and went wherever I told him, for the most part. Kelli had told me—none too gently—that if the horse wasn't doing what I wanted, it was probably because I wasn't asking right, but Gambit and I were getting along pretty well. My main problem now was that everything—and I mean *everything*—ached.

Luke guided his horse down a shallow embankment and plodded through the stream, and I dropped in right behind. The water was up to the horses' knees and running fast and cold from the spring

snowmelt. Some of the cows had balked at it when we crossed earlier, but we'd checked all along it pretty thoroughly when we pushed
them onward. How could one have gotten lost? I craned my neck and
twisted around in the saddle to look around the bend, but I didn't spot
anything.

We'd just stepped up to the rocks on the other side when Luke held
up his hand and stopped. "Wait. Can you hear anything?"

I held my breath and strained my ears. "I just hear water splashing
and rocks rolling in the stream."

He shook his head. "That's not rocks rolling. This way." He turned
upstream and urged his horse into a trot.

I groaned and felt my leg muscles die. Seriously? "Okay, Gambit," I
hissed through my teeth. "We'd better catch up." I gave the best kick I
could, and he lurched into a bone-jarring trot after Luke's horse.

"There he is!" Luke disappeared behind the boulder where the
stream turned. I could just see his horse's tail swishing and the swing
of his foot as he jumped out of the saddle. "Hey, come on over here. I
might need a hand."

He was assuming I'd be able to walk when I got off! I stopped
my horse next to his and winced as I made my legs do the unthink-
able—move at my bidding without collapsing. I slid down from the
saddle, hoping to touch down gently, but my foot was so numb I
slipped on a river rock, and my hat flipped off.

"Ah!" I yelped, grabbing for Gambit's mane. It would be just my
luck to roll my ankle right now, nine hours from civilization with no
way out but horse or helicopter. But before my feet could sweep out
from under me, before I could lose my balance and fall, I felt Luke's
arms close around me. His chest was solid behind me, his hands steady
at my waist, and he pulled me back to my feet.

"You alright?" he asked in my ear.

I nodded, my hands drifting down to cover his. "I think so."

He didn't let me go all at once. He just held me, his chin close to my cheek. His breathing hitched, and I heard him swallow before he blew out a sigh. "Right. Well. Uh, turn around and grab my shoulders. Let's make sure your ankle's okay."

I inched around and found myself embracing Luke Walker. His hands were still at my hips, keeping me close, while mine seemed to find their way around his neck. His Adam's apple bobbed, and his eyes drifted to my mouth.

I sucked in a breath. "I think I can walk."

He blinked, and a few seconds later, he nodded. "Okay, good. Let's check that calf." He stepped back, his hands sliding away, and I wobbled a little as he let me go.

This just wouldn't do. I was rapidly losing a grip on whatever sanity I had left—which couldn't be much because I'd agreed to come on this crazy trip. And now, my heart was racing, and my brain was turning to mush whenever that cowboy looked at me.

I clenched a fist and closed my eyes. "Come on, Audrey," I scolded myself. "Keep it together!" I'd just enjoy this for what it was—a chance to get out and do something I'd never done before with a guy who was too cute not to like. I couldn't let my imagination run wild and fall for a cowboy on a cattle drive. How cliche would that be?

"Audrey, can you get out here okay? I might need you to pull his hoof out." Luke had scrambled over some rocks in front of where the horses were standing, and he was bending over a little black form. "Looks like he tried to walk through here and got stuck."

The rain was running down my face now, but I didn't take the time to go back for my hat. I put my arms out for balance and tiptoed over the wet rocks after him. The calf had collapsed on his chest, half in the water, with a hopeless look on his little black face. "He looks cold," I said.

"Probably is. I just hope his legs are okay and he hasn't had too much of a shock." Luke came around to the calf's right side and gestured with the brim of his hat. "Side your hand down that front leg there. When I say 'go,' I'm going to roll this rock out of the way. If he kicks free on his own, let him go, but he's probably been here a good forty-five minutes, so he might need help. Ready?"

I nodded.

"Okay. Go." Luke grunted, and his boots scrambled in the riverbed as he hefted the rock.

I felt down the leg and gave a pull, and the foot popped free. But the calf didn't jump and run off, like I hoped he would.

"Dang. Other leg must be stuck, too." He had to slosh through several inches of water to go around. "Watch out. He'll either fall or jump when I get this."

I straightened and waited as Luke reached into the water. He felt around, and then his shoulders jerked as he gave a pull. Freed, the calf writhed and leaped, crashing into Luke's chest and splashing away. Luke flailed, his arms spiraling to keep his balance.

I don't know what made me do it. He'd saved me, so I guess I thought I could save him, and I reached out to grab the front of his rain slicker. I'm not sure which one of us actually fell into the other, but there I was, rocked in that cowboy's arms and staggering to keep my feet in the rolling creek. Rain was running down my hair and dripping into my eyes, and it seemed like the best idea in the world to duck under the shelter of his hat.

Luke just froze for a few seconds. Then his hands came up and cradled the sides of my face, his thumbs caressing my cheeks. This time, when his gaze dipped to my mouth, I didn't shy back. I tasted sweet rain and Luke's warm lips and the kind of wild abandon I'd always run from. It was like a cage around my heart had broken open, and I clung to that cowboy for all my life was worth.

Chapter 16

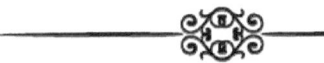

Luke

"Toes getting warm yet?" I walked around behind Audrey and passed her a cup of hot joe. She was huddled under a thick blanket I'd thrown into my pack saddle just for her, and her stockinged feet were stretched toward the campfire to dry out.

She tipped her face up to me with a smile and scooted over on the log to make room for me. "Much better. Meryl's stew sure helped."

"Yeah, except Marshall hogged half of it," I said with a chuckle. "Got your tent all set up. There's a lantern in there and an extra bed roll underneath your main one for more padding. You should be comfy enough."

"Why do I get the feeling that you're spoiling me?"

I touched my hat and winked. "Maybe because I am."

Audrey tucked her hands inside my collar, against my jaw, and pressed a kiss to my lips. "Thank you," she whispered.

"Is that all I get?"

"Are you accusing me of being stingy?" Her fingers wrapped around the back of my neck, snaking into my hair, and she pulled me down for a deeper kiss. She really did taste like espresso and chocolate—rich and velvety and exquisite. Too good for me, really, but I wasn't complaining.

She kissed her way down to my chin, then let her hand drop, but I couldn't stop staring. How had a guy like me managed to turn the head of a smart, classy woman like Audrey Livingstone? I didn't even feel qualified to guess the answer.

"Hey, are you alright?" she asked.

I made myself nod. No, I wasn't alright, but I'd pretend. "Yeah. Just fine. So, did Dad and Meryl crash for the night?"

"Just a few minutes ago. You know, it's kind of humbling that Meryl's twice my age, and she acts like she could easily do another five days of this."

"You ought to try keeping up with my dad. He runs circles around all of us." I stretched my boots out and looked up at the stars. This was one of my favorite things about coming up here—the view.

Audrey followed the direction of my gaze and laced her fingers through mine. "Beautiful. It's nice that the rain stopped when the sun went down."

"Yeah, and pretty soon, we get to see a real show." I pointed up at the sky, where a few straggling clouds were clearing away from the moon. "Get away from the campfire, and the stars up here are like nothing you've ever seen."

She closed her eyes, letting the fire warm her face, and drank in a breath of that clean mountain air I loved so well. "Oh, this is amazing. How can I feel so miserable and so incredibly satisfied all at once?"

I nodded. "That's kind of where I live most of the time."

Audrey laughed and sipped some coffee. "I shouldn't drink this so late at night. I'll never get to sleep."

"Trust me. After a day like today, you could drink five cups and still sleep like a baby." I tugged the blanket up a little higher around her shoulders. "Sure you're warm enough?"

Her eyes dropped to the blanket, then she bit her lip, and a playful look dawned on her face. "Yes, but I know a way to get warmer." She stretched her arm out and tossed half the blanket over me.

That was too good of an idea to pass up, so I snuggled a little closer, slipped my arm behind her inside the blanket, and wrapped us up like a burrito. "There. Comfy?"

She buried her head against my shoulder and nodded. "Thank you for inviting me up here, Luke. This is... I'll never forget this as long as I live."

I turned to brush a kiss against her hair—still damp from our little splash in the creek. "Me neither."

"Hey, Audrey," Kelli called from the darkness. We could see the flash of her tin coffee cup and the glint off Marshall's belt buckle as they approached the fire after setting up their tent. "Need some ibuprofen?"

Audrey lifted her head a little, but she didn't pull away. I liked that—she wasn't too proud to be seen cozying up to me. "I already took a handful! Thank you, though."

"Sure thing." Kelli plopped down on the opposite log and Marshall draped another blanket around her shoulders. She looked up and caught his hand as he stepped away. "Thanks, babe."

Marshall squeezed his wife's fingers, then walked over to grab a few more pieces of firewood. "How you feeling, Audrey? Still walking okay?"

"I'll let you know tomorrow, Marshall. So, with the fire pit and the tent clearing over there, it looks like you guys camp here often."

"Twice every year," I said. "Evan and I are the ones who cut and stripped these logs back when we were… oh, I think that was the summer I turned thirteen. There's a good pocket over that rise for the cows to get out of the weather, and that stream we crossed earlier cuts back over that way so they have water through the summer. We'll let them stay up here till the end of August before the grass runs out, then we'll push them back down. Hey, Marshall, think it's going to rain any more on our way back down?"

"Hopefully not. We should get home quick tomorrow." Marshall lowered himself to the log beside his wife and heaved a long sigh. "Anyone know where Evan went?"

"Last I saw him, he was pitching his tent," Kelli said.

Audrey pointed. "He walked into the trees a few minutes ago. He was carrying a lantern and a notebook or something, and he looked like he wanted to be left alone."

Marshall met my eyes, and we both shook our heads. "He did," I said. "He ain't been right since he lost Anne and his daughter Emma. Likes solitude better than people. And that wasn't a notebook. It was a little sketch pad."

Audrey rested her chin on my shoulder. "What does he draw?"

"He isn't the artist. Emma was."

Kelli was frowning now. "I didn't know that."

Marshall tucked himself into Kelli's blanket and pulled her under his arm. "I forgot about it. Yeah, Emma got to come up here a couple of times that last summer. She was determined to draw everything she saw, but she only got about six pages done. She told Evan that she'd bring that same sketchbook back every year until all the pages were full. I think he decided he'd finish it for her."

Audrey was covering her mouth with her hand, and I caught the gleam of a tear in the firelight. "I had no idea."

Kelli didn't say anything—she just stared at the fire, her lower lip puckered in a pout and her expression broken.

I tightened my arm around Audrey and leaned my cheek on her head. I hadn't meant to make her sad, tonight of all nights. She had come up here to switch up the monotony and stress of her life, and for some reason I still couldn't describe, she'd let me be the one to pull her away from it all. Evan's story broke all our hearts, but it didn't need to break hers, too.

"Hey," I murmured into her hair, "did you want to check out the stars before we hit the hay?"

She turned into me slightly, and her soft smile in the firelight's glow said it all. I grabbed her boots from beside the coals and helped her tug them onto her feet, then stood and offered her my hand.

"Good night, you two," Kelli said. I'm pretty sure she stifled a giggle, but Marshall nudged her, and she made her face go straight.

I didn't care what they thought. I had my arm around the most gorgeous woman I'd ever encountered—a woman who challenged everything about me and made me long to be the kind of man she wanted. The kind of man she needed and deserved. I didn't plan on letting go anytime soon.

I led her away from the light of the fire into the shadow of the tent I'd set up for her and pointed to a couple of stumps we could use for seats. Audrey narrowed her eyes. "Luke Walker, if I didn't know any better, I'd say you were planning this."

"Of course I was. I'm not ashamed to own up to it."

She wrapped her arm through mine and laughed. "Well, I hope I don't disappoint you."

"I'm more worried I'll disappoint you." I pulled her close and traced the full outline of her lips with my fingertips. Her breath was warm on my skin, and my pulse was racing like it hadn't done since I straddled my last bull. She was just so perfect, and if I knew me at all, I'd find some way to mess it up.

"Luke?"

"Yeah?"

"Are we going to look at the stars, or are you going to kiss me?"

I grinned and pointed. "Stars are right there, see? But I think I'd rather kiss you."

She nodded and grabbed my face. "Same here."

Audrey

"You did it, didn't you? You kissed yourself a cowboy."

I dropped my keys on the kitchen counter and turned to face Jess, my mouth open in shock as I shook my head. "I'll never tell."

"Liar!" she laughed. "So? How was your trip?"

I blew out a sigh. "I don't even know where to start. Who knew that a cattle drive could be the most unforgettable couple of days of my life?"

"Well, me. I knew that."

I gave her a playful push in the shoulder. "Get out. Really, I'm just... everything seems new now. All the crap of normal life seems like such a petty waste of time. Who needs a real job? I'll just give it all up and go wrangle cows for a living."

"Uh-huh. And what about the cowboy?"

I sank into a chair at the kitchen table. "I think I'm going crazy. *He's* crazy, and I can't get enough of him. But what in the world would I actually do with so much crazy in my life?"

Jess sat across from me and shrugged, rolling her eyes to the ceiling. "I mean, it's not like your life now is sane. It would just be a different kind of insanity."

"Right!" I propped my elbows on the table and buried my face in my hands. "Yeah, I'll just give up on New York and my career. Do you know how many years I spent in school? I'm still paying off loans, and at this rate, I probably will be until I die."

"But it's not like you can't use your degree here," Jess reasoned. "I'd even go so far as to say our town needs you. You have something to offer that no one else around here does."

"Jess, I'm not just a dentist. I'm a specialized oral surgeon with a sterling reputation, and job offers pretty much anywhere I want to go. In just about any city in America, I can earn well over a quarter million dollars a year. But here? I'm lucky to pay the bills."

Her mouth dropped open. "Oh." She blinked. "Wow, my friend is super smart!"

"Not smart enough. I'm losing my head over a cowboy who barely graduated high school, and I'm enjoying every minute of it."

"Luke might not have been an academic, but he's far from dumb," Jess said defensively.

"Oh, I..." I held my hands up. "I didn't mean it that way at all. I have every respect for him and his abilities. He can do things I've never even dreamed of! It's just so far out of my sphere that..." I drummed my fingers on the table. "I just don't know how our worlds would really fit together. And I can't afford to lose my heart to a relationship that might be doomed before it gets off the ground."

Jess chewed her lip. "I guess you just need to figure out your priorities. You know me—I read romance novels, and I have this silly notion that love will always find a way. I really do believe that, but if you don't, then you owe it to Luke and to Lizzy and yourself not to get carried away. I'd hate to see you hurt each other."

I heaved a breath and nodded, my eyes drifting to the window beyond Jess. "Sometimes I wish God would give me a big road sign. 'Go that way.' Something like that."

"I think He does. You just have to pay attention, but with the way you drive, you probably ran over it."

I snorted a laugh and pressed the heels of my hands into my eyes. "Shut up. How is Kat?"

"Asleep. I just looked in on her right before you pulled in. Oh, and a nurse was here today. She said she'd left you a voicemail."

I straightened and pulled my phone out of my pocket. "Is that what that was? I saw the notification when we got back to cell service, but I didn't recognize the number, so I didn't listen yet. What about Lizzy?"

"She was kind of upset that you didn't get back before her dad came to pick her up. She wanted to hear about your adventures."

"Oh, man. I really thought I'd make it, but James *would* choose this week to actually pick her up on time."

"Of course, he would." Jess got up from the table and walked around to put her arms around me from behind. "I need to get home. Dusty will start thinking I forgot about him."

I wrapped my hands over her arms and gave her a squeeze. "Thanks, Jess. You really didn't have to do this, but I'm so grateful."

"I'm glad you went. And don't worry about Luke. He's a big boy. Just take your time, enjoy the crazy, and see where it leads you."

I laughed. "That's about the worst advice I ever heard."

"And there's more where that came from! See you tomorrow?"

"Yeah." I pushed up from the table to give her a real hug. "I'm going to visit the ranch tomorrow."

"Atta girl."

Kat was still asleep when I got out of the shower. I scanned the log chart beside her bed—Jess had been meticulous—and checked her heart rate on the monitor she was wearing now. It was low, and so was her oxygen level. I swallowed, and my eyes started to sting.

"Oh, Kat," I breathed. I sank into the chair beside her bed and took her hand in mine. "What are we going to do?"

Her fingers felt cool, but they stirred to life when I cupped them between my hands. Her chest rose a little more, and slowly, she opened her eyes.

"Hey," she rasped.

"Hey, yourself. I'm sorry, I didn't mean to wake you."

Her mouth turned up. "How was it?"

What could I tell her? I couldn't rub it in her face that I'd just had an incredible time with a sweet, fun-loving man who made me want to forget everything and become a cattle rancher. But all the pleasure in Kat's life now was vicarious—she was living through me, whether it was for my part in her daughter's life or the dreams I still had the hope of chasing. Romance and adventure were forgotten memories for her.

I sniffed and wove my fingers through hers as I searched for the words. "It was amazing," I managed.

"And Luke?" came her ragged whisper.

Despite my blurry vision, I couldn't help the giddy blush that came over my face. "He's amazing, too."

Kat's eyes closed, but she was still smiling. "Don't make my mistake, Aud."

Her mistake? The only place Kat had gone wrong was trusting the wrong guy. Did she think Luke was like James? "What do you mean by that?"

She tried to pick her head up. "Don't..." She gave up and dropped her head back to the pillow. "Don't settle," she sighed.

Don't settle. What did that mean? Don't just take up with Luke Walker because he was here, and he was sweet and a good kisser, and he was the kind of guy to take care of a girl for the rest of her life? Or don't settle for a cold, faceless career where I could be replaced at any moment by the next hot shot, when I could have the kind of love they make movies about?

"Kat, I don't understand. What..."

I broke off. She was asleep again, her head tipped to the side, and her fingers slack in my hand. The heart monitor was staggering along with its slow beeps, and the room eerily still.

I tucked her blankets a little tighter around her legs, checked her over one last time before leaving the room, and closed the door behind myself. I could use some sleep, too. Just a quick text to Luke to say goodnight...

Except I'd forgotten about that voicemail. Jess said it was from a nurse, so I should probably listen. I touched my screen as I wandered back to my own bedroom, and the message started playing.

"Hello, Doctor Livingstone, this is Julianne Walters at Mercy Medical Center. I work with Doctor Andrews, and he would like to discuss palliative care options for Katherine. Doctor Andrews feels that discon-

tinuing the dialysis may be in her best interest at this time, and he would like to schedule a call with..."

My phone slipped out of my hand.

Discontinue dialysis! So, this was it, then? We were just giving up? My throat closed, and I crumpled to my knees beside my bed. What would happen now? If we discontinued everything, Kat would simply vanish in a matter of weeks or even days. I tried wiping my eyes, and my nose, but the shock just kept running down my face.

How could I give up on my sister? On Lizzy's mother?

But how could I ask her to suffer any longer just because I couldn't let her go?

I leaned on my bed, my head buried in my arms, and sobbed. It wasn't fair! Kat had so much to live for. No one remembered anymore that she could sing like a nightingale or that she was voted the homecoming queen, or that she used to play dolls with me when I was little, and she was "too old" for that kind of thing. Nobody knew that she'd once dreamed of playing on Broadway, and nobody knew how much she gave up for Lizzy.

Time was just too short, and it seemed like so much of the little time Kat had been given was just wasted. What could I do to make the rest of it everything it could be?

The only thing I knew was that I couldn't lose another minute. And I shouldn't have gone to the mountains with Luke.

Chapter 17

Luke
Three weeks later

"Luke, Dusty, give me some slack!" Evan shouted. He was trying to reposition a young steer we'd just roped out in the lower eighty so he could doctor a wounded leg, but the little devil was fighting him tooth and nail.

"I *am*," Dusty shot back. "It's Luke's end. Luke, wake up over there!"

I nudged my horse a little farther forward. "I ain't asleep at the wheel. I thought you wanted me to keep him tight so he couldn't kick you in the face."

There was a reason Evan usually did the doctoring—he was fast. He reached in with a quick dab of the antibiotic ointment, pulled the ropes, and stepped out of the way. "Let him go. Is that the last one we needed to check?"

"Sure hope so. I'm starved, and Jess's dad is coming over for burgers, so I need to go help her." Dusty coiled his rope and tied it back to his saddle. "Luke, is Audrey coming up this evening?"

I flicked the kinks out of my rope, but I didn't put it away yet. "Doubt it. She's staying with her sister a lot."

Evan lifted his hat as he walked toward us. "How is she doing?"

I shook my head. "Not good. She's on hospice now."

Evan looked down. "I'm sorry. Terrible for her daughter."

My jaw tightened. "Yeah. I can't do much about it, either."

"I'm sure Audrey appreciates you just being there," Dusty suggested. "A listening ear, you know?"

"I'm tired of folks sayin' that. I don't deserve a girl like Audrey, you all know that, but I'd give my eyeteeth to be able to fix somethin' for her. All anyone says is 'Just be there,'" I mimicked sarcastically. "It's the stupidest thing I ever heard."

"Well, Luke, that's all you can do." Evan took a swig from his saddle canteen and spat some of the dust out of his mouth. "Unless you somehow learned to walk on water, the best you can offer is to be the guy who'll walk through the trials with her. Audrey doesn't expect anything more."

"She should," I muttered as I put my rope away. "She's got nothin' to look forward to right now. Wish I could give her that."

Evan looked up at me with a thin-lipped smile and clapped my horse's neck. "You'll know when there's something she needs. Now, come on, let's get back to the barn."

We waited for Evan to swing into his saddle, and the three of us struck up a ground-eating jog. The grass had come in nice this year, and the last rains we'd had were at the end of April. After today, all the kids would be out of school, and we'd be able to hire plenty of help fixing fences and running irrigation pipes for the hay fields. This was my favorite time of year—we were still feeling the freshness of spring, but we got all the perks of summer, too.

And speaking of something to look forward to... "Hey, Dusty," I said, jogging a little closer to him, "did you make up your mind about that roping jackpot this weekend? About time we tested that pretty mare of yours with some real competition."

Dusty didn't look at me for a few seconds, and when he did, he wasn't smiling and eager like he ought to have been. "Yeah. You know, Luke, I've been thinking. Maybe we wait till you find you a new heading horse? Dozer's getting up there."

"No, he ain't. Most of the top horses in the pro circuits this year are over fifteen. They're seasoned and reliable, and Dozer's as fit as a fiddle."

"Yeah, but there's your knee. You were limping yesterday after that colt bucked with you."

"So what? I limp all the time, but that don't stop me from throwing a rope."

He sighed and looked up to the skies. "What I'm trying to say is that I'm not sure I want to compete this season."

My jaw about hit my saddle horn. "Not compete? Why in blazes not? You're the fastest heeler this side of the range! Every header there hopes to pull you in the afternoon draw, and we just about always win the first go together. Why wouldn't you want to go?"

"I just got married, Luke. I'm always working, and we're late getting started on building our house. I just don't think I should burn up my spare time going to jackpots this summer."

"But you've finally got the horse for it! She ain't no backyard pony tryin' to keep up. You're riding roping royalty, and she needs to rack up some winnings!"

Dusty sighed and glanced over at Evan. Evan just held up a hand—he didn't want any part of this conversation. "Luke, I—I know. And I know you found Duchess and had big plans for her, and I want to help make all that happen. But my wife's got to be my priority right now. Maybe I don't sit out all season—we could still get to some events to stay sharp. But I finally got a guy to come pour the foundation for our house, and he's doing it as an after-hours favor for me. He's coming on Saturday."

Well. That... that was just... I looked away and ground my teeth for a minute. Blast it, Dusty! Of course, I got it, and I couldn't blame him for picking his house over a roping, but I'd been counting on him! I screwed my mouth closed and sniffed. "Fine," I decided. "I'll go alone. Plenty of other heelers to go around."

"Luke..."

"Nah. You do what you gotta do. I'm going roping."

From the corner of my eye, I saw Dusty glancing at Evan again. This time, Evan looked back, then just shook his head.

We got up to the barn, and I hopped off and had my saddle stripped, and my horse put away before Dusty'd even hung his hat up. No sense in hanging around to chit-chat. I put my gear away and then stalked off to pay a visit to Two Bits before I went up for some chow.

He trotted over to the fence when he saw me coming. I was the only one he'd do that for—probably because I always had food for him. I'd started keeping little peppermint candies in my pocket when I found out he liked them, but I wasn't going to have a stallion learning to sniff me down for treats. That wouldn't end well, so I'd taught him to bow before he got his peppermint. He was a smart son of a gun, and as soon as he heard me crackling those candy wrappers, he plunged a foreleg out and started diving his head down.

I chuckled and patted his neck as I offered him the peppermint. "Good boy." He was putting the weight back on, that was for sure. Once the weather warmed up and he was able to eat all he wanted, the difference was like magic. He'd lost all that rotting winter hair, and his new summer coat was almost glossy. Not bad for a horse that stumbled in here two months ago at death's door.

Doc Burns had been astonished. "What are you feeding him?" he'd demanded. "This is more than just good hay."

Darn straight it was more than just good hay. I had a whole supplementation regimen going. Two Bits got more goodies in his meals even than Five Iron and Maserati, our two most valuable horses, and it was really starting to pay off. Vitamins, flax, gut support supplements, joint supplements, hoof supplements, a custom mineral blend, and lots and lots of the best hay we grew. He was still on the thin side, but he wasn't a skeleton anymore, and he was feeling good.

So good, in fact, that he'd broken out of his pen the other night and was trying to jump into the broodmare pasture. I was the first one down the next morning, so I got him put up without too much fuss, but I started keeping an extra clip on his gate after that. No sense in everyone getting all riled up about him being a problem stud.

He was nibbling on my hat brim, trying to get me to pet him, so I scratched his belly like he liked. "Watch your manners, son," I warned him. "I won't have you gettin' pushy. You gotta be a gentleman."

Two Bits just stuck his upper lip out to show how much he liked the scratching. "All right, that's enough," I said with a pat on his rump. "You go eat your dinner, and I'm gonna go eat mine." He followed me to the gate, and I secured both latches, then reached through to stroke his forelock. "Behave yourself, now."

Audrey

"No more school for the summer. Are you excited about that?" I glanced over at Lizzy as we pulled away from the school parking lot.

She nodded, but she didn't look at me.

Hmm. I didn't turn my head to stare at her, but I kept flicking my gaze that direction, to see what expressions might be crossing her face. Lizzy had been withdrawn lately, and the reason wasn't much of a mystery.

The school had finally asked a counselor to step in, and for the last two weeks, Lizzy had been spending daily time in her office, either talking about what was going on in her life or just doodling on a piece of paper if she didn't want to talk.

It didn't seem to be helping anything, and my theory was that it was too little, too late. Lizzy had been struggling for the whole school year, and no one had paid attention. And now, when things were getting worse, they finally tried to do something about it, but Lizzy hadn't had time to build a trust relationship with the counselor.

"Hey. If you look in the back seat, there's a surprise for you," I said.

She didn't rouse herself to respond for a few seconds. When she did, it was with a dull look, and she eyed the colorfully wrapped present without saying anything.

"Well, open it!"

She turned back around. "I'll do it when we get out of the car."

I chewed my lip and pressed the accelerator a little harder.

"Are we going up to the ranch?"

I didn't answer immediately. "Not today, Lizzy. We have to go home."

"Because Mom's dying."

I veered off the road, squealing tires and burning up a spray of gravel as we turned onto the shoulder. The car rocked to a stop, and I still had a death grip on the wheel. "Lizzy..." I swallowed. We'd talked about this, but she'd never been so blunt. So emotionless. That scared me. "Lizzy, we need to—"

"I don't want to talk anymore," she snapped, crossing her arms. "That's all we do. Talk about this, talk about that. I'm *fine*."

I drummed my fingers on the wheel and glanced in the rearview mirror at that present she wouldn't open. "Lizzy, what you're going through is understandable. It's normal that you'd feel frustrated. Sad. Maybe even angry or helpless. If you want—"

"I don't." She turned away to stare out the other window. "Stop telling me what to do. I just want to go to my room and be left alone."

Yes, that was part of the problem. Lizzy spent entirely too much time alone in her room these days.

I'd been trying to give her as many opportunities as I could to be with her mother, but she didn't seem to want to make the best of them. James had agreed—grudgingly—to let Lizzy stay with Kat on the weekends for now, since she didn't have many left. And now Lizzy blamed me for keeping her away from her dad.

We'd also stopped going to White Pines for the after-school program, and she hadn't forgiven me for that, either. It wasn't like I was asking her to make all the sacrifices—I'd cut my work hours and hardly left the house so I could be with Kat more. I had people I wanted to see and things I'd rather be doing, too. But for now, I just felt that I should cherish every second I could with my sister.

The problem was that for Lizzy, more time with her mother didn't equate to... *more*. I stuffed my foot into the clutch and ground the gears as we pulled onto the road. "You know, Lizzy, someday you will wish you had this time back."

She hugged her arms tighter around herself and shrugged. "Don't care."

That comment shot a bolt of anger through me. How dare she get hostile with me? "*Excuse* me?"

"You heard me. You keep saying stuff like 'I'll regret this when I'm older,' but you don't know anything about it. Just leave me alone!"

I glared at her in horror. Where had this disrespectful brat come from? And what could I do to get through to her?

I wasn't stupid. I'd put up walls like this when my parents died, too, but I wasn't twelve when it happened. Of course, someone her age would struggle more with losing her mom, and Lizzy had been watching it happen, bit by bit, for a couple of years now. She was done. She'd kept her chin up, stayed cheerful, and tried her hardest, and she just didn't have anything left.

The only thing that had brightened her lately was time at Walker Ranch or White Pines. The horses drew something out of her that I couldn't, and the people she found there cared about her without asking for something she couldn't give. Luke had skyrocketed to hero status in her eyes, but we hadn't been seeing much of Luke or the horses lately.

Not that I hadn't wanted to. I just... I couldn't leave Kat. And I wasn't sure I should lead him on when I didn't know how much I could really give him. What would happen... after?

But there was something else I could do. I pulled into the driveway and stayed in the car as Lizzy got out and trudged into the house without her end-of-the-year gift. I'd thought she'd be excited. I'd been excited to give it to her. Silly me, I guess. I thought she'd go nuts to have her own real cowboy boots.

Luke had offered to teach her to ride this summer, so the boots were really his idea. On the one "date" he'd talked me into—we went out to chilidogs at the Burger Shack—he took me on a late-night shopping trip to the farm store. Hardly romantic, but it was one of the sweetest evenings I've ever spent with anyone. We just wandered through the aisles with a shopping cart, picking up grain for his horses and a first pair of real western jeans for me and those boots for Lizzy. We didn't really talk about anything important, and we didn't do anything all that special. It was just nice to be with him and to let someone put a smile on my face. However briefly.

And Luke was the one I needed right now. He'd be able to get Lizzy out of her bedroom, and he'd talk up all his big ideas for the summer with her until she was laughing and plotting mischief again. It would be nice to hide my face in his chest and just let him hold me for a few minutes, too. I pulled my phone out of my purse and dialed his number.

Chapter 18

Luke

"Hey, sweet thing. You look tired."

Audrey rubbed her eye and tried to laugh. "No more than usual. Thanks for coming over."

"Aw, come on. I wouldn't miss a chance to do this." I hitched my arm around the dip of her waist and leaned my forehead on hers until she broke out of that stressed-looking frown she was wearing. I hadn't worked up the guts yet to play with her hair the way I really wanted to, but I twisted a hunk of it around my finger and brushed the silky locks over her soft cheek. "Are you gonna kiss me, beautiful, or just keep me waiting?"

She did laugh this time. And then she slid her hands up my chest and pulled on my shirt collar until her lips tumbled into mine. Ah, this was heaven. Just a little corner of it, maybe, but I was pretty sure there were angels singing somewhere. Kissing Audrey wasn't like other girls. She kissed me like she meant it. Like she needed for me to mean it. She kissed like she was exploring me, trying to know more of me, and not just having a little fun for herself. How could I not just serve my heart up on a platter for a woman like that?

"I still can't believe that tooth doesn't hurt," she murmured against my chin as she slipped down from her tippy toes.

I grinned. "Why do you think I'm dating a dentist? Hoping I can get a deal on the filling."

She snorted a laugh and covered her mouth. "You're terrible!"

I grabbed her hand and pulled it away from her face. "And you're smiling for a change. My work here is finished."

"You wish." She sighed and gestured to the house. "I was hoping it would cheer Lizzy up to see you. Do you mind?"

I tucked her hand under my arm and led her toward the house. "Sure thing. I brought a two-pound bag of chocolate kisses for her."

Audrey stopped following me, her mouth turning down and her eyebrows climbing her forehead. "Luke Walker."

"I'm kidding! It's only half a pound. Come on, I..." I stopped and stiffened when a rebuilt blue Dodge pulled onto the street and turned straight for us. "Hey, isn't that James Tracy?"

She turned and groaned when she saw the truck. "Ugh. Yes."

"What's he doing here?"

"Nothing useful or helpful. I'll talk to him."

I glanced at her—the lines of fatigue around her eyes, the grim clenching of her jaw. I couldn't let her fight all the battles alone. I steered our steps so I was between Tracy and her. "I'm sticking around."

Audrey gave me a doubtful look, but she didn't say anything. Tracy got out of his truck and marched straight for her with a withering scowl on his face. I made a little sidestep, putting my shoulder in his path so he'd have to go through me before he could confront her.

Tracy never was a real swift one, but he finally registered what was going on. He stopped and spat on the sidewalk. "I didn't come here to talk to you, Walker."

I crossed my arms. "But I'm here, all the same. You don't look too mannerly today, Jimmy. I got a rank old bull that walks up more polite-like than that."

His lip curled. "Still the big-headed buffoon, huh, Luke? Mind your own business and let the grown-ups talk."

I couldn't remember the last time I saw red like that. I wadded up a fist and took half a step forward. "Wanna rephrase that?"

"Luke." Audrey put her hand on my arm. "It's okay. Just go on inside."

I looked down. Her face was dead serious, and she'd be furious with me if I didn't take a hike now. But leave my girl out here alone for him to yell at while I ran and hid in the house? It wasn't in my genes.

"Actually," I decided, "I'm just going to pop the hood on your car right there and see what's been making that noise. I think you need a new fan belt. Is it unlocked?"

She let go a sigh and frowned at me, nodded and said, "You know it is."

I gave Tracy a look that any guy with half a neuron would understand loud and clear—"You mess with her, you deal with me." Then I walked to the driveway where I could keep an eye on him but still let her do what she needed to do.

He didn't waste time complaining as soon as he got her to himself. "You turned me in!"

Audrey stood up a little taller. "Yes, I did. It's sort of the law that I'm supposed to report SNAP benefit fraud."

"For what, you petty cow? So you can make me look bad in front of a judge?"

"You don't need my help doing that. Did you ever think there might be a reason your own benefits ran out? Go get a job, James."

He stabbed a finger toward her, making the adrenaline slam through my veins. I didn't move, but I had a pair of fists ready for him. If that varmint threatened her...

"I have rights, too! That's my kid you're hiding in there, and you don't get to keep her from me. I'm picking her up right now."

"James, you agreed to let her stay with her mother this weekend."

"That was before you went behind my back! Now I've got these social workers breathing down my neck, and I haven't seen my kid in two weeks. Tell her to get her stuff."

"James, please! You can't take Lizzy away from her mother right now. Kat's—"

"Kat won't even know she's gone," he snarled. "She's practically dead already."

Audrey's pained gasp was all it took for me. I rounded the edge of the car and pushed my sleeve up. "Time to go, Tracy," I bellowed. "You've overstayed your welcome."

I wasn't really planning on decking him. I'd never started the fight in my life, but I'd finished a few, and James Tracy looked like the kind of guy who needed a little finishing. If he had the guts to tackle me, that is.

"Oh, don't do it, Walker. I'll call the cops."

"No, you won't. You've got more to hide from the law than either of us do." I hooked my free hand through Audrey's elbow. "Are you okay?"

She was tight, angry, her mouth screwed up into a bitter scowl. But she closed her eyes for a few seconds and took a sharp breath. "I'm not afraid of James. He's just a bottom feeder with delusions of grandeur."

Hah. That was my girl. I shot Tracy a stare that would make his hair turn white if he knew what I meant by it.

"Here's what's going to happen, dude. You walk away right now with your jaw still hanging where it's supposed to be. Go cool off. No one's trying to violate the custody arrangement, but you've been asked to show a little human decency and let the kid be with her mom. Do you really want to be the one to take her away if it should end up being Kat's last weekend here? Your own daughter would live with that for the rest of her life, and you'd be the one she blamed. Think it over."

James Tracy was almost purple in the face. He looked from Audrey to me and then back at her again, and then he spat a brown stream on the driveway. "This ain't over. I'm making a few calls."

"Go ahead," Audrey dared him.

He glared at her for a few seconds longer, then pivoted and stomped back to his truck, muttering a string of oaths and slamming the door when he got in.

That meant it was time for me to face the music. Audrey wasn't a damsel type of girl, and she wouldn't appreciate a guy trying to be all tough for her. I couldn't have done less—it wasn't in me—but that didn't mean she wanted me to step in. She'd drag me into the house and dress me down for interfering in her business.

If she invited me in at all. She'd probably just kick me off the property.

"Audrey," I began. "Look, I'm sorry for—"

That was when she cut my breath off with a hug so swift and fierce she almost broke my ribs.

I put my hands on her back and held her tight. "Well, that was unexpected," I wheezed.

She buried her head a little deeper into my chest, and I heard a faint sniff. "Thank you, Luke."

"Of course, sugar. I can't let a numbskull like him bully my girl."

She sniffed again and pulled away, pointing her finger at me. "Just don't do it again. Ever. I'm not into cavemen."

I laughed and turned her under my arm to walk her into the house. "I know, darlin'. You don't even like cowboys."

Audrey

"You sent my dad away? Why? I wanted to go with him! I *hate* you!" Lizzy turned and ran for her bedroom, slamming her door so hard that the rest of the doors in the house rattled.

"Let me handle this," Luke said, gently restraining my shoulder to keep me from storming after her. "I'm not quite so close to all of it, you know?"

"I don't have any better ideas," I sighed. "What are you going to do?"

He gave me a thin-lipped smile and brushed my cheek. "I'll just chat with her through the door. Should work."

I raised a brow. "You haven't been around that many teenage girls, have you?"

Luke put a finger to his lips. "Might be best if she doesn't hear you talkin' to me."

"Fine. I'll sit with Kat. If you can get Lizzy to come out of her room without more drama, I'll buy you dinner."

"You're on, sweet thing."

Luke walked down the hall and knocked on Lizzy's door. "Hey, Dead Eye. It's me, Luke."

He waited for at least two minutes while she didn't answer, but he didn't look too concerned. He just squatted with his back to her door like he had all the time in the world. He was either more stubborn or more patient than I would have been. I just opened Kat's door across the hall and sat with her while I listened and waited.

Kat was awake watching television when I went in. She'd been feeling a little better lately because she wasn't going through the stress of dialysis several times a week. It couldn't last—I knew that—but just for a little while, it was nice to see her a little more alert.

"What is Lizzy upset about?" she asked.

I held my breath before confessing, "She's angry with me because I asked her dad to let her stay here this weekend."

Kat puckered her lips, then gave a slight nod of understanding. "I see. Is that Luke Walker I hear outside?"

"Yes. He's trying to talk to her. Who knows." I shrugged. "He'll probably have better luck than I will."

My sister's eyes returned to the television. "She can't stay in her room all the time."

"I know. I'm trying to get her out to the living room, or even in here, but—"

"No, I mean she needs to get out. Just because I'm stuck here doesn't mean she should be. Let her go, Audrey."

"To James's house? But we agreed..."

Kat shook her head. "Go with Luke. Both of you. Take her to the ranch tomorrow or something."

"No. That's out of the question, Kat. I don't have a nurse, and the whole reason I asked for James to let her stay was—"

"To watch me die?"

I sucked in my lower lip and stared at the floor. "Kat..."

"She's just a kid, Aud. I love her too much to watch her break like this."

I raised my eyes to my sister's. "I just don't know if that's a good idea. What if... what if we're out, and you can't call for help, and—"

"Audrey? I'll be here when you get back. I promise."

I reached for her hand and gave it a squeeze. "Okay, Kat. I'll take her."

Luke didn't look happy about that idea.

"Tomorrow? That won't work. No, I don't think you should. And anyway, didn't you just tell old James that you wanted Lizzy to stay with her mom?"

"Her mom is the one who asked me to get her out. Come on, Luke. I thought you'd be the first to jump on this idea."

He squinted and scratched his ear, and I'd learned that meant he was thinking about something he didn't know how to say. "Yeah, but tomorrow? How about Sunday, or next week?"

"I suppose no reason, except you've told me before that Saturday is the easiest day for you to work around having her come up."

Luke shuffled his feet and stared at the ground. "Uh-huh. It's just that..."

"If you're busy, just say it, Luke. I get it. You have a life and things to do. I wouldn't want to interfere with your work."

He shook his head. "It's not ranch work. Well, not exactly. I'm going to a roping over in Twin Falls."

I'm not sure why, but my heart dropped a little. I couldn't expect him to arrange everything around us. I wasn't even sure I wanted him to, because that would mean... things I wasn't ready for it to mean yet. But he was the only person who'd really taken the time to invest in Lizzy—who seemed to see her the way I did. It had started to feel like he was in the fight with us, but that was probably just me. He had his own rainbows to chase.

"I see." I took a breath. "Okay. I'll just keep her home. You go."

"It's just that I've got to stay sharp, you know. I haven't gone in too long, and the top guys, they're there every time. Honest, I'd love to have her come up, and I'd put her on a horse and—"

"Really, Luke. Just go. Lizzy will be fine."

"Well... So how about you guys come up for an hour or two this evening? She can help me groom Two Bits and pack the trailer. I'll call Meryl and ask her to throw a couple of extra burgers on the grill. How 'bout it?"

I thought for a second, then nodded. Kat would tell me to say yes. "That would be nice."

Chapter 19

Luke

Audrey and Lizzy didn't stay long. It was such a pretty evening, and I tried to talk them into hanging out on the porch eating Meryl's potato salad and drinking sun tea. I couldn't sit with them because I had things to do, but no reason they couldn't just take it easy for a bit. But Lizzy was restless and cranky, and none of the usual stuff interested her. I even let her walk Two Bits from his stall to his field so she could watch him play, but after about ten minutes, she was bored and wanted to go home.

"I think I'd better just take her," Audrey said. "I'd hoped it would cheer her up to get out of the house, but I guess not. Besides, you have to get ready to leave in the morning."

"That won't take too long. My rig's almost always ready. I've got a little time." Some of that was true. All I had to load was my horse and my gear. It was my usual chores that wouldn't get done tomorrow while I was gone that were calling me away now.

She folded her arms and frowned at her toes. "It's fine, Luke. Tonight just didn't work. You're busy, and she's probably tired. I don't want to try to force something when we've all got other stuff going on. I'll see you when you get back." She kissed my cheek and called for Lizzy, and a few minutes later, they left.

I didn't like watching them go. I just sat on the porch for a few minutes, where I could see the long tail of the driveway heading out to the road, and waited for them to be completely out of sight.

What was the deal? Lizzy was usually pretty easy to perk up. She had to be gloomy because of her mom—she wasn't stupid, and it was pretty understandable. But this was one of her favorite places, and she loved being around the animals. I'd always been able to pull her out of a funk before, just by making space for her.

Oh.

Was that it? I'd told her before they even got up there that I was busy, heading somewhere else tomorrow, and didn't have a lot of extra time. That was life! Audrey was a big girl. She understood that.

But Lizzy was a kid—a kid about to lose everything she'd ever known. And she'd spent the last couple of years being an afterthought, an inconvenient complication to a family with enough troubles already. A problem for someone to try to solve.

And I'd just told her she was a problem for me, too.

I laced my fingers over my chest and tapped my thumbs as I leaned back in that porch chair. And suddenly, I had an idea.

"You're not going roping?" Audrey's voice over the phone the next morning sounded confused rather than pleasantly surprised like I'd hoped. "But I thought this was a huge deal to you. Jess told me about all your plans for building a breeding program for rope horses and how good you and Dusty are. Why wouldn't you go?"

I tugged my boots on as I headed out to throw hay for the morning feeding. "I changed my mind."

"Luke. You didn't cancel because of us, did you?"

"So what if I did? Can't a guy change his plans? I can go roping some other time."

She was quiet for a few seconds. "I don't know what to say. You didn't have to do that."

"I didn't have to. I wanted to. So, I guess come up whenever you're ready, and we'll have us some fun. Oh, and make sure she unwraps those boots. She's gonna need 'em."

We hung up, and I sped down to the barn in the side-by-side to start getting things ready. Lizzy wouldn't feel like an afterthought today. That was for darn sure. I'd made a few calls last night and got my dad and my brothers on board—all except for Dusty because pouring the foundation for his house was a pretty fair excuse.

Dad and Meryl were going to stage a four-alarm chili-dog cookout, and Marshall and Evan got to work late last night to put together a corn-hole set. Kelli raided the attics for a bunch of patriotic bunting, and I pulled some old Fourth of July supplies out of my stash. Morgan was probably more helpful in getting things pulled together than anyone else. She knew all the right people to call on a moment's notice, and she could wrangle kids and volunteers like nobody's business.

I hopped out at the barn and clapped my hands in eagerness to get started. The sun was already warm, and summer was finally underway. It was Memorial Day Weekend, and we were going to have us a private, impromptu kids' rodeo.

Audrey

"I can't believe it. You organized all this just since last night?" I covered my mouth and scanned the entry yard at Walker Ranch. It was full of cars. Kids were running everywhere with squirt guns, parents were standing on the grass with fresh lemonades and iced tea, and I think every cowboy in the valley was rolling in with a horse trailer full of ponies.

Luke grinned and shrugged. "I had a lot of help."

"I see that! How did you talk everyone into this?"

"It wasn't as hard as you'd think. Everyone's ready to get out and kick up their heels, and we've got some pretty good connections. So? What do you want to do first? We got Stick Pony Cutting—Cody's in charge of that, and he's got a bunch of ducks. You gotta watch it, it's a riot. Oh, and over there, we got Cow Dog Racing, where the kids lead a dog around a little track we set up and see who wins. That's a gag, really, because half the dogs here don't even know what a leash is. Marshall's teaching some trick roping in the round pen—don't let him fool you, he ain't that good. Let's see... Oh, Evan's got the older kids over there trying their hand at a little chute dogging, and they'll have pony rides later. That'll be fun to watch. Or you can just pull up a chair and park yourself in the sunshine and watch it all from the porch."

I turned around, my mouth hanging open in wonder. It was like the whole town had turned out for a festival, the kind of thing that takes a year of planning and dozens of volunteers. And it had been put together overnight by one crazy cowboy.

"I... I don't know what to say. I'm just astonished!" I clapped my hands to my cheeks and laughed, just trying to take it all in. "Luke, this is incredible."

"Yeah, but will Lizzy have fun? That's kind of the whole point."

I looked over at my niece—at her big grin as she grabbed a squirt gun and raced off after some of the kids she knew from White Pines. "I think you succeeded, cowboy. I can't wait to see her enjoying this."

"Oh, my gosh. I can't watch this!" I covered my eyes, but I couldn't help peeking through my fingers. Some of the cowboys had saddled horses in the big outdoor arena, and they'd staged a race. Except for this race, they each had a rope dragging a kid on a burlap sack. The kids would lay down on their stomachs and hang on like a water skier for dear life, spraying dust and skidding wildly as the cowboy tore off down the arena till they crossed the finish line. And then they'd get up and do it all over again.

"This is insane!"

"They're wearing helmets," Luke protested. "What can go wrong?"

"Death, that's what can go wrong! You're not putting Lizzy on one of those things."

"Why not? All she's gotta do is let go if she gets scared. She'll be fine!"

I stared at him. "You're nuts!"

"Yeah, but you already knew that. Come on, Aud. She'll be okay, I promise. I guess she could get a tooth knocked out, but I know a gal who could fix it for her."

I rolled my eyes. "Luke Walker, you're as bad as those kids! How in the world I let you talk me into these stupid ideas, I'll never figure out."

He leaned in to nuzzle my cheek, resting his elbow on a fence rail and putting his arm around the small of my back. "It's because you're wild about me, sweetheart."

"Oh, is that what it is?" I asked dryly. "Were you planning to tell me this?"

"Ah, I figured you'd put it together sooner or later." He kissed me softly, then tugged me upright. "Come on. Let the kid get her blood pumping. It'll be the best thing in the world for her."

"As long as that blood stays inside her body."

He winked. "No promises, doc. Hey, Lizzy! Come on, let's show 'em how it's done!"

And so, I watched from the fence rail in horrified amazement, my hands over my eyes half the time. Lizzy plopped down on a little chunk of tarp and grabbed the end of Luke's lariat. He looked back at her, waited for the thumbs up, and jumped his horse into high gear. And my niece, the child I'd sworn to raise and protect in my sister's place, squealed in terrified delight as Luke dragged her at probably twenty-five miles an hour through dirt and sand and dust.

When they crossed the finish line, Lizzy jumped up, spitting sand out of her mouth and whooping for joy. She ran to straight to Luke, and he caught her up and pinwheeled her through the air—just like a dad would do with his own daughter. They were laughing like crazy people, and I heard her beg to do it again.

I couldn't figure out the appeal. It looked painful! She had to be covered in bruises from head to toe. Her jeans were probably stained forever, and her elbows were freshly skinned up.

But she was smiling bigger than I'd seen in months.

Luke

"Seriously, though. You've got to admit that Meryl's homemade chili is just as good as Beaufort's. And when's the last time you had hushpuppies like that?"

Audrey set a hand on her hip and shook her head. "Never. I didn't even know what hushpuppies were until two hours ago."

"No way! You've got some catching up to do." I dipped my hand into the basket and pulled out a couple more to drop them on her plate. "They're kind of a southern thing, but Grandma Walker came from Texas, and she wouldn't call it a proper cookout without a side of hushpuppies. I like to dip 'em in barbecue sauce."

"That? Sounds terrible."

"Don't knock it till you've tried it, sister. Let's go sit under the tree there."

I grabbed a mason jar of lemonade, and we wandered to the shady spot I'd picked out. What no one else had noticed all day was that I'd stuffed a picnic blanket up over a branch, so it was ready and waiting for us when we wanted to use it. I set the plates down, gave the picnic blanket a shake, and we had a ready-made oasis.

"Wow. You really thought of everything."

I grinned as I helped her settle on the blanket. "Actually, I sorta stole a page out of Cody's book. He took Morgan on a picnic for like their second date. I suggested something different, but he didn't like my idea. Just as well, because she ended up marrying him, and she might not have if he'd done what I told him to do."

Audrey sipped some of her lemonade as she gazed up at me. "Dare I ask what your idea was?"

"Nope." I kicked my dirty boots off and joined her on the picnic blanket. "But if I'm lucky, maybe I'll get to show you someday."

"Oh, now I'm really curious. Does it happen to involve the back of a pickup truck?" She picked up a hushpuppy, swept it through a puddle of barbecue sauce, and nibbled on it while giving me the kind of look that could boil a guy's blood.

I just blinked and stared.

Audrey's mouth turned up into a little smirk, and she took another dip of the sauce. "Did you know it's better for your oral health if you breathe through your nose instead of your mouth?" she asked casually.

I closed my mouth and swallowed. "Yeah. I know something else that's better for my..." Well, I'd better not say *that*. Either it wouldn't make any sense, or it just sounded plain wrong. But when she was being all smart and coy like that, my brain turned to jelly. "Oh, just come here." I pushed her plate away, bundled her into my arms, and we toppled sideways together.

"Luke!" She pounded on my shoulders with the flats of her hands, then she gave up and wrapped her arms around my neck. The whole time, she was laughing so hard she could hardly breathe, but she managed to kiss me pretty thoroughly.

I loved her laugh. The girl I'd once thought never cracked a smile, but she had a laugh that could make my heart sigh just hearing it. Maybe because she only laughed when she was truly happy. And she didn't laugh at just anything—she knew how to tell when I wanted her to laugh with me and when I needed her to take me seriously. It made me want to huddle under a blanket with her and just tell her all my secrets.

"Luke, there are kids around here," she giggled against my neck. "We should try to act respectable, you know?"

"They're all playing with the ponies. They couldn't give a hoot about us."

She quirked a brow and pushed my chest. "We're going to get people staring and gossiping."

Reluctantly, I sat up and helped her do the same. "Rain check, though?"

"Rain check." Audrey leaned back with her arms behind her and drank in a sigh. "Luke?"

"Mmm?" I was still gazing at her with a stupid smile I wasn't bothering to wipe off.

"What are people saying?"

I shrugged. "You mean about us?"

She sat up straighter. "You have to admit, we don't make much sense. No one in their right mind would think that you and I..." She pointed between us and stopped.

"Well... maybe that means I'm not in my right mind, because it seems to me that we get on good where it counts."

She smiled. "We're complete opposites. I never even saw a live horse outside of the Macy's Thanksgiving parade until I moved here. My idea of a romantic date was dinner at a five-star restaurant and a Broadway play. A wild adventure was ice skating in Central Park. And here I am, sitting on a blanket on the ground, eating fried cornbread dipped in barbecue sauce!"

"So... you don't like the hushpuppies?"

She laughed and shook her head. "I do. I love them. I love it here, and you've shown me things I could never have imagined! But I've got..." She looked down, her forehead wrinkled. "There's a whole other life I left behind in New York. I sort of always thought I'd get back to it."

"Now, that's what I call crazy. Who would want New York when you could have all this?" I gestured to the yard full of laughing kids, neighbors chit-chatting on the lawn, and dogs rolling around playing in the grass. "No comparison."

She rolled her head to the side. "You have a point, but still, we're pretty different, Luke."

"Aw, that's all just superficial stuff. I say we actually think a lot alike when you get right down to it. And besides, who said we have to sign a contract? I like being with you, and I think you like being with me. Isn't that enough for now?"

Her lips pressed into a tender smile. "Yeah. It is."

Audrey

Luke followed me home that evening. He said he wanted to say hi to Kat and to thank her for letting Lizzy come up to the ranch, but I knew he had other motives, too. Lizzy had asked for and gained permission to ride in the truck with him, so I had the car to myself. I watched his headlights in my rearview mirror and tried to figure out why my heart was rattling around inside my ribs.

It made no sense. I'd always liked classy, sophisticated men—guys who knew their wine and appreciated opera, and owned a collection of real ties. Luke would probably choke himself if he tried to tie a tie. And taking someone like him to the opera? He'd hate it so much that I'd have to drag him out of there and never show my face again.

But there was something about that cowboy that I'd never met anywhere else. It was true—he wouldn't know a Chardonnay from a Riesling, but he seemed to know *me*. He knew just when to tease me and when I needed him to step in to my rescue. And with Luke, I knew I was always getting the unvarnished truth. He wouldn't change to try to be someone different just to please me. He was simpler than that. He had more integrity than that.

My eyes darted to the mirror again. It was still stupid of me to be dating him. Was it dating? It was something. But I shouldn't let it carry on. I might not even be living in the state for much longer. I needed to tell him. Tonight, before I lost myself completely. I'd started to earlier, but then I lost my nerve. It was pretty hard to keep my wits about me with Luke Walker trying to steal my heart.

Right when I pulled into the driveway, my phone rang. Luke and Lizzy were still a block behind me, so I stole a second to glance at the screen and see who it was. My stomach dropped when I saw Peter's name.

I didn't have time to talk to him right now! My breath came short and shallow as I watched his name flashing on my screen. Should I just answer and tell him I'd have to call him back? I owed him at least that much.

But the longer I hesitated, the less I wanted to talk to him. Finally, the decision was made for me, and the call went to voicemail. And about twenty seconds later, a message popped up. I swallowed and held my phone to my ear to listen.

"Audrey, it's Peter. I thought I'd try you here because I hadn't heard back from the messages I left at your work. Darling, I really need an answer about the job. I have a stack of referrals on my desk—some of the top candidates in the country, but I want you. I know you said you needed time, but I was hoping we could talk about things. It's not only the job. I miss you, beautiful. Call me when you can."

I squeezed my eyes shut, my heart hammering in my ears. Peter still thought about... about us? There'd hardly ever been an us. We'd been seeing each other for six months before I left, and not seriously. But there had been the thought of something serious. We liked the same things, and we had the same goals. We could have been a power couple, both professionally and on a personal level.

Peter and I made sense.

But as those headlights from that lifted Ford swept into my driveway behind me, I couldn't even remember what my feelings for Peter had been. I just tossed my phone back in my purse and got out to greet my cowboy.

Lizzy was so proud of her bruises and skinned elbows that she spent ten minutes telling her mother all about them. How she'd been towed behind a running horse, how she'd eaten six hot dogs and ridden a pony that was the color of caramel corn and doused every boy there with a squirt gun—except for Dustin, because she didn't want to pick on Dustin. I just leaned on the door frame and listened, smiling through the proud tears trying to prick my eyes.

Kat was fairly glowing tonight. She brushed Lizzy's tangled and dirt-streaked hair out of her face and just listened, a look on her face that went beyond happiness. "Oh, baby girl," she said when Lizzy had finished talking. "It sounds like you had a wonderful day. I'm so pleased."

"Yeah, and Luke's going to teach me to ride a horse this week. I have to earn my lessons by working at the barn, but he says I can sweep and clean stalls, and he'll teach me to throw a rope like he does. Mom, have you ever seen a dog herd cows? It's amazing! Dusty just whistles, and they know which way to turn, and..."

She went on for a few minutes longer, and all the while, Kat's smile just kept growing. Finally, I touched Lizzy's shoulder. "Honey, let's let your mama rest. You can tell her more tomorrow. Why don't you go get ready for bed?"

Lizzy hopped down from the chair and kissed her mother. "Good night, Mom. See you tomorrow."

Kat let her hand slip out of her daughter's as she left the room, then she rested her head back on the pillow and grinned at me. "Thank you, Audrey. And tell Luke thank you for me. That was so sweet of him to do all that for her."

"He's waiting right outside. I can invite him in so you can tell him yourself."

Kat looked like she was considering it, then she shook her head softly. "I think he'd rather hear it from you. Go on."

"Bet you've never been kissed in the bed of a pickup before."

I stretched my feet out and leaned back into Luke's chest as I gazed up at the stars. We were still parked in the driveway, but a short little goodnight at the front door had turned into over an hour of talking and kissing and just enjoying holding each other under that dappled sky. "I have now. I begin to see the appeal of a pickup."

"Yeah? So, four stars?"

I shrugged and gave him a teasing smile.

"Five?"

"I'm feeling generous, so sure."

Luke lifted his hat and grinned. "Boy, howdy. Wait till I tell Dusty."

"Luke Walker, you wouldn't dare!"

"Oh, heck yes, I would. You know they're taking bets about us. It's tradition. For example, I'll guarantee you that Marshall thinks you'll break my heart, and Dusty's betting that I'll break yours. I think we ought to make both of them wrong, don't you?"

I rested my head on his shoulder. "That would be something." I drew a deep breath. "Luke, there's something I've been meaning to talk to you about."

"Oh, yeah? What's that?" He leaned his cheek on the top of my head as one of his hands caressed mine, and his other hand stroked my hair.

If he kept doing that, I wouldn't be able to form a coherent sentence. My brain was flooded with endorphins, and all I could think was that I didn't want him to stop playing with my hair and holding me against his chest, and letting his voice rumble against my skin. I had to close my eyes and count to three to try to establish some sort of order out of my rioting senses.

"You know," I began haltingly, "I don't... I don't know what's going to happen in the next few months."

"What, are you talking about...?" He jerked his head toward the house.

"Yes, exactly."

"Well, Lizzy will still need you, won't she? More than ever, I'd say. What do you figure on doing about that?"

"I don't know what I'll be *able* to do." I looped my fingers through his and tightened my grip. I knew what I wanted to happen. What I *should* want. I should want full custody of Lizzy, so I could move her to a better town, a better school, and I could give us all the advantages that my years of hard work had paid for. But her own mother hadn't even been able to get that. The reality would probably be far messier.

"Her dad won't give up custody easily," was all I managed. "And I'm not saying he should. I'd be furious with him if he didn't try to fight for her, but I also don't think he's the right person to raise her."

"So, seems pretty simple to me. One way or another, we just keep on keepin' on. Even if she lives with him, she'll still need you in her life. You spend time with her whenever you can, and she can come up and work for me at the ranch if she wants. We'll help her keep her feet on the ground. Let's not borrow trouble from tomorrow, huh?"

There was still so much I needed to tell him—about New York and the job, about how I'd never planned to stay here. In fact, if James got full custody—and I knew he would because he was her father and I was just an aunt—I'd planned to go back to New York without Lizzy.

What more good could I do her? I could offer to pay for her college someday, but she probably wouldn't even choose college. The truth was, I just didn't know if I had it in me to be torn apart any longer. And I didn't know if I should keep forcing Lizzy to live in two worlds.

Just let her go to her dad and have one home to put down some roots in, rather than trying to fight with me and all my expectations for her.

But I just couldn't bring myself to say any of that to Luke. Not now, not when everything else was so right, and I finally had a few minutes of peace in his arms. Instead, I sighed and nestled a little deeper into him. "You know, for a former bull rider, you make a lot of sense sometimes."

"You should hear me when I'm working the branding pen. Sometimes I think I'm the only one who does make sense."

I laughed and kissed him. And I stayed out there in that pickup with my cowboy until the crickets quieted down and the stars had swung a quarter of the way around the sky.

Finally, I made myself uncurl my stiff legs, and Luke helped me hop down from the pickup bed. He walked me to the door, his hands lingering at my hips, and leaned his forehead against mine. "Good night, Audrey."

I pressed my lips to his. "Good night, Luke. Thank you for the day you made for us."

"Anything for my girls." His fingertips grazed my cheek, then he turned around and walked back to his truck. I stayed there, watching him until he backed out of the driveway, then slowly closed the door.

My girls, he'd said. Could Lizzy and I really belong to him? Because that sounded delicious and safe, and like the kind of life I'd never dared to imagine. Maybe it was the hangover of a day full of dreams come true. Or maybe I was just living in denial, refusing to face the realities of tomorrow. But right now, the best thing I could ever hope to be called was Luke Walker's girl.

What was wrong with me? I knew from the beginning this was a crazy idea, but I couldn't help it any longer. I was head over heels for that cowboy. What that meant for all the decisions I'd have to make soon, I couldn't know. But I knew one thing. I wanted him, and I had to tell someone. Out loud.

I tapped lightly on Kat's door and slipped inside. She slept at such odd hours that half the time when I checked on her in the night, she was awake. "Kat?" I whispered.

She didn't answer. Well, I shouldn't be surprised. It was almost two in the morning. I'd tell her tomorrow. But as I tucked the blankets back up under her chin, something felt very wrong.

"Kat?" My voice cracked with alarm, and I grabbed her hand. It was cold.

My sister, the one who'd always looked out for me when I was little, the strong one who'd taught me so much about life, was gone.

Chapter 20

Luke

Flowers are stupid.

You're supposed to buy all these useless flowers for someone to cheer them up when they're sick or sad, or tell a woman you love her, or send to the family when someone passes. They're pretty, but I can think of lots of prettier things. And they just wither and die and smell bad when the stems turn brown, and then the people you wanted to do something nice for just have a mess to throw away.

But here I was, buying flowers for Audrey because I didn't know what else to do. Jess had told me what kind to get, and I knew I wouldn't even remember, so I had her write it down for the florist. I ended up with some ruffly pink roses with little white things stuffed in between them. These weren't for the service. They were just for her, so I probably should've given them a little more thought.

But what were flowers supposed to do, anyway? They couldn't give her her sister back. They couldn't fix any of the broken stuff in her life. Nothing could fix it, and that was why I gave up and just bought the stupid flowers.

I stopped by her work to drop them off for her. I'd figured she'd have taken the rest of the week off after the funeral because it seemed like when something that big just ends, the rest of life ought to stop for a little while, too. But there was her car in front of the dentist's office, just like always, so I swung into the parking lot and shut off the engine.

The receptionist looked up brightly when I opened the door. "Good afternoon, Mr. Walker. Can I help you?"

I held the flowers aloft. "Is the boss lady free?"

"I'm sorry, Mr. Walker, but she's with a patient now. She has the next half hour blocked out for this procedure. May I give her those for you?"

"Fine." I shrugged and dropped the flowers on her desk. It wasn't about the flowers, anyway. I wanted to look into her eyes and know that she was alright. To take her in my arms and promise that I'd try to make it better, or at least try to make the ache dull a little bit.

"Tell her I'll call her later, will you?"

"Of course, sir. Did you want to take a moment and schedule your filling while you're here?"

I rolled my eyes. "Some other time."

Doc Burns's truck was parked in front of the barn when I got home. I walked inside to check out what was going on, and I found Evan standing in the aisle holding Pistol, his retired bulldogging horse. Pistol used to be an NFR champion. Now, he was twenty-seven and hadn't been ridden in about two years, but Evan still went out and pampered him every chance he got.

I nodded toward my brother. "Is he lame again?"

Evan's expression didn't change. "Still, you mean. It's been over a year, and we've tried about everything."

Doc was checking out a computer monitor of some fresh x-rays and shaking his head. "I don't know, Evan. I thought we had him on a good path, but this is a pretty sharp rotation of the coffin bones. The left is worse than the right, but both are bad. Has he been out on spring grass? All that sugar can set off an episode like this."

"Nope. Dry lot and no changes to his hay."

Doc looked grim. "It's up to you. We can keep trying to save him. We can go back to the heavy padding on his shoes to make him more comfortable, and I'll give you a prescription for some better pain relief for him."

Evan stared at his horse, his face a mask. "Will he ever get better? I don't mean for riding. I just want to know if these front feet can improve so he'll be sound in the pasture again."

Doc sighed and glanced at me. "No. They won't."

I figured Evan would make the call right there. We'd all had to do it at least once with our favorite horses. You take the best care of them you can, you do all in your power to keep them healthy and sound, but in the end, you don't let an animal suffer.

Evan's jaw muscles clenched, and he smoothed his hand over Pistol's neck. "Is he in pain right now, Doc?"

"Yes, but with the measures I'd prescribe, we can make him comfortable. It won't fix anything, and it'll be temporary, but he could have a few good months, at least."

Evan nodded. "Do it. I'd like him to have one nice summer. He can just rest and watch the world go by and get lots of pets and scratches. He deserves a happy last chapter."

Doc Burns closed his computer. "Sounds good to me. I'll write up a plan for the farrier. Oh, Luke, could I have a word with you before I go?"

"I wasn't rushing off, but I'll hang around for a bit." I scratched Pistol's neck while we waited for the vet to go back to his truck.

"You're wondering why, aren't you?" Evan asked. "Why don't I just let him go now, why go through the heroics for just another couple of months."

I shook my head. "You said why. That's a good enough reason."

He heaved a sigh and gave Pistol's forelock an affectionate tug. "Life's too short as it is. I just figure if I can give him even another week, I'll do whatever it takes."

I was staring at the ground, and I gave a bitter little laugh. "Like Audrey, practically killing herself to give her sister a little peace at the end. Wonder how much good it did."

"It was everything, Luke." Evan's gaze grew unfocused as he stroked Pistol's bony old head. "Everything."

"Luke, I'm going to Idaho Falls tomorrow to testify about the seizure case. I was wondering if you'd like to write out anything for me to say."

I scratched the back of my head and frowned. "What, about the stud's condition? Sure, I'd like to give them a piece of my mind. I hope they spend twenty years in jail for what they done to these horses."

"They won't. It's a plea deal, Luke."

My jaw dropped. "No way. They'd better not come off scott-free."

"Oh, they'll at least get their wrists slapped, but it might not be much more. Animal neglect is a tricky charge. If it's serious enough, and the DA thinks he can make the charges stick, he'll go for a felony. But these guys are claiming personal disability and financial hardship, so they'll get some pity. If I had to guess, I'd say they'll probably get charged with five counts of misdemeanor neglect for the horses that had to be put down. They'll pay a fine, and that will be it."

I threw my arms in the air. "That's ridiculous! What happens to the rest of the horses?"

"That's why I'm going to testify. I'd like to see them all forfeited so they can be adopted into safe, loving homes. You've been the one rehabbing this horse. I told Morgan to do the same thing, so write down everything you can think of. Before and after pictures, behavioral oddities, any evidence of abuse that I might have overlooked. I'll finish preparing my statement this evening. Doctor Childers and Doctor Brainard are giving statements as well, so hopefully, between all of us, we can present a clear picture of what happened."

I growled and kicked the gravel. I wanted to head over to Audrey's as soon as she got off work, so I'd have to hurry up and get this done before that. Writing stuff never was my strong suit, though, and I didn't know anything about making a legal statement. Maybe I'd ask Dusty or Morgan to help me. "Okay, Doc. I'll email something this afternoon. Anything else?"

"I don't think so. Oh, wait, yes." Doc fished a bunch of exam sheets out of his clipboard. "I actually didn't come up here to look at Pistol.

Evan grabbed me just as I was finishing these. Dusty had me out to preg check the rest of your broodmares, and here's a list of the results. You have twelve more nice, healthy-looking foals coming next year. Only one of those I checked didn't take so far, and it's... this one." He pulled one paper out and put it on top. "Bella, that's the one. You'll find approximate due dates and all that on each mare's exam sheet."

"Thanks, Doc."

I started leafing through the papers as I wandered off. I'd head upstairs to Dusty's office so he could file these, and then I'd make him help me with that statement. I climbed slowly, checking all the mares' names. It looked like all the show-type mares we'd bred to Five Iron were safely in foal. Our ranch stud, a handy old using horse named Bobby, was getting up there and was starting to have trouble settling his mares, but even most of those had taken. That made twenty-five foals coming for next year, including the thirteen that Doc had checked earlier in the month.

Wait a minute. I flipped back through the papers. We only had twenty-five broodmares. If one wasn't pregnant yet, I must have miscounted somewhere. I walked over to a bench and started spreading the papers out in alphabetical order to see where I'd slipped up. Ariel, Bella, Copper, Daisy...

Duchess.

"What do you mean, 'you suspected'? Why didn't you say anything?"

Dusty had his elbows propped on his desk, and he was trying to hide his chin behind his fists. It wasn't working because I could see that he was about to bust a gut laughing. "Because I knew you'd blow your lid like this. So, asked Doc to check her when he was examining the broodmares. I was out at the house site getting trusses delivered, so I couldn't stick around for the exam. But I have to say, I'm not surprised."

I flung the papers on his desk. "She didn't get pregnant all by herself. What did you do, go over to Bud Wilkins' stud behind my back?"

Dusty raised his brows and shook his head. "Guess again."

"Well, what, did she get left in the field with Bobby and his mares overnight or something?"

"Nope."

I rocked forward on his desk, getting eye level with him. "What happened?"

He leaned back in his chair, still chuckling. "What happened is that black stud of yours got into her pen a few weeks ago. Jess and I heard a commotion outside the bunkhouse, and when we went to check it out, he'd just flipped the latch and let himself in with her. I didn't think they'd been together for more than a few seconds. Guess I was wrong."

"And you didn't say anything? 'Hey, Luke, you need to chain that stallion's corral so he can't do that again.' Nothing?"

"It was the middle of the night! I closed Duchess' run after that so she was locked inside her stall, and he couldn't get to her in case he escaped again. The next morning when I came out, there was already an extra clip on his pen. I figured you had it handled, and there wasn't any good that could come from getting you all riled up until we knew."

I crossed my arms. "*I* put that clip there because he *did* escape again. I found him running loose the next morning. You still shoulda said something. What are we gonna do now?"

He frowned and shrugged. "We're going to wait for Duchess to have her foal, I guess. Actually, it should be an incredibly nice baby. Exactly the kind of foal you're wanting out of her."

"But we don't own that stud! We can't file a breeding report, we can't get papers. We'll be waiting all year, and a mare that should be dropping foals worth tens of thousands of dollars will be carrying a grade colt worth a grand, if we're lucky."

"Yeah. So, call your buddy Joe. Maybe he can help out, since he used to own that stallion."

I narrowed my eyes and pointed. "You'd better be right."

"I always am."

Audrey

I tapped lightly on Lizzy's bedroom door. "Hey. Need any help?"

All I heard was a sniff, but at least she wasn't shouting for me to go away. I slid the door open and found her sitting in the middle of the floor, her clothes strewn everywhere but inside her suitcase.

She looked up. "None of these fit."

I pushed some t-shirts aside and squatted on the carpet beside her. "We'll have to get you some bigger clothes. I think you grew about two inches in the last month."

She shrugged and stared at the empty suitcase.

I waited for her to say something, but she just reached through the pile, scattering underwear and socks and t-shirts until she found her oldest, most stained nightgown and pulled it into her lap. "Mom bought me this before she got sick."

I watched to see what she would do. "It looks like you've worn it a lot."

She sniffed and wadded it into a ball like she was going to toss it in the corner, then stopped herself and just set it down beside her. "I can't wear it anymore. It's too little."

"Lizzy," I said softly, slipping my arm around her. "Do you want to talk about anything?"

She hesitated, then shook her head.

"Because I'm here, you know. I'm always here. Even if you have to call me to talk, I'll always listen. And it's okay to cry."

Her throat worked, and she looked up with a sheen over her eyes. "I just want my mom back."

I pulled her close, tucking her head under my chin. "Oh, sweetie, so do I."

She let me cuddle her for a few seconds, then stiffened and pulled away. She wouldn't look at me, and she was fighting tooth and nail to keep any real expression from showing up on her face.

She needed more than just a hug and a little sympathy, but I didn't know what to offer. I chewed my lip and shifted to get more comfortable. "Did your dad say what time he was coming?"

"I don't know."

"Well, maybe we can go right now and get you some jeans that fit. What do you say?" I tucked a lock of hair behind her ear and studied her face. She looked so much like her mother at that age.

Lizzy pulled away from my touch and shook her head. "I don't want to go anywhere."

"What if I take you sometime next week? I can ask your dad if it's okay, and I'll take the afternoon off if necessary. I'm sure he wouldn't mind me buying you some clothes." As if. James would be happy if I'd keep buying all the groceries and paying the light bill for him, too.

Lizzy picked up a pair of mismatched socks, folded them together, then pulled them back apart. "It's not your job."

"I think it is. You're my only niece. I'm allowed to take you shopping, aren't I? It's the rules."

She folded the socks together again—one black with pink stripes and the other pink with black stripes. "These are fine."

I watched her fiddling with the socks. "Don't you have the correct mates for those anymore?"

"They can go together. See?"

"I see they don't match. The colors are wrong."

"But they're made the same, and they fit the same. I like them together."

"Okay... but you'll need more than one pair that fits. Come on. I'd like to take you. How about on Wednesday? I'll arrange with your dad to pick you up. We can leave early enough in the afternoon to get some frozen drinks from Kelli's coffee wagon and drive to the city, and—"

Her eyes flashed, and she threw the socks across the room. "I don't *want* you to! Just leave me alone."

I sat back on my heels. "Lizzy, I understand if you're upset right now, but you may not raise your voice to me."

"You're not my mom! You can't tell me what to do. The court said so. I'm going to my dad's, and I don't have to listen to you anymore."

"Lizzy! Where did all this come from? I know you're upset, but please, if you'll just talk to me—"

She snatched a loose pile of too-small clothes and hurled them at my face. "I'm done with stupid talking, and I hate you! Just go away!"

Instinctively, I raised both hands to shield my face, and then I stared at her in stricken silence. "I hope you don't mean that."

"I said it, didn't I?" She hopped to her feet and stomped to the door to fling it open and point me down the hall. In the light from the window, I could see the red rims of her eyes and the dried streaks of tears. "Just get out and leave me alone!"

In all the time I'd been living here, I'd been careful never to let Lizzy see me cry. It wasn't that I didn't close my door and have a quiet sob whenever all the grief overflowed. I'd just never believed that I had the right to make her carry my sorrows. But right now, the tears were streaming, and there was nothing I could do to stop them.

With all the dignity I could muster, I got shakily to my feet and walked toward the door, staring at her the whole time. She wouldn't meet my eyes—she just stood there with her arms crossed. I tried to swallow the knot in my throat, but I wasn't very successful.

"You know, Lizzy," I rasped, "I'm not perfect. I've screwed up some, and I know you didn't always like following the rules here when your dad didn't make you do that. But I do love you, and I've done my best."

She wouldn't look up. Because, apparently, my best wasn't good enough.

James didn't even bother getting out of his truck when he came to pick Lizzy up. That infuriated me, probably more than it should have, because I'd already spent the last hour weeping in my bedroom. The court had awarded him temporary custody pending a hearing, and he was pretty stinking smug about it. He just stared at me through the windshield and honked for Lizzy to come out.

I probably shouldn't have done it, but that snapped my last raw nerve. I marched out to his truck and pointed for him to roll down his window. James gave a sarcastic roll of his eyes, then hit the button.

"Don't bother, you spiteful old biddy. I'm gonna feed her whatever I want now because she's my kid, and you can't tell me not to give her junk food. And I'm sick of that nine o'clock bedtime rule. She's old enough to stay up later and watch R movies, and you aren't her parent, so shove off, Audrey."

I tried to bite back my temper, but some of it must have flashed across my face because James got a triumphant grin.

"What, you don't like that? Too bad. You don't get any say because it's not your place. So, go on and leave me alone."

"I'm not trying to tell you what to do," I said between clenched teeth. "I just wanted to remind you that Lizzy has a summer job and riding lessons scheduled at Walker Ranch. You won't forget to drop her off in the afternoons, right?"

He sputtered and shook his head. "You don't seriously think I'd take my kid up to the Walkers' place, do you? Those guys are a bunch of blow-hards who think they're God's gift or something."

"They're good people, and they've done a lot for Lizzy."

"Yeah, well, I'm her dad. She don't need those jerks." He honked the horn. "Lizzy! Come on, let's go!"

"James, I'm asking you. Please, for Lizzy's sake, let her go see the horses. I won't be there, and I'm not trying to trick you. She needs—"

"She needs to get her tail out here before I have to go in and get her. If you wanna get in the middle of this, you go tell her that. And then stay out of the way, Audrey. You've got no business here."

I folded my arms across my chest and screwed my mouth closed. Oh, how I wished I was a man, and I could flatten him! The law was on his side, so I couldn't call the cops or a social worker just because he'd insulted me. But Lizzy...

She appeared at the front door then, toting her suitcase. She barely looked up at me and got into the passenger side of James's truck without a word. I walked to that side so she wouldn't have to look past her dad when I waved at her. She glanced up, just long enough to acknowledge my existence, then her eyes fell to her lap again.

James put the truck in gear, backed out of the driveway, and they were gone.

Two hours later, I was sitting at the dining room table with my laptop, researching family law. Kat had done everything possible in her will to provide for Lizzy, but there was so much she couldn't do. James was right—I didn't have much of a leg to stand on when it came to continued shared custody. It didn't matter that I could prove he was always behind on child support and didn't have a job. The courts always liked to err on the side of the biological parents, even if those parents were dead-beats.

And I suppose there was a reason for that. It shouldn't be easy to take someone's child away. But really, when I reasoned out what I thought would be best, I didn't want to take Lizzy away. James was a worthless low-life, but he was her father. I'd hurt her all over again by robbing her of the only parent she had left.

But I did want to be able to be there for her—legally and personally. Unless the judge forced him to, James wouldn't let me do that. And from the way she'd sounded this afternoon, Lizzy didn't want me, either.

Everywhere I looked, I hit a dead end. There were special cases all over the place, but our situation seemed pretty cut and dried. He would have to voluntarily share custody, or at least permit me to be in her life on an informal basis. He'd never do that. And proving he was an unfit parent was out of the question because I found cases of really, *really* terrible human beings who should've lost their kids and didn't. James was nowhere close to bad enough for the courts to revoke his parental rights.

I rubbed my eyes and closed the laptop cover. There just didn't seem to be much I could do. Maybe it was time to surrender. Let James and Lizzy live their lives and stop trying to interfere. That was what she'd just asked me to do, wasn't it?

I knew it was the grief talking. She was at a tough age for any kid, and she'd just been through hell and back with no idea what was around the corner for her. She didn't even know what a stable home should look like, and my efforts at giving her a taste of one hadn't won her over. What kid would want the kind of rules I'd enforced for her when she could live like a wild thing with her dad? And really, was it so bad that he wasn't as strict?

It was humbling to confess it, but almost two years in this town had taught me something: my way wasn't the only way. Would he parent her the way I thought he should? Absolutely not. But she wasn't my kid to raise, and even if she were, she'd already made me re-evaluate some things I'd have thought were best. I'd have valued school more. I'd have taught her to dress more professionally and eat her vegetables better and read more books, and play an instrument.

But those things weren't really right for Lizzy. And maybe I wasn't right, either. If I loved her, maybe the best thing for me to do would be to back away.

I started to get up from the table, and my eyes landed on that bouquet Luke had dropped off at my work. I smiled and touched one of the petals. Light pink roses, for sympathy and affection, mixed with delicate, orange-scented syringas for new beginnings and love. Oddly enough, the New York state flower and the Idaho state flower blended together.

There was no way he'd picked those out by himself. He must have asked someone to help him, and my money was on Jess, the incurable romantic. Once, I would have scoffed at him for that. If a guy didn't know how to choose flowers for his woman, it was a sign of laziness and failure to understand, or at least make an effort.

But Luke had obviously swallowed his pride and asked for help from someone who knew me because he thought it would make me happy. And maybe that was sweeter by far than a guy who knew it all on his own.

He'd called earlier, asking if he could come over and see me tonight. I'd almost said yes. I really wanted to see him, to press my ear to his heart and let him play with my hair and to lose myself for a little while. To forget all my worries for an hour and just be with the guy who made me happy.

But that would only prolong the inevitable. Kat was gone, Lizzy was where she said she wanted to be, and I was facing all the decisions I'd been putting off. There was nothing keeping me here any longer. It was time to really think about the future and stop just wishing and hoping that things were different. Time to admit what I'd been denying all spring.

I was crazy about Luke, but I'd only known him for a few months. He would always have something of a wild streak that I'd never understand and could never fully adapt to. He was the most amazing man I'd ever met, but could I trust a crazy cowboy like him with my future? I *had* a plan once. A good plan—one I'd sacrificed so much for, and one that wouldn't keep waiting forever.

Lizzy didn't want me in her life anymore. Luke... well, Luke was all gas pedal and no brakes. I could cling fast to him and hold on for the ride, hoping and praying we didn't crash and burn. It sounded intoxicating and brilliant—the chance to chase rainbows and sink my roots deep into good soil and watch them grow.

Or it could be the worst decision I ever made.

The life I'd left behind was safer. It was known, well-traveled, and it made sense. By every measure, I'd be stupid to turn my back on it now, since my job here was finished.

I leaned forward to drink in the sweet scent of the syringas one last time, then I sat back and opened my laptop. I didn't really belong here. I might as well start looking for apartments to rent.

Chapter 21

Luke

I pounced on my phone on the first ring. "Audrey?"

"Not unless I got a lot purtier overnight. Whatch'a been up to, you old windbag?"

I let go of the breath I'd been holding and found a smile. "Hey, Joe. I was expecting someone else."

"Obviously. Is she good-looking?"

"Better than you can imagine. And don't try to imagine her, either, because I'm not sure I'd like a dirty old scoundrel like you thinking about my girl."

"Ouch!" he laughed. "Hey, I got your message last night. Seems you're in a bit of a pickle with a pregnant mare."

I stuffed my phone in the crook of my shoulder and grabbed a broom to tidy up the barn aisle. "You could say that. Dusty said I should call you, but honestly, I'm not sure what, if anything, you can do."

"Well, it's funny you should mention that. I pulled my records on that horse."

"And?"

"Let's see, I sold him almost three years ago. Same buyers, so he didn't change hands again. They paid a mint for him because he was just coming on strong that season in the roping pen. My cousin Gage won a pile of money on him that summer, so we didn't sell him cheap. It's funny, you know. You figure one of the best protections you have in selling a horse is selling him for a high dollar so someone will be forced to appreciate him."

"Yeah, you'd think. That's crazy. What else?"

"Okay, so here's where it gets weird. They went to the sale down in Texas right after they picked him up and got themselves a bunch of broodmares. From what I found out, none of them were anything special. Sounds to me like they were running out of cash, and they thought that lots of mediocre mares could cross on one quality stallion and make them a lot of money."

"Also stupid. Mares contribute more than fifty percent. Anyone will tell you that. They'd have been better off with two good mares than twenty bad ones."

"You're assuming they did their homework, but if they did, they'd have found out nobody gets rich in this game. I don't really know what their deal was, but the guy got hurt and couldn't work anymore. Things got tight for them, and then they didn't try to re-home all those horses like they should've. But are you ready for the real kicker?"

"Oh, sure." I set the broom aside and plopped down on a bench.

"They never transferred him."

I squinted and leaned forward. "What?"

"According to the breed registry, he's still in my name. I signed off on all the papers; they had the transfer report. They just never sent it in. One wonders what they were planning to do with all those babies they were raising, but I know they're not registered because they never filed any reports."

I shook my head. "So, what now?"

"I guess that depends on what happens with the case. On paper, he's still my horse, but that's not actually true. Since they've still got the signatures and everything, and I don't have possession of the horse, it would be unethical for me to file a lost papers affidavit. They could take me to court over that if it came out."

"No, Joe, I'm not asking for you to do anything like that." I kicked back on the bench and scowled. "The way Doc Burns is talking, we don't know what's going to happen. He's testifying about it today, but it's not impossible that these creeps could get their horses back."

"That's what I'm afraid of. Maybe if they do, we could talk them into selling him back. Think that would work?"

"I guess it's possible if they're hard up for money. I hate rewarding them for just about killing this horse, but I'd do it if that was what it took to keep him out of their paws."

"Yeah. Well, keep me posted, will you?"

"Sure thing. Thanks for digging into it, Joe."

"You got it. And hey, if you ever get tired of ranching, you let me know, will you? I'd hire you in a heartbeat. We could use a guy who knows his stock and can schmooze with all the bigwigs."

I rolled my eyes up to the ceiling like I was thinking about it. Once, that would have been amazing. But I was pretty happy where I was, and even happier with where life seemed to be going. "Appreciate the offer, Joe, but I'll have to pass."

"I figured you would. Take care, bro."

Audrey

"Dustin, I promise, this won't hurt. Please let Doctor Livingstone take a look, and then we can go home."

I stood in the far corner of the little treatment room, my hands empty and my manner as unassuming as I could make it, as Meg Truman tried reasoning with my patient for this afternoon. This wasn't the first time she'd brought her son Dustin in for a checkup. He had some sensory issues, so he couldn't stand brushing his teeth the way he really needed to. And that meant he had a lot of trouble with cavities.

But Dustin didn't want to get in the chair, and we'd been trying to reason with him for ten minutes already. He just hung back in the open doorway, his eyes roving distrustfully over the chair and all my equipment. I couldn't really blame him. All those drills and picks and rinsing tools probably looked pretty horrifying to a kid who didn't even like a toothbrush.

"Come on, bud," Meg pleaded. "Just a quick peek. Doctor Livingstone won't do anything to surprise you. You remember that, right?"

Dustin's eyes slid to me and narrowed. He shook his head and hugged the wall.

Enough of this. My stomach had been gurgling and unsettled since before lunch, I had a headache coming on, and I had other patients coming after him. I couldn't argue with him all day.

I sighed and pulled off my gloves and tugged the mask off my face. "Dustin, do I look more familiar now?"

He glanced between his mother and me. "I know who you are."

I tossed my PPE in the trash and moved forward to stand by Meg. "You know me as Doctor Livingstone, right?"

He nodded.

"And do you remember your friend Lizzy from your class?"

"She's not from my class. She's a year ahead of me because I stayed back in kindergarten."

"Okay. But you remember her, right? She's been up to White Pines with you, and you guys played at Walker Ranch a few times."

Dustin's jaw locked, and he gave a single nod.

"Well, did you know that Lizzy is my niece? That makes me more than just Doctor Livingstone, doesn't it?"

I could see the gears turning as he stared at his shoes. I risked taking another step forward, then crouched and offered my hand. "My other name is Audrey."

Dustin peered suspiciously at my hand. "You're still a dentist."

"That's right, I am. But I'm also your friend, and I'd like for you to be my friend. And friends don't hurt each other, so Dustin, I am promising that I won't hurt you."

He hugged the wall a little tighter. "But sometimes it does hurt. It pokes, and it's cold."

"Yes, I know. But here, take a look." I reached slowly for a cleaning pick and held it level in the palm of my hand. "Okay, poke my finger with it."

His gaze darkened. "That would hurt you."

"Only if you're mean, but I don't believe you're a mean person. Go ahead and try it."

Dustin looked at his mom, then carefully reached for the pick I offered. He examined it for a few seconds, then slowly pointed it into my index finger and pushed. *Hard.*

It took all I had not to wince, and I was actually surprised I wasn't bleeding. As it was, he left a sharp divot in the pad of my finger that was still bright red for several seconds afterward. Meg cleared her throat and peered over my shoulder. "Oh, my," she gasped. "Are you okay?"

I forced a grin at Dustin. "Just fine. See, you pushed pretty hard, didn't you? I won't be pushing at all, just scraping. May I show you?"

He stuck his hand out, staring eagerly at the pick. I gently swept it over his palm, following the grooves of his hand, and he laughed. "It tickles."

"Yes, it does. What do you say? Will you let me tickle your teeth?"

Dustin took the pick from my hand and clasped it tight. "Can I keep this?"

"Sure. I have another one just like it." I picked it up to show him that it was exactly the same. He examined it, and he must have approved because he climbed into the chair.

The rest of Dustin's checkup went pretty smoothly. "No new cavities this time," I told his mom. "But watch out for those back teeth. He had a fair bit of buildup starting there, so he needs to work on his brushing."

Meg grabbed both of my hands in hers. "Thank you, Audrey. He was so nervous to come today! I don't know what we'd do without you."

"Oh, I'm sure he'd be fine. It seemed like he just needed a few minutes to think about it." I unclipped my fresh mask and tossed it in the garbage.

"I wish that was all it was. You have a gift, Audrey. I've seen lots of other people try the same sorts of things to get Dustin to trust them, but he almost never does. There's something about you."

I smiled as I typed up his treatment report. "That's really sweet of you to say. You know, there's a really top-ranked children's clinic over in Idaho Falls. I know it's a drive, but they employ several specialized pediatric dentists, some of whom are trained in special needs."

"I'm so glad we don't have to drive to Idaho Falls! He'd never be able to hold it together for such a long car ride, and then be able to see the dentist on top of it? He'd fall apart. We're blessed to have you in our town."

I stopped typing. "Meg, I have to tell you that I'm thinking of selling the clinic."

Her eyes widened. "Oh, please don't do that. Why?"

I squeezed my hands between my knees and sucked my upper lip between my teeth. How much should I tell Meg? She'd be one of the few who would understand the struggles of dealing with an explosive tween under stress. Except she was Dustin's real mom, and custody had never been a problem. Frankly, I was too embarrassed to tell her that my niece had been refusing to take my calls and wanted nothing more to do with me.

"Oh, it's just business," I lied. "I've decided to take a job in New York that's exactly what I've always wanted. I'd have been there two years ago if Kat hadn't needed me, and the longer I cool my heels here, the fewer opportunities I'll have to move back to where I really ought to be."

Meg sank in the guest chair of the treatment room, her expression so broken that my heart squeezed for her. I couldn't possibly be so important that I could make her cry by leaving town! But her brow crumpled, and she looked like she was trying not to lose her composure. She sucked in a breath, then pasted on a brave smile.

"You're right. You need to follow that opportunity while you can. I'm just so sorry to hear we're going to be losing you."

"Meg," I said gently, "it's not like I'm irreplaceable. There are lots of dentists around. Someone new will come to buy the clinic."

She smiled sadly and shook her head. "No, Audrey, you're one of a kind. It's not easy to find someone who understands Dustin, you know? When you have an autistic kid, you figure out pretty quickly which people you can trust. We're really going to miss you."

I sighed. Great. I'd crushed poor Meg. I'd never thought of myself as special like that. I didn't think any of my clients would even miss me, but here was Meg, fighting back the tears. I reached for her hand to give it a reassuring press.

"Don't tell anyone yet, please. It's not set in stone yet—I'll stick around until all Kat's and Lizzy's affairs are settled. Besides, there are some people who should hear it from me before anyone else knows."

Meg squeezed my fingers. "Do you mean Luke Walker?"

I stiffened and put a hand to my mouth. "Oh, dear. Have I been that obvious?"

She just smiled. "Yeah. I, for one, was really thrilled for you. He's a great guy, Audrey, and the way he looks at you..." She shivered and closed her eyes, thumping her chest like her heart was aching. "Pure deliciousness. You're really going to leave that cowboy behind?"

I blew out a sigh. "It's complicated, Meg."

"Most things are, on the surface. But underneath? Usually, the answer is pretty simple." She got up from the chair and took my hand again. "I'm really going to miss you, Audrey. Take care of yourself, will you?"

I nodded. "I will. Bye, Meg."

Luke

"Hello, Luke."

My stomach filled with butterflies when I heard Audrey's voice. I'd missed talking to her yesterday, and something about hearing her voice just made everything else disappear, and I felt warm and fuzzy all over. "Hey, sweetheart. Busy day?"

"You could say that. You called?"

Straight to the point, huh? "Yeah, I called because Lizzy didn't come up this afternoon. Is everything okay?"

I heard a sigh on the other end. "She's with her father now. I don't think he planned to bring her."

"Oh." I found a chair and slid into it. "Maybe in a few days or something."

"Or... maybe not. He said he doesn't like you, Luke."

"Well, the feeling's mutual. I might'a busted his jaw once or twice back in high school."

She gasped softly. "What for?"

"I don't like bullies." I kicked my boots on the floor. "But that stinks about the kid. I had a horse all picked out for her and everything. He'll still get her up to Morgan's place once in a while, won't he?"

Audrey was quiet for a few seconds. "I wouldn't count on it. Luke, things are going to be kind of different now. I don't think I'll be able to visit her too much."

"What do you mean? Of course, you will. James can't raise that kid on his own. He doesn't even want to. You remember how he left her at the house. The dude's a terrible dad."

"But that's not enough to... Luke, what I'm trying to say is that there's no way I'll be able to keep her now. And I shouldn't." I heard a sniff. "I'm just her aunt."

Something prickled at the back of my senses. This was wrong. Very, very wrong. "Audrey, come on. You can't give up on her."

"It's not giving up if she doesn't want me. James is going to get full custody, and Lizzy is happier there."

"I don't give a hootin' holler what she *wants*. She needs *you*!"

"We don't always get the things we need."

"What?" I stood up and started to pace. "This doesn't sound like you. What's going on?"

Another sniff. "Nothing. I'm just coming to terms with facts—something I should have faced months ago. Luke, there's something I need to tell you."

The tone of her voice, the hesitation, and the choked-back tears behind it all, made the hair stand on the back of my neck. "Why do I get the feelin' I'm not gonna like it?"

"Luke," she whispered. "Please don't make this harder than it is. There's a... a job. In New York."

"New York! But what about Lizzy? You're just going to leave?"

"I'll wait until the hearing, but... Luke, we both know what's going to happen. Lizzy deserves one home, not two, where she's being pulled back and forth all the time. It's not fair to her."

"Fair, you talk about fair? What was all that about being there for her and trying to do what her mother couldn't? And what about me? You're walking on me, too?"

"We aren't engaged, Luke. We... I don't know what we were... are. But we've been together for a couple of months. I'm talking about something I've been planning for half my life!"

"So? I was thinking about a lot longer than that, and I thought you were, too."

"We both knew this was going to come someday. I should have said something long ago, but... I just couldn't. I tried, so many times I tried to say it, and I didn't know how to make the words come out." She drew a ragged breath. "I'm sorry, Luke. We'll only end up hurting each other if we aren't honest now."

"Hurting each other! Audrey, I'd never hurt you. I love you!"

She fell silent—so still I could hear my own heartbeat in my ears. I'd blurted it out, hadn't I? All those secrets that had been bubbling up in my soul, they'd finally spilled out of my mouth, and now I couldn't take the words back. And I didn't want to.

"Luke." Her voice broke. "I can't... I... I have to go."

"Audrey, wait! I—"

The line went dead.

Audrey

My hands were shaking as I dropped the phone. My legs were trembling, my head was spinning, and I couldn't see through the tears. How could I? I deserved the stabbing ache in my ribs where my heart should have been.

Because only a heartless shrew could dump Luke Walker.

He loved me. I covered my mouth with my hand and tried to choke back a sob. Had he really said that? He couldn't mean it! It had to be just words. He cared for me, I knew that. Wasn't I crazy over him, too?

But... *love?* That was so much bigger than anything we'd even dared to hope. That sounded serious. Permanent.

It sounded like everything I'd ever dreamed of.

I wiped my face and tried to get to my feet, but I was quaking too much to trust my legs. I couldn't let myself be distracted, no matter how much I adored Luke Walker. It couldn't last! I'd be a fool to hang my heart on the delights of the moment and turn my back on the goal of my lifetime. Twelve years of higher education, and I barely had anything to show for it!

But Luke... the pain in his voice had nearly broken me. And when I thought about everything I'd have to give up to chase that old ambition, I had to wonder...

Was it worth it?

Chapter 22

Luke

A steaming mug of coffee appeared on the table between my elbows. I lifted my head from my hands to see Evan taking a seat beside me and sipping his own cup. He wasn't looking at me—just leaning back in his chair and staring at the wall.

"Have you come to try to make me feel better?"

"Nope."

"Good. Because I don't want to feel better."

He shrugged. "Figured."

"And I don't need you looking all wise and supportive. You can cut it out now."

"I'm just drinking my coffee. There was enough for two cups. Thought you might want some."

"Well, I don't."

"Fine."

"Fine." I gave the cup a push with my index finger and slid it across the table.

Evan didn't flinch. He just pulled his phone out and started check-ing the weather report. I squeezed my eyes with my fingers and heaved a sigh.

I'd known it was too good to last. Why would a sophisticated, educated, beautiful woman like Audrey Livingstone want a cowboy with dusty jeans, sloppy grammar and too many old scars to count? She always was way out of my league.

But I'd never thought she'd just up and leave town when her sister died. Yes, now that she mentioned it, I did remember her talking about New York and all she'd left behind. But going back? Never even occurred to me.

Jess had taken one look at my face after that phone call, and she'd dragged me out to the barn to beat a confession out of me. Then she told me some things I'd never put together before—how Audrey could be the lead surgeon at a fancy new clinic back east and how hard she'd worked for that kind of opportunity. And now, after all the waiting and the tough things of the last couple of years, the job offer had landed in her lap. I think Jess thought it would soften the sting for me to hear that, but it didn't.

I knew what it was to want something big like that, and I'd also had it slip through my fingers. Maybe the difference was that by the time it came back around for me, with Joe trying to get me on board with his stock company, I'd already found what I really wanted somewhere else. I guess I hoped Audrey had, too.

But why wouldn't she at least stick around for Lizzy? That was what I couldn't figure out. Heck with me. We were just enjoying each other's company for a while, right? We'd made no promises. But everything she'd been to that kid for the last couple of years—well, that seemed to me like a promise. The kind you live out, even when things don't turn your way.

A chair shifted across the table, and I figured it was Evan finally giving up and leaving me alone. But no such luck. It was Dad, settling in with his crossword puzzle and a pencil stuck behind his ear. I propped my cheek on my fist and ignored him, toying with the handle of the coffee cup.

What was I going to do now? I'd been thinking long and hard about the words that tumbled out of my mouth last night. The forever kind of words—the ones I'd never said to any other woman. I never really figured on saying them to that sassy dentist, but I meant them. And now that I'd meant them, shouldn't something happen? What kind of man pours his guts out to a woman and gets turned down flat?

The latest issue of *Stockman's Magazine* slid onto the table beside me, and Dusty pulled out the closest chair. Like the others, he didn't look at me. Just sat down like he was minding his own business and started thumbing through the pages.

I sighed and dropped my fist on the table. "You know, y'all are pretty obvious."

Dad looked up from his crossword, his mouth slack and his gaze foggy. "Beg pardon?"

"I mean you, all of you, just sitting here waiting to gang up on me like some self-appointed Happiness Committee."

Evan set his empty cup down. "Nobody's saying anything, Luke."

"Well, good. Because you don't need to."

Evan shrugged. "Good."

I glanced around at each of them for several seconds. "So, why are you all still sitting here?"

"It's the dining room table," Dusty said. "Everybody sits here."

"'Cept I notice Meryl and Jess are curiously absent."

"Went to the store." Dusty licked his index finger and turned over a slick page of his magazine. "And besides, if you really wanted to be left alone, you'd have gone somewhere else."

I narrowed my eyes at my youngest brother. Dusty had me pegged, alright. I didn't want lectures, and I didn't want platitudes. The last things I needed to hear were, "I told you so," and "These things happen for a reason." But I also wasn't quite in the mood to lock myself in a dark room because I'd just end up bawling like a little kid.

I guess there are worse things than having your brothers and your dad just sit with you. I eyed them each one more time, then spun the handle of that coffee cup around and tipped it back. I might get through this with my heart intact, or I might not. But at least my family was in it with me.

Audrey

I thought by morning, I'd feel a little lighter. The decision was made, the important people informed. Of course, it was all pending the custody hearing and the settling of Kat's affairs, but those were just formalities. I knew what was going to happen, so I should have felt relieved that I'd finally made the call and set things into motion for the next phase of my life.

But by morning, I was sick.

Not sad-sick. Casting-up-my-accounts sick. Shaking-hands-with-the-commode sick. I'd found a clean sock from the laundry basket, and I was using that to wipe the queasy sweat off my forehead, but it didn't help the rest of me. After an episode at five that left me shaking and crawling back to my bed on all fours, I managed to pull my brain together enough to text Kari that I wouldn't be in today.

Then, I slept for four more hours, but it wasn't a nice kind of sleep. I had my head in the popcorn bowl a couple of times, and the rest of it was a delusional, restless kind of lethargy. I kept hearing Luke's voice in my head, seeing him in punctuated snippets of dreams. Every time, I'd try to reach for him, only to wake up heaving again.

What had I eaten? This felt a lot like food poisoning, but I couldn't think of anything that might have caused it. There was probably something in my medical textbooks about psychosomatic illness. Hah! It would serve me right if I'd done this to myself. It was less than I'd done to Luke.

Luke...

I groaned his name as I flopped over on the bed, half buried under the covers and half bare to the blowing ceiling fan, because I couldn't decide if I was freezing or about to burn up. That was how my brain felt, too—each foot in a different world, and me being ripped apart in the middle.

Shouldn't it have gotten easier now that I'd come clean with my plans? I'd checked those mental boxes, and now I could move forward. But it just didn't feel that way. In fact, it had gotten harder, and I'd barely found the enthusiasm to call Peter yesterday to accept the job. He was happy. Shouldn't I be?

But there's no point in trying to reason with a brain that's too scrambled to even put together a few sentences. I tossed and turned a few times, and after a while, I must have fallen back asleep. It must have been sleep, because it felt better than being awake. Because I dreamed about Luke.

Luke

I almost dropped my coffee mug when Cody slammed into me, coming out of the tack room. He was toting about six training headstalls and a handful of colt-starting flags, and he was dragging so much stuff that it was a wonder he could walk at all.

"Shoot! Sorry, Luke. I didn't see you there."

I stumbled back a few steps and flicked the wet coffee from my hand. "Dude, what are you doing? You look like you're about to run a horse training clinic. Aren't all the colts started already?"

He shifted his shoulder because some of the headstalls were slipping. "Ours, yeah. But this is for White Pines. I've got some volunteers coming today, and we're going to start groundwork and retraining the rescue horses. Didn't you hear? I thought Morgan called you last night."

"Yeah, she did. I figured it was a sympathy call or something so I didn't answer."

Cody cracked a grin. "Well, you should check your voicemail. The neglect case settled yesterday."

"It did?" I perked up. "So? Are they going to jail?"

"No. No fines, either."

My fists curled. "*What?*"

"Don't get all bent out of shape yet. They agreed to forfeit all claims to their animals, and they're prohibited from owning anything, even a dog, for ten years."

I felt my eyes grow wide. "Wait, does that mean...?"

"Yep! All the horses are going to be legally available for adoption. So, we're starting the process of getting them ready for their new homes. Morgan already has some interested folks lined up, and she's hopeful that the horses can all be placed. How about that, huh?"

"So, what about the stud?"

"You should check your messages, dude. Morgan pulled some strings for you."

"For me? What's that mean? I just want to know what I'm supposed to do with him now."

"Come on, Luke. Everyone knows you want to keep him. Morgan got the paperwork started already, and because he's got that brand, a positive identification with the breed registry, and a viable home already located, she got the usual adoption requirements waived. He's your horse."

"What, already?" I gulped. "Just like that?"

"Just like that. Are you going to help me load this stuff in my truck, or what? I could use a hand unless you have something better to do today."

"And what would that be?"

Cody tossed the gear in his pickup and adjusted his hat. "Well, you know Morgan. She hears things. Sometimes I think she has a hotline to everyone in town—it's scary the stuff she's able to find out. Audrey's sick today."

Sick? My heart gave a funny little thump, but I made myself shrug it off. There wasn't anything I could do about that. She didn't want me. "That's too bad."

"Yeah. She sounds pretty miserable. Throwing up all night, can't even get out of bed today. Been there, right? It's the worst feeling. Especially when you're all by yourself."

I put my hands on my hips. "What are you drivin' at, Cody?"

"Me? Nothing. Help me grab some saddles, will you?"

I went after him, scuffling my boots on the concrete. "You say she can't even get out of bed?"

"As of five this morning. That was four hours ago. Grab that roping saddle, please. I might need to hop on a babysitter horse to ride along with the greenies."

"But who's taking care of her?"

Cody had his arms full of saddles and a saddle blanket between his teeth. He turned around to look at me and just shrugged. "Herself, I guess," he mumbled around the blanket. "Bring that short-skirted cutting saddle, too. It's nice and light."

I threw a saddle under each arm and followed him out to his truck, my eyes on the pavement. I didn't like hearing about Audrey being sick and alone. She might not want me forever, but it sounded like she needed me for now, at least. She needed *someone*, anyway.

"Can Morgan go check on Audrey?" I asked as I threw the saddles in the truck.

Cody closed the door and leaned on his rig, shaking his head at me. "Why don't you just go, Luke? You know you won't be satisfied until you've made sure for yourself that she's okay."

I stuffed my hands in my pockets. "She broke up with me. Why would I go over there and hurt all over again? It's not like I'm going to change her mind and make her stay just because I take soup over."

"Not if it's *your* soup, that's for darn sure."

I curled my lip. "You're a jerk."

Cody clapped a hand on my shoulder. "Luke, I know you care for her, so just go do what you need to. Why did you pour yourself out taking care of a horse you were probably going to lose? Why did you spend so much time investing in someone else's kid? Love isn't about what you can get back. It's about what you can give."

I scowled at the ground for a full minute and a half. "Cody? I hate it when you're right."

Audrey

The blanket fell off my face as I rolled over. Light stabbed my eyes and made me flinch, and I cast my elbow over my face. Ugh. My head felt like it was double its usual size, and my tongue was thick and sticky.

This wasn't food poisoning, and it wasn't stomach flu. I used to get this when I was a kid, but I hadn't experienced it in years, and supposedly I'd outgrown it. This time was worse than ever before, and when it hit me in the middle of the night, the idea of food poisoning made sense. But by now, I was pretty sure that what I had was an abdominal migraine the size of Texas.

It was rare, the doctors used to tell me. So rare that it took two years of my mom hauling me to the doctor and Kat fussing over me at home before they ever got a diagnosis. I used to get this after cramming for tests—brought on by stress and fatigue and running low on emotional reserves.

Yeah, that sounded about right. When had my tank ever been lower? The hazy aura fogging my vision when I tried to sit up just confirmed it. My head swam, I felt queasy again, and I flopped back on the pillow.

With symptoms this bad, I should go to the hospital, but obviously, I couldn't drive myself. My hand bumped around on the bedside table, searching for my phone, but when I felt it, I accidentally knocked it on the floor.

Oh, well. I'd get it later.

Sometime later—I wasn't sure how long—something cool touched my forehead. Then I felt an ice chip pressed to my lips. I groaned and tried to grab more of that cool feeling.

"Easy, sweetheart, you're going to choke. Plenty more where that came from."

My eyes fluttered, and I squinted to block out the swirling images and bring them into focus. And I think I smiled.

"Luke?"

"Yeah, baby. I'm here. You look awful."

I fumbled around for his hand and squeezed it. "Thanks."

"You smell awful, too."

I swallowed and felt how raw my throat was. "Any more nice things you want to say?"

"I'm sure I'll think of something. Do you need a doctor?"

I tried to swallow again and nodded. "Please."

The medicine helped. After fluids, anti-inflammatories, nausea drugs, and migraine medication, I was starting to feel a little more like a human. Not a fully functioning one, but at least I wasn't doubled over anymore.

Luke took care of everything. He talked to the doctors, wrote down what I needed to do for follow-up care, and arranged for the nurses to help me take a shower before I checked out of the hospital. He'd even packed a pair of clean yoga pants and a sweatshirt that didn't smell like puke.

I was so loopy half the time that most of those details barely registered, but there was one thing I never doubted. All afternoon and late into the evening, no matter the need or the time, Luke was my hero. A scruffy-looking hero in faded Wranglers and a cowboy hat... the best kind.

The hospital sent me home late in the day, but I didn't care enough about the time to check the clock. Luke pulled into the darkened driveway and carried me into the house. I just let him drape me in his arms, clinging to his neck like a pillow. He was warm and strong, and he was the only place that made me feel better.

"Are you thinking about food yet?" he asked after he had me settled on the couch. "Because I could eat a whole quarter of beef right now."

My eyes crossed, and I clutched my stomach. "Oof, don't make me think of heavy stuff like that. Maybe just some soup. Do I have any cans in the pantry?"

He held up a finger. "I'm way ahead of you." He walked back to the porch and returned with a Dutch Oven carried with a hot mitt. "I asked for someone to bring this by when I knew what time we were heading out. Dad just dropped it off a couple of minutes before we got here."

I sat up a little. "Is that the famous cabbage stew I've heard so much about?"

Luke scoffed. "Are you kidding? I wouldn't feed you that. I only make that stuff because everybody hates it. I got out of a lot of cooking that way."

I narrowed my eyes. "Wait. So... you've been pulling everybody's leg for years? That soup is the stuff of myths and legends, and you made it as a joke?"

"Pretty much. But this is the good stuff. Good old farm-style chicken and vegetables with homemade stock and those awesome thick noodles. I think Meryl made it, so you're safe. Feel like giving it a whirl?"

I leaned my head back against a couch cushion and laughed softly. "I think you could talk me into trying just about anything."

The soup felt like a steaming bowl of comfort—hearty and hot and easy on my poor stomach. Luke carried away what I couldn't eat, and I heard him in the kitchen, meticulously storing the leftovers in the fridge. Then, he came back and sat on the edge of the couch beside me.

"Anything else you need?"

I shook my head. "Just sleep. I'll feel a lot better in the morning. Luke... I don't know how to thank you."

Those purple-blue eyes roved over my face—soft and searching and tender as a caress. "You don't need to thank me. I'm just glad I came over when I did. You looked pretty rough."

"But why did you come to check on me in the first place? No one would do that. I broke up with you over the phone, like a coward, and you still rode in to my rescue."

His face clouded, and he looked down. "I know maybe I wasn't what you wanted, but I figured for now, I could be what you needed. That's all."

That made my throat choke up all over again, and I reached for his hand. I couldn't even think of any words, but just touching him felt like something. But not enough. I pulled his hand to my mouth and kissed it. "I don't deserve you, Luke."

"Don't talk like that. Carin' for people—it's not about deserving or owing debts or being good enough. It's just being there."

I touched his cheek and smiled. "And here you are."

His lips thinned. "Come on, sweet thing. Let's get you more comfortable so you can get some sleep. Think you can walk straight, or do you want me to help you back to your room?"

Something in me deflated. I supposed he had to go home sometime, but I wasn't ready to let go of him yet. Could I even manage on my own? I didn't want to, but I probably could.

"I think I'll stay here," I said after a minute. "It's a little easier to get up."

"Okay." Luke shoved off the couch and disappeared down the hall. I assumed that was it—he was putting my medicine out for me or something, and he'd be gone. But a few minutes later, he came back with his arms full of blankets and pillows. "So, how do you want to do this?"

"Well... doesn't the pillow go under my head, and the blanket goes on top? Just toss me one of each, and I'll figure it out. Thanks for grabbing those for me."

He dropped the bundle and cocked his head. "Should I crash on the chair or the floor? That's what I was talking about. That chair looks like a widowmaker if a guy has to sleep in it overnight."

My mouth fell open. "You're staying with me?"

"Well, I'm sure as heck not leaving you alone yet. Unless you'd rather have someone else come over. I could probably get Jess here. Would you rather have her?"

Numb, I just shook my head, fresh tears sparkling in the corners of my eyes. "No. I want you."

"Okay, then, move over a little." He shook the folds out of a blanket and laid it over me, then came back with two pillows. "I got an idea. Sit up a bit."

Luke sat beside me and turned so his back was facing the arm of the couch. Then he fluffed a pillow in the corner by his shoulder and held out his arm, inviting me to lay back on his chest. That... that looked like the best place on earth. I kicked my feet toward the other end of the couch and let him wrap me in his arms. And I learned all over again what peace felt like.

"Comfy?" he asked as he tucked the blanket under my chin. "How's your stomach feeling?"

I snuggled my cheek against his chest. "Better."

"And your head?"

"Also better. It's not pounding anymore."

"Good. Just close your eyes, baby. Get some rest." His fingers found the base of my skull, just at the edge of my hairline, and began slow, comforting circles. The tension just bled out—all the anxiety and pain and stress I'd been carrying, melting away because of Luke's touch.

I sighed and sank a little deeper into him. "Luke, you're breaking my heart."

"Shh. Don't fret about me." He kissed the top of my head. "Just relax."

"No, there's something I need to tell you. The other night, the things I said to you—"

"I'm not tryin' to change your mind, Audrey. Jess told me how hard this decision was for you." I heard him swallow. "I love you, but you're right. We've barely gotten to know each other, and you'd be a fool to turn your back on that opportunity."

"No. I'd be a fool to turn my back on you."

His arm tightened around me. "What?"

"I mean, a person's dreams can change. I spent so long regretting what I lost that I almost didn't see what I had in front of me. And it's so much better than anything I could have made up on my own."

He was quiet for a few seconds. "I'm not sure what that means. Are you thinkin' straight right now?"

"Straighter than ever."

"Well, what was all that about breaking your heart? I didn't come over here to hurt you."

I chuckled softly and turned a little so I could drink in his scent, pressing my cheek to his chest. "Luke, there *is* a good way for a man to break a woman's heart. You found it."

"I still don't get it."

"That's okay, cowboy. Sometimes you have to break something that isn't working the way it should so you can put it back together right."

His chest rose and fell in a sigh. "That sorta makes sense. But I still think it's the migraine talking."

"Hmm." I let my eyes drift closed. "Guess I'll save the 'I love you' speech till tomorrow. Good night, Luke."

He kissed my hair once more. "Sleep well, Audrey."

Chapter 23

Luke

When I woke up, I couldn't feel my legs. Except for my bad knee—my knee was screaming, but everything else was numb. My right arm was shot through with tingling pains, and my neck felt like I'd put my head in a vise and bent it backward. But Audrey was still sleeping on my chest, and that was well worth suffering a little for.

She must have felt me squirming to restore the circulation to my hand because she drank in a deep breath and moved her head. "Luke?"

"Still here, sweet thing. How'd you sleep?"

She pushed off my chest—I think she cracked a rib or two in the process—and scrubbed her face with her hands. "Was that sleep? How long was I out?"

"Long enough for the sun to come up. Head feeling any better?"

She crunched up her face and screwed up her eyes against the sunlight, then she turned to squint at me. Her hair was a rat's nest, and her face was crisscrossed with creases from my shirt. But she'd never looked more gorgeous to me.

"I think it's okay. For now, anyway." Then, her eyes flew open. "Oh, my goodness, I need to call Kari! I'm probably late for work already."

"Nah, she called yesterday when the doctor was checking you out. I talked to her and told her you'd need today off, too."

"It's not about that." Audrey stuck her foot out, searching for the floor, and then an arm followed until she was crawling, spider-like, off of me. I appreciated how careful she was not to elbow or step on anything... delicate. Once she was free, she stood up, and I was able to shake my own legs out and try to restore some blood flow.

She was turning around, brushing the hair out of her eyes as she tossed through the blankets and searched the floor in front of the couch. "Where's my phone? I need to call the office, right now!"

I massaged the kink in my neck and stood up. "Over on the entry table. What's the rush? Get some food into you and take a breath. You look like you're going to fall down."

She waved me off and stumbled to the door to grab her phone. "No, you don't understand. Two days ago, I told Kari and Lucy both that I was planning sell the clinic. I thought Lucy was going to faint, and Kari actually started crying." She punched the phone screen a few times until it started to ring. "They'll be trying to get their resumes together and searching for other jobs. I need to tell them I've changed my mind!"

I stepped over to her and pushed her phone down. "Wait, does that mean... what you said last night?"

She nodded, and a smile blossomed on her beautiful face. "I'm not going anywhere, Luke."

It was like a light exploded in my brain, and I was tingling everywhere. "You mean it? You're staying in town?"

"I'm staying with you."

I grabbed her by the waist and picked her up for a kiss that made me see stars. "You really mean it?" I gasped when we came up for air. "You're not going to New York after all?"

"No, I'm not!" she laughed and kissed me again. "I'll call and decline the job as soon as I talk to the girls. Oh, wait." She put a finger to her lips and tucked her phone to her ear when someone answered. "Kari? Is Lucy in this morning?"

I listened for a minute, and then I stepped outside to let her finish her business. As I soaked in the morning sunshine, all the newness of the day warmed me all the way from my lungs down to my toes. This was good. Everything was good.

Audrey wasn't going anywhere, and that meant I'd need to make a forever place for her in my life. I was ready to do that. I didn't know what it would look like yet. Would she want to get married soon? Or spend some time just going on as we had been? And would Lizzy be a part of our lives? Audrey didn't seem to think so, but there had to be a way for things to get sorted out. Something *had* to work.

But the important thing was Audrey had picked me—over New York, over all her other dreams and ambitions. For some crazy reason, she'd turned down the bright lights of the big city in favor of the twinkling stars over the mountainside. And I'd make sure she never regretted that.

The door opened behind me, and Audrey slipped out to wrap her arms around my middle. I clasped her hands at my chest as she rested her head on my back. "I think I'm overdue with telling you something."

"Oh, yeah? What's that?"

She fisted her hand on the front of my shoulder and pressed a kiss to the back of it. "I love you, cowboy. And I want to build tomorrow, right here with you."

I grinned and turned around, taking her in my arms. "You're on, sweetheart."

Audrey

"So, have you guys talked about getting married? Wedding dates? Oh! I know a great little church. It's about five miles up the road, and it has these big open beams in the rafters. Perfect for hanging those little twinkle lights!"

"Kelli, let me take a breath!" I laughed. "I just turned down the job offer, and I'm still figuring things out." I blew the steam off the coffee Kelli had just brought me and took a sip. We were gathered around the dining room table at Walker Ranch because I still needed to take it easy today, but I was tired of sitting at home. So, Luke had brought me to his house, and I'd been immediately surrounded and welcomed. Just like I was already family.

"You really did it," Jess sighed over her coffee cup. "I was so hoping you would. I've never seen Luke look prouder, by the way."

"Hah." I rubbed my eyes. There was still just the littlest bit of ache and fatigue lingering. I wouldn't have wanted to be anywhere else, putting myself out and trying to make a brave face in public. But this felt like home, and I didn't have to fake anything. "He proposed about five times between my house and here."

"Five? Didn't you accept the first time?" Kelli gasped.

"Yes, but he wanted to hear it again. He's such a goofball."

"That sounds like Luke," Jess giggled. "Hey, do you know what this means? We're all going to be sisters!"

I sat back a little. "Oh, wow. I hadn't even thought that far ahead." I blinked and shook my head a little. *Sisters!*

"That's right! Oh, and just so you know, Morgan counts," Kelli informed me. "Cody's basically Blake's son, so that makes Morgan our sister, too."

My heart cried a little bit, but at the same time, I felt a silly grin spreading on my face. "I just lost the only sister I had, and now I'm getting three new ones. That's..." I huffed. "Is it okay to be happy about that? I'm so confused!"

Jess reached across the table to squeeze my hand. "Do you think Kat would be happy for you?"

I pressed my lips together, thought for a second, then nodded. "Yeah. Yeah, she would."

"Then it's okay to be happy. She'd want you to live, Audrey. So, live for Kat, no regrets."

I nodded. "For Kat. Right." My gaze fell to the table, and I toyed with my coffee cup. "I just wish I knew if there was something I could still do for Lizzy."

Luke

Two Bits liked having his ears scratched. He'd tip his head way to the side and stick his upper lip out, and his eyes would roll back in their sockets. The clown would shake his head and sneeze at me when I stopped scratching, then tilt his ear toward me again, asking me to do it all over.

"Enough, you crazy horse," I said, patting his shoulder. He was all slicked out now, with good healthy flesh covering his ribs and hips, and if you didn't know his history, you'd never guess he'd been a near-dead rack of bones a few months ago. He looked good, he felt good, and Doc had cleared him to start reconditioning. A few more weeks, and I'd throw a leg over him and see if he could ever make it back to the roping pen.

But even if he didn't, I had big plans for this fellow. Joe was sending me his registration papers, and I already had a few friends talking about what a great outcross he would be for their own programs. He was one in a million—the diamond in the rough I'd been searching for for years, and he'd landed in my lap when I wasn't even looking.

Funny how a wrong turn in life can end up so right. I slid Two Bits' stall door shut and headed for the side-by-side to drive up to the house. I found Audrey in the living room, laughing over a cup of tea with Meryl, Jess, Morgan, and Kelli. They stopped when I walked in the door.

"What's going on in here? Is it safe, or should I tell the guys to steer clear?"

"We were waiting for you, Luke," Meryl said, standing up with a bundle in her hands. "I didn't see any sense in holding on to this any longer, so here." She passed me the bundle. It was soft and bulky, wrapped up in a bit of tissue paper.

I took it and held my breath. "Is this what I think it is?"

"Open it and find out."

I glanced at Audrey, but she only gave me a teasing smile back. She probably knew what it was already. My hands shook as I tore the paper off to reveal an old quilt.

"Your mom made that for you," Meryl said gently.

"I know." I sniffed and unfolded it so I could see it all. Mom knew me, alright. Lots of red and blue, my favorite colors, and asymmetrical quarters. Not like the ones she'd made for my brothers. They all looked even and balanced with regular squares and points. Traditional quilt blocks. This one was a riot of shapes and sizes, blended colors, and mismatched lines. But if you looked at it right, those colors and shapes shadowed together to make a wandering path over the surface, starting in one corner and meandering to the opposite one.

Yeah, Mom knew me. She must've known that I wouldn't take the easy road and that I'd be chasing my life's ambitions in a dozen wrong places before I found the right one. But down in that last corner, she'd sewn a single red heart.

And that was it. I'd tried everything, hunted all the crazy ideas that came my way until I finally discovered what I'd been looking for all along. One little heart was all it took to bring my world into focus.

Audrey came to stand beside me, and she pulled the bottom corners up so we could both see the face of the quilt. "It's beautiful."

"Yeah. It fits." I tugged the quilt from her hands and rolled it up into a neat bundle once more. "Guess we'll have to build us a house to put it in, huh?"

She laughed and tucked herself under my arm. "We can do that."

"Good. Say, how about you and I take off and go to Beaufort's for dinner? I've never actually taken you out on a proper date, so it's about time we fixed that."

She frowned thoughtfully. "Ooh, great idea. Meryl's been feeding me for two days now. She's probably ready for me to get out of her hair."

I pulled her close to kiss her temple, and I didn't care that all those girls were still watching and snickering behind their hands. "Alright. I'll go get changed, and you..." I stopped when Audrey's phone went off. "Do you need to get that? Might be work or something."

She sighed impatiently. "Right, a dental cleaning emergency. It can probably wait." She dug her phone out of her pocket, then her eyes widened when she saw the number. "Oh! It's Lizzy's case worker." She looked at me, her expression fragile. "I have to take this."

Audrey

"Miss Livingstone? Thank you for coming so quickly." The case-worker came out of the house with her hand extended to greet me. "I'm sorry for calling you out here on such short notice."

I shook her hand. "That's alright. Is everything okay? Where's Lizzy?"

"She's inside with an officer. Miss Livingstone, your former broth-er-in-law is being held in the county facility pending bail, and Eliza-beth needs a safe place to go for tonight. Are you willing to take her now?"

"Yes, yes, of course." I was straining to see over her head, to find out if Lizzy knew I was here. She must be so scared! But all I saw was the curtain darkening the windows.

"Sign here, please." The caseworker thrust a clipboard at me, and I scribbled on the bottom without even reading it.

"What happened? You didn't give me any details on the phone except that James had been caught driving under the influence."

"That's all I can give you for now, Miss Livingstone. The officer can fill you in on the rest. If you'll follow me?"

She led me up onto the porch and opened the door to the saddest sight I'd ever witnessed. I recognized Sheriff Wyatt because he was one of my patients. Nice man, usually smiling, but right now, he was sitting on the couch with his forearms resting on his thighs and a long, weary expression on his face. And huddled on the floor in front of him was Lizzy, with her arms wrapped around her legs and her head buried between her knees.

I probably shoved the caseworker aside, but I didn't care. "Lizzy! Lizzy, are you okay?"

She lifted her head, and her eyes rounded. "Aunt Audrey!" She clambered to her feet and dove into my arms, hiding her face against my sleeve. I'll never forget how hard she was trembling. "I'm sorry! I'm s-so s-sorry!"

"It's okay," I soothed. "You're fine. You're safe. You don't have anything to be sorry for."

She shook her head and sobbed, coughing and gulping back tears. "It's my fault! I'm so sorry!"

"Nothing is your fault. Honey, you're going to be okay." I looked over her head at Sheriff Wyatt to see if he could clear it up for me. He shook his head and pointed outside—he didn't want to talk in front of Lizzy. All I could do for now was pat her back and hold her until she could catch her breath.

Oh, where was Luke? He'd waited in the truck because we weren't sure if this was something that should involve him or not. I needed some answers from the sheriff, but I couldn't leave Lizzy yet.

That was when a touch at my shoulder told me that he was already by my side. "Is she okay?" he murmured.

I just shook my head helplessly. "I don't even know what's wrong. Can you talk to the sheriff?"

He squeezed my shoulder and met Wyatt's eye. "Yep. If he'll talk to me."

Luke

"Aren't you the one who popped the fire hydrant and flooded the parking lot back in 2011?"

I rolled my eyes. "Yessir. Not proud of it."

"And the football stadium lights. That was you, wasn't it?"

"I was seventeen."

He narrowed his eyes and started to nod, then; "Wasn't there something to do with a billboard? Or was that one of your brothers?"

I set my hands on my hips and sighed. "We gonna keep regurgitating all my misdeeds, or are you gonna tell me what's wrong with Lizzy?"

He studied me for a few seconds, chewed the inside of his cheek, and apparently decided I wasn't the delinquent he remembered. "We picked James Tracy up last night on a DUI violation. He blew way over the limit, and his vehicle was impounded. Unfortunately, he became belligerent with the officers and attempted to evade arrest while still in his vehicle. Due to the degree of his actions, it will be a felony charge in this state."

"Whoa." I scratched my chin. "You said this was last night?"

Wyatt nodded grimly.

"How come we're just now hearing about it?"

"There was a passenger with him, a young woman whose behavior was somewhat hostile and uncooperative upon initial contact. She was not placed under arrest and was escorted home, but she said nothing at the time to the attending officers."

He hooked his thumbs over his duty belt and leveled a heavy look at me. "Two hours ago, she called the station to advise us that James Tracy had a child at home who was likely left unattended. Upon our arrival, we discovered the child had barricaded the door and locked herself alone in a room because she was afraid."

"Holy moly," I breathed. "But she's got a phone. Why didn't she call for help?"

"Her father took her phone. I don't pretend to know why, but she had no means of contacting anyone. There is no landline at the house, and she was afraid that if she walked to the neighbor's house, we would be called, and her father would get in trouble."

I growled under my breath. "Still protecting him, huh? The dude deserves whatever he gets."

The sheriff's face softened. "It's self-preservation. I've seen this in kids before, and it breaks my heart every time. Doesn't matter what she feels for her father. She depends on him for safety and protection, so she'll cover for him." Wyatt glanced back at the house, and then his voice grew even more serious.

"Right now, he's charged with felony evading arrest, driving under the influence, and child endangerment. I understand there is already a hearing scheduled, as Miss Livingstone is the late Mrs. Tracy's designated guardian for her daughter?"

I nodded.

"I am taking Elizabeth into emergency custody. Given the circumstances, I am placing her in the care of Miss Livingstone rather than seeking a foster care provider. The hearing will probably be moved up due to the nature of the situation. It is probable that Mr. Tracy may be facing jail time and the temporary suspension of his parental rights. Is Miss Livingstone prepared for the possibility of assuming long-term care for Elizabeth?"

That was the first time I'd smiled. "I'm sure Miss Livingstone will be agreeable to that."

Audrey

Lizzy was still breathing fast and dashing tears off her face when Luke helped her into his truck. She clung to his hand like she wasn't going to let go, and for a minute, I didn't think she would. But once I got into the back seat beside her, she turned loose of Luke and held on to me so tightly I thought she was going to crack my ribs.

I brushed the hair out of her face and cradled her head to my shoulder. "You're not hurt, are you?"

She shook her head.

"Did anyone frighten you?"

Lizzy hesitated, then shook her head again.

I glanced up and met Luke's eyes in the rearview mirror. "Well... what's the matter?"

She flexed her grip on my t-shirt. "I was all alone. Everyone left me, and I was alone." Her face crumpled, and a little sob squeaked out. "And I was so scared when they didn't come back. I don't want to be alone!"

Oh. That did make sense. Lizzy had been afraid of being alone for months, and I'd attributed it to the fracturing of her home and the loss of her mother. The volatile emotions, the highs and lows, and the deep insecurity she expressed at times—of course, she felt frightened and anxious.

It had to have been much worse at her dad's house. No rules meant no stability, nothing predictable in her life to hang on to. And with no way of calling anyone or knowing why her dad hadn't come home last night, it probably sent her already-fragile emotions into a panic attack. Little wonder she was so frantic that she wouldn't let me go.

"It's my fault he left," she choked. "He always left when he said I was rude. I yelled at him because he said I burned dinner, and then he didn't come home. I didn't mean to make him leave!"

"You didn't make him do anything, Lizzy. He's an adult who makes his own choices. I know you can't believe me right now, but I'll keep saying it as often as I have to. This was *not* your fault. It wasn't right for him to leave you like that."

She was quiet for a minute. "Am I coming back home?"

Home. That was like putting the screws to my heart and giving them a twist. Angry words had passed between us, but she still thought home was with me. I sighed and brushed my fingers through her hair again. It looked like it hadn't been combed in a week.

"For now. The court will decide what happens in the future, but I've been saving evidence for a while. I'm going to hire a lawyer and fight for you to stay with me for good."

Luke raised his chin to look at Lizzy in the rearview mirror. "Me too, kiddo. I talked your aunt into marrying me, so it's kind of a package deal. Think you can live with that?"

She loosened her grip for the first time and lifted her head to gape at both of us. "You mean it? Really?"

"Yes, really," I laughed. "Can you believe it? Me, marrying a cattle rancher! I'm going to need lots of help, you know. I haven't even learned how to brush a horse yet."

"I want to live with you guys," she announced. "The officer said the court would ask me what I wanted because I'm old enough. I'll tell them I want you. They have to let me live with you if I say that, right?" Hope glowed in her eyes as she gazed up at me, but then her face clouded. "Is it okay if I say that? Will there be room for me after you guys get married?"

"Sweetheart, I'll always have a place for you. In my heart and in my home. My world isn't the same without you."

"And I'll need lots of help around the place." Luke peered at her in the mirror again with that playful twinkle in his eye. "Know anyone who'd be interested in working around the barn and taking care of the animals?"

She sucked in a breath and nodded, her eyes wide, as she grinned at me. And when Luke reached into the back seat, Lizzy grabbed his hand like a lifeline. "Can I call you Uncle Luke?"

"Call me anything you want, baby girl. Ain't nobody gonna mess with my ladies, I can guarantee you that." He winked at her in the mirror.

"Promise?" She looked from Luke to me and back again. Luke glanced at me, and there was that little wrinkle in his cheek—that look he'd gotten before, when I first noticed that we really did think alike. He gave a small nod, letting me answer her.

I reached out and cupped both their hands in mine. My girl and my cowboy—three aimless and fractured people, now one family. "Promise. We take care of each other."

She gripped our hands a little tighter, but her breathing was starting to even out, and she was getting brave enough to smile again. After a minute, she whispered, "Okay."

From our hearts to yours

T hank you for spending a little time with the family at Walker Ranch.

I hope you've enjoyed getting to know everyone. I'd love it if you would share this family with your friends so they can experience life on the ranch with these swoony cowboys and sassy cowgirls. As with all my books, I have enabled lending to make it easier to share. If you leave a review for *Taming the Cowboy* on Amazon, Goodreads, Book Bub or your own blog, I would love to read it! Email me the link at **TheCowgirlWrites@TessThornton.com**

Would you like to read Blake Walker's romance? Dive into Blake and Meryl's story, and stay up to date on upcoming releases and sales by joining my newsletter: https://dashboard.mailerlite.com/forms/ 249660/75244350638917199/share

And now, keep reading for a sneak preview of Evan and Meg's story!

Epilogue

Evan
One month later

"Luke, there's another one!" I waved my brother down and held the gate as the last steer scampered through. He reined in that big black stud of his and circled around to scoop up the stray.

"How many is that?" he called.

"Twenty-seven. That's all of them. Can you guys take it from here?"

He tossed a gloved hand at me, then cupped it to his mouth. "Audrey, move on up to the left flank. Nice and easy, and we'll get these fellers pushed out to pasture. Wait, Lizzy, don't run! *Walk that horse!*"

I chuckled to myself as I latched the gate and turned my horse back toward the barn. Luke could handle the cows and the kid just fine without me. It was a sweet touch of irony that Luke was now parenting a teenager who was every bit as rowdy and reckless as he'd ever been. He was always in trouble and never slowed down at that age, and she was just like him. I often wondered how Audrey survived living in the same house with those two.

I cut through the broodmare pasture on my way back so I could take a look at the colts. They were all getting big, and some of them had already started to shed out their fluffy baby hair on their legs and muzzles. It was a hot and dry day, and the band of mares were all grouped under the shade trees, flicking flies off each other's faces and resting from the afternoon sun.

I halted my horse about fifty yards out and just gazed at them from a distance. When we had nursing foals, I came down here every day, without fail, and parked my horse in the same spot that I had for fifteen years. I came alone these days, but it hadn't always been that way. I sighed and rested my forearm on my saddle horn, scanning the group for any signs of trouble—lameness, sickness, anyone not thriving.

And, like always, one little face pushed its way out from the center of the herd to the outskirts. I grinned as I settled in to watch him. That little palomino colt of Goldie's tossed his head at me, then stood staring back with eyes bright and alert. A fly buzzed his nose, and he snorted, half-reared, and spun around. Then he whirled back to stare down my saddle horse. He was a picture, that one. Long, clean legs, chiseled muscles, and floating gaits, and all at just three months old.

"That's the age," my dad used to tell me. "You want to know what they'll look like as adults? Look at them at three months, and you'll see."

I'd said the same thing once to my daughter Emma. She was three at the time, and we were sitting in this very spot. I'd put her on in front of me that day so I could bring her down here to see the babies grazing, and she'd been captivated by a flashy buckskin colt she called Biz.

"See how he watches you?" I'd asked her. "He's curious and bold. He'll be friendlier than the others."

"He's special," she'd informed me. "Please, I want that one, Daddy."

I'd hugged her close, my heart swelling with pride. "Good choice, cupcake. I'd picked that one out for you, too. You guys are going to do amazing things together."

But the years hadn't played out the way I'd planned. Emma and Anne had left me to run down their dreams without them. I'd done my best, trying to check off the boxes and build the castles in the sky that we'd dreamed up together as a family. But without them to share the victories with, life was just hollow.

I watched that yellow colt for a few minutes more. He was so much like his uncle Biz in the way he would trot toward me with that springy stride, then stop and snort, then run off chasing butterflies like he wanted me to follow him. Emma would have loved this little guy, and I had my eye on him, too.

Finally, I picked up my reins and headed back toward the barn. I had to drive out to the hay fields this afternoon to decide when to harvest them, and I still had that one field sprinkler to finish repairing. I'd probably be working well after dark, but I'd take that over being bored. Keeping busy kept my mind from spiraling.

Cody was closing the door of the horse trailer as I trotted into the yard, and he tipped his hat to shield his eyes from the sun. "Oh, hey, Evan. I'm heading home. We're hauling out to that show in Tucson in the morning, so I'm going to go spend the evening with my wife before I go."

I gave a single nod as I hopped off my horse. "Fine. Say hi to Morgan for me."

"Yeah... uh, she's... she's not feeling well." He walked over and rested his hand on my horse's hip. "She asked me to pick up some ginger ale on my way home."

I was pulling my cinch, but when he said that, I stopped and stared at him. The smug look on his face said it all. I just grunted and finished loosening my saddle. "Anyone else know?"

"Not yet. She wanted to wait until I got back from this show, and then invite the family up for a barbecue to break the news."

TESS THORNTON

"Well, cool. Congratulations."

"Thanks. I hate asking this, but would you mind stopping over there once or twice this week? Just to check on her. She won't ask for help, but she'd confide in you."

I looked up. "Why me? Why not Kelli or Jess or somebody?"

"Because you know how to keep a secret."

My mouth twisted into a frown. Yeah, he was right there. I *was* good at keeping secrets. I yanked the saddle off my horse and threw it over the wooden rail we had set up there. "Fine. What does she need?"

"Gosh, I don't even know." Cody pushed his hat up and scratched his head. "Any ideas? I've never done this before. Isn't she supposed to start craving pickle juice and watermelon?"

"Depends. She might start chowing down on Mexican food or ice cream, or she might not be able to eat hardly anything."

"See, I knew I came to the right guy. At least you know something. I'm completely clueless."

I blew out a sigh and untied my horse. "I don't know what you think I can tell you. Morgan's the one you need to listen to, not me."

"Yeah, and Morgan has a history of trying to do everything for herself and refusing to let anyone help her. She could be flat on her back with morning sickness but she'd tell me over the phone that everything's peachy. Just check on her once or twice, that's all I ask."

I shrugged. "Sure."

"And whatever you do, *don't* tell Kelli. Jess or Audrey, maybe, if you really need to. But Kelli would blast it on a loudspeaker in the middle of town, and then I'd have your dad calling me up to come home early from the horse show, Meryl trying to plan a baby shower in the first trimester, it would be a mess."

I smiled a little. "Sounds about right."

Cody stuck out his hand to shake mine. "Thanks, Evan! This means a lot to me."

"No worries. Ride 'em good and get your tail back home soon."

He started walking backward toward his truck. "You betcha. Maserati's on top of the world right now. You're going to have another champion this year, or I'll eat my hat!"

I pointed at him. "I'm holding you to that."

Meg

"Dustin, here's a fresh set of sheets. Please put them *on* your bed this time, okay? I don't want to find them crammed under the headboard again." My son was sitting at his desk with his back to me, his shoulders bent over something, and his feet swinging.

"Dustin, did you hear me?" I walked closer. "Please respond."

He straightened and meticulously set his carving tool aside. "Mom, I can't talk when I'm detailing. It's too squiggly."

"Fine. You're not detailing right now, so did you hear me about the sheets?"

"Yes." He picked the tool back up and resumed scraping at the block of wood on his desk. I couldn't tell what this one was going to be yet, but knowing Dustin, it would take my breath away when he was finished. He liked to work in sections, so while most of the block was still rough-cut, the corner where he was working had been carved away to reveal what looked like sweeping hair or waves or something.

I knew better than to touch one of his creations while he was working on it, so I leaned close and tucked my hands between my knees. "That's incredible. What is it?"

He sighed in exasperation and put his tool down. "It hasn't told me yet."

My eyebrows raised. He had the oddest way of talking about his sculptures, as if they were living things. "Well, has it told you to clean up the shavings off the floor when you're done?"

He didn't answer this time. He just picked his tool back up and studied the corner where he'd been working, his tongue sticking out a little as he turned the piece from side to side. I shook my head and backed out of the room.

Nobody understood how Dustin could work the way he did. He started carving when he was two, with a kitchen knife on my dining room table legs. I still had that dining room table, and it was quite the conversation piece. By the time he was in preschool, he was creating chess pieces out of soapstone while most kids were still mastering the basics of play-doh. Oh, and he was beating all the local chess players down at the retirement center with his home-carved pieces.

At the time, his teacher thought he was a child genius—some kind of art prodigy descended to live among us mortal folk. Then the next year, another teacher discovered that he couldn't read, and suddenly he was no longer a genius. He had a learning disorder.

But could you call it a learning disorder when a kid could extract masterpieces from wood and clay and stone? He didn't start with a plan, he didn't begin on a large scale and hone in on the details later. The finished product just revealed itself bit by bit, and he spoke of it happening almost in spite of him rather than because of him.

Two years ago, I'd taken him to the university to ask an art professor to watch him work and help me decide how to guide his efforts. The art professor watched Dustin for an hour, then just shook his head and threw up his hands. "I don't even know what his concept is, let alone how to instruct him. You need someone trained in working with special needs students."

And so, there it was. Everywhere my brilliant, sensitive son went, he was labeled as different. A problem. That kid that no one understood and no one wanted to take the time to know because he intimidated them. Everywhere, that is, except for one place.

I made a pass through the kitchen and slipped three sandwiches into baggies. The same three sandwiches every week—turkey, turkey, and turkey. Dustin liked having choices, but he didn't appreciate variety, so this was my small way of actually getting him to eat his lunch instead of smashing it in the back seat of my car. I dropped my own sandwich in after them, zipped up the cooler bag, and walked back to Dustin's room.

"It's eleven-thirty," I said through the door. "Time to get ready to go up to White Pines."

There was the usual deliberate pause, then, "Okay."

I always held my breath until he said that "Okay." Because there was once a time when getting him to go anywhere at all was a fight—one I didn't usually win.

But then Morgan had come into our lives with her therapy horses and her love of people and her faithful troop of volunteers. And Dustin, the kid who didn't use to even get out of the car when we went places—assuming I could get him in the car in the first place—was now the poster child for the whole facility. It was the only place he went where he was made to feel equal and capable, and respected, just like every other kid.

He got in the car and put on his seat belt, and then asked the usual question. "Will Morgan let me ride Biz today?"

"I guess you'll have to see. Biz has lots of people who love him, you know. We have to share him."

"But I like him better than all the other people do," Dustin said. It wasn't up for debate. "I'm going to ride him today."

I sucked in a breath as I wrapped my fingers around the wheel. *Please let Biz be available today* was my usual prayer. "Okay. Here we go."

Keep reading about more sweet cowboys from the Walker Ranch! Grab your copy of *A Heart for the Cowboy* and find out how these two mend each other's broken hearts.

A Winter Surprise for the Cowboy

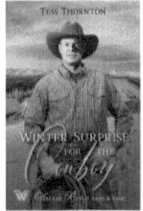

Blake Walker has built a legacy in his family and his ranch. His five boys are starting to find love and build their own lives, and he's beginning to wonder what adventures are left for him.

Meryl Justice has raised everyone's kids but her own, and now she's looking forward to retirement from the job she's had for thirty years. She loves her home and her farm animals, but is that all there is?

Find out when these two hearts set out to discover if wintertime might not just be the best time of all to fall in love!

Click HERE to get your story.